After graduating with degrees in English and Political Science, **Eva Shepherd** worked in journalism and as an advertising copywriter. She began writing historical romances because it combined her love of a happy ending with her passion for history. She lives in Christchurch, New Zealand, but spends her days immersed in the world of late Victorian England. Eva loves hearing from readers and can be reached via her website, evashepherd.com, and her Facebook page at Facebook.com/evashepherdromancewriter.

Also by Eva Shepherd

Those Roguish Rosemonts miniseries

A Dance to Save the Debutante
Tempting the Sensible Lady Violet
Falling for the Forbidden Duke

Rebellious Young Ladies miniseries

Lady Amelia's Scandalous Secret
Miss Fairfax's Notorious Duke
Miss Georgina's Marriage Dilemma
Lady Beaumont's Daring Proposition

Rakes, Rebels and Rogues miniseries

A Wager to Win the Debutante
A Widow to Defy the Duke

Discover more at millsandboon.co.uk.

A MARRIAGE TO SCANDALISE THE EARL

Eva Shepherd

MILLS & BOON

All rights reserved including the right of reproduction in whole or in part in any form. This edition is published by arrangement with Harlequin Enterprises ULC.

This is a work of fiction. Names, characters, places, locations and incidents are purely fictional and bear no relationship to any real life individuals, living or dead, or to any actual places, business establishments, locations, events or incidents. Any resemblance is entirely coincidental.

Without limiting the author's and publisher's exclusive rights, any unauthorised use of this publication to train generative artificial intelligence (AI) technologies is expressly prohibited. HarperCollins also exercise their rights under Article 4(3) of the Digital Single Market Directive 2019/790 and expressly reserve this publication from the text and data mining exception.

® and TM are trademarks owned and used by the trademark owner and/or its licensee. Trademarks marked with ® are registered with the United Kingdom Patent Office and/or the Office for Harmonisation in the Internal Market and in other countries.

First published in Great Britain 2025
by Mills & Boon, an imprint of HarperCollins*Publishers* Ltd,
1 London Bridge Street, London, SE1 9GF

www.harpercollins.co.uk

HarperCollins*Publishers*, Macken House, 39/40 Mayor Street Upper, Dublin 1, D01 C9W8, Ireland

A Marriage to Scandalise the Earl © 2025 Eva Shepherd

ISBN: 978-0-263-34526-1

07/25

This book contains FSC™ certified paper
and other controlled sources to ensure responsible forest management.

For more information visit www.harpercollins.co.uk/green.

Printed and Bound in the UK using 100% Renewable Electricity
at CPI Group (UK) Ltd, Croydon, CR0 4YY

To Archiebald the Cat,
who kept me company as I wrote this book,
even if he was asleep most of the time.

Chapter One

London 1898

Lucy stared at the clock slowly ticking on the mantelpiece, waited for her father to finish writing yet another sermon and wondered whether time could move at different speeds.

It surely could. How else would one explain the way sometimes every second appeared to stretch out to an eternity when at other times the entire day would pass by as if in a flash? And given that time had this peculiar quality, why was it that when one was happy and enjoying oneself time moved quickly, but when one was bored it slowed down to the ponderous pace of a somnolent snail?

Surely it would be better for the good times to move slowly and the dull, dreary times to pass at such a rapid rate one hardly noticed them fly by.

She watched the clock's second hand click one beat forward and released a despondent sigh.

How much longer?

Her father's pen continued to scratch across the paper while she sat and stared into space as if she had nothing better to do with her time.

She should be out enjoying herself, not stuck here in this stuffy study trying to work out esoteric problems like the contrary nature of time. She turned to face the window, covered with heavy lace curtains as if to stop the world outside from intruding into her father's cloistered sanctum. She was finally here, in London, the most exciting city in the world, and yet her life was just as tedious as it had been when she'd been stuck away in that small Cheshire village. Beyond the front door, life was happening. People were having fun, laughing, dancing, falling in love and living their lives to the full.

She could almost hear life's siren call, urging her to break free, to run outside and take hold of all the pleasures she had been desperately wanting to experience during her last long, lonely twenty years.

Instead, she turned back to the mantelpiece to watch the second hand in its slow progress around the clock face. She held her breath as the hand seemingly paused in midair, taunting her, then ticked forward one more step in its endless journey.

'Well, my dear,' her father said as he slowly replaced the lid on the ink-well and screwed back the top on his fountain pen. He picked up the papers and shuffled them into a neat pile, placed them to one side and then, finally, turned towards Lucy.

'I invited you into my study because it is time we had a little talk.'

Lucy groaned inwardly and hoped he would be true to his words because her father's *little* talks could be as long-winded as his sermons.

'Now that you've been presented to Queen Victoria, you are about to embark on a new chapter in your life. One where you will be out in Society.'

That was hardly news to Lucy. When she'd been informed by her uncle that as the daughter of the third son of an earl she could have a coming out and be presented to Her Majesty, she had been ecstatic, as if handed the keys to her prison door.

The event itself had been somewhat of a disappointment. The old queen had appeared to sleep through the entire occasion, but the idea of being *out in society* and all that entailed gave Lucy so much pleasure it was almost impossible to contain herself.

'Yes, Father,' she replied with as little enthusiasm as possible in case a show of exuberance caused him to rush her back to their Cheshire home where she could be subjected to the supposedly calming effects of the countryside.

'Why anyone would want such a thing I struggle to understand.' His thin lips curled with disdain. 'Working at the side of a clergyman and providing support and comfort for his parishioners must be the most rewarding life a young woman could have.'

Lucy kept her face as expressionless as possible lest she reveal her true feelings: that the thought of such a life filled her with horror akin to the idea of being buried alive.

Twenty years confined to the countryside, being forced to study theology, Greek and Latin, while outside people laughed, loved and enjoyed the sunshine had left her desperate to experience all the good things life had to offer. And by the end of the Season she would have experienced them all, then would hopefully fall in love, marry and never have to see the inside of a vicarage again.

'But my brother has deemed you should attend a Season and find a suitable husband, and as he is the head of the family, we have no choice but to comply.'

Lucy said a silent prayer of thanks to her uncle for being her saviour and offering her this tantalising promise of freedom.

Her father's bushy grey eyebrows drew together over his deep-set eyes. 'I just hope you are ready for the...' he leant towards her '...moral challenges that may present themselves.'

'I believe I am, Father.' She nodded solemnly while rejoicing internally. Her debut had been delayed two years, her father claiming she was not yet mature enough to cope with the temptations that being out in

Society would present, but finally he had been forced to acquiesce to his brother's directive.

'I know you are a good girl and will be on your guard against...' here his eyebrows pressed even closer together '...against men who try to take advantage of a young lady's innocence.'

Lucy sat up straighter. *Men who try to take advantage?* This was starting to sound somewhat naughty and decidedly interesting.

'You must keep a watchful eye out for such men.'

Rakes. That was who he was talking about. She was sure of it. Their maid-of-all-work back in Cheshire had given her a forbidden book that detailed the exploits of such men, and Lucy was curious to discover if such creatures really were as devilishly handsome and deliciously decadent as those portrayed in the novel.

She nodded and gave a suitable frown of concern. 'Yes, Father. I certainly will be watching out for such men.'

'Good girl. You are unfortunately a pretty young woman, and that can sometimes attract a certain type of man.'

Really? This was becoming more interesting by the minute.

'Your dear departed mother was just the same. A prettier lass you would never see. But she was also a sensible young woman. She did not require a Season and was most amenable when our parents arranged our marriage.' He waited for Lucy to say something.

'Yes, Father, most sensible,' she replied.

Whether it was sensible or not, Lucy did not know, her mother having died giving birth to her, but it seemed the appropriate thing to say. As for being pretty, Lucy had to agree with that. The miniature portrait her father always travelled with did depict an attractive young woman, one with Lucy's blond hair and blue eyes, and the kindest smile she'd ever seen. A smile that always filled her with sadness that such a smile had never been bestowed on her.

'You must follow your mother's example, my dear. You must be ever vigilant so that you only attract the right sort of man, respectable men, men who are seeking an equally respectable wife.'

'Yes, Father.' Lucy mirrored his frown. 'So what sort of men should I be avoiding?' she added, trying to not sound too interested in this taboo topic.

'Has your aunt Harriet not discussed this with you?'

'No, Father.' Her maiden aunt had kindly taken on the role of chaperone for the duration of the Season, but as she had no experience with men as far as Lucy was aware, no such talk had occurred, and Lucy doubted it ever would.

'I believe you will find unacceptable men easy to spot. Be wary of men who are known to gamble and have a reputation for frequenting the theatre, especially the ones in the less salubrious parts of town. Avoid the men the ladies whisper about. If you deem any man overly handsome, then judge him to be a dandy. Such men are best given a wide berth as they are often aware of the effect they have on impressionable young women and are apt to take advantage if given the opportunity.'

Lucy nodded. *Gambling, theatres, handsome, whispers*. Those points were easy enough to remember. Her father was perhaps right. If she were to make a good marriage it *would* be best to avoid such men, but she could not deny she was intrigued and hoped she at least got to see one of these alluring creatures before the Season was over.

He reached over and lightly patted his daughter's hand. 'I know that you will not be drawn to such men, but predators can hide their true selves behind a façade of genteel behaviour. I urge caution.'

'I shall keep in mind your good advice at all times,' Lucy said, supressing a little laugh as she briefly pictured herself on the arm of a handsome man and causing all the ladies to whisper about them behind their fans.

'I know you will, but hopefully you will not need to concern yourself with such trials.' His thin lips stretched into a semblance of a smile. A rare event, one that was surely a cause for concern.

'There is a very good chance you will be lucky enough to marry even before the first ball of the Season.'

'Marry?' Lucy choked out. 'Before the Season starts?'

'I know, my dear. You have every reason to be thrilled by this good news. The Earl of Rothwell has invited us to his house for the weekend.'

'Who?' Lucy recoiled in her chair, hardly able to believe such cruel fortune could befall her.

'The Earl of Rothwell. He is in need of a wife. His aunt was a childhood friend of your mother. She had heard you were coming out this Season and thought you would make him an exemplary wife. She has written to me and suggested this arrangement. He has a vast estate in Dorset.'

Her father paused and made another of those seldom seen smiles as if there were even better news to impart. 'And if he finds you acceptable, which I am sure he will, then you two can be married at once and you won't have to go through the ordeal of a Season and all its perils. You will be able to get away from all the hustle and bustle of London and retire immediately back to a quiet and contemplative life in the countryside.'

No! Lucy wanted to scream. *I've only just got away from the crushing quiet of the countryside. I want hustle. I want bustle. I want to finally have some fun. I want to spend my time at balls and theatres. I want to finally live. And when I do marry I want it to be to a man who loves me and I love in return, not to some earl chosen for me because he 'is in need of a wife'.*

Instead, she forced herself to remain silent and give nothing away. If her father thought for one second that she was looking forward to breaking free from his restraining influence, she would be back in the countryside before she had time to catch her breath.

'I can see this is causing you some anxiety,' her father said.

Lucy cursed herself for failing to keep her emotions completely in check.

'But there is no need.' He once again patted her hand. 'I know our circumstances might be, well, a bit straitened.'

He waved his hand in a circle to indicate the townhouse they had leased for the Season, one that had obviously seen better days and was in the slightly less fashionable end of Bayswater.

'It matters not. The earl has made it clear he cares nothing for his bride's dowry. All he cares about is that she is a chaste and virtuous young woman, who seeks a quiet life.'

This was getting worse and worse. She might as well have stayed in Cheshire if she wanted a quiet life.

'I am perhaps committing the sin of pride when I say this,' her father said, with a self-satisfied expression, 'but I believe the earl is unlikely to find a young lady more virtuous and chaste than my daughter.'

On that her father was probably right, but only because Lucy had been given no opportunity to be otherwise.

'When you meet the earl, I want you to remember at all times that you not only possess those treasured qualities he seeks, but even though you are only the daughter of the third son of an earl, you have excellent connections on both sides of your family.' He nodded his head slowly. 'Yes. Any man after a wife will know that if he pledges his troth to Miss Lucinda Everhart, he is courting a woman from an impeccable background.'

'Yes, Father,' Lucy said in a manner she hoped was suitably demure and contained the required hint of humility expected of a young lady from said *impeccable background*. 'But should I not find him acceptable, will I still be expected to marry him?' she asked tentatively.

'Why would you not find him acceptable?' Those eyebrows approached each other once again.

'Well, perhaps there might be no love between us,' she said quietly.

Her father glared at her, and Lucy wished she had not spoken.

'Love? I would think a daughter of mine would not be so foolish to have such flighty, romantic notions.' His nostrils flared with disdain. 'Do not give me reason to think you are still an immature young woman who should not be out in Society.'

'Of course not, Father,' she said lowering her head and cursing herself for making such a foolish and candid revelation.

'I have every reason to believe the earl will be exactly what you are looking for in a husband,' he continued, still glaring at her.

'Yes, Father,' she said in her most humble voice.

'But I'm afraid I also have some bad news,' her father added.

What? There was worse news?

How much worse could this get? Her Season was all but over before it could begin. There would be no fun, no dancing, no flirting. She was expected to marry a man who, according to her father, could not possibly be unacceptable, and she was going to be confined back in the countryside before she'd seen one single site in London or attended even one ball.

'Once our visit to the earl's estate is over, I'm afraid I will have to return to Greyton.'

Lucy caught herself in time before she smiled at this wonderful news. 'You will?' she said with a forced note of disappointment.

'Yes, I fear my parishioners will be missing my guiding hand, and I am loath to be away from them for too long in case they resort to intemperate ways.'

'Of course, Father. I understand completely. Yes, you must return to your parish.' A little twinge of guilt nipped at her conscience, but she firmly pushed it away. She had no doubts the parishioners were pleased to have a break from her father's moralising and criticism, but their loss was her gain. She would try and find some way to make it up to the long-suffering parishioners, but right now it was more important that she grab on to this one elusive chance at freedom before it slipped through her fingers.

Her father continued to stare at her, and Lucy feared he could read her mind. If he knew how much she longed to dance, to laugh, to be surrounded by people all determined to enjoy themselves as much as she was, she was sure she would be subjected to a lecture on the danger of vain imaginings and the sin of impure thoughts.

She held her breath and waited for him to chastise her. When he finally nodded, relief flooded through her.

'I'm sure all my teachings will serve you in good stead. And Aunt Harriet will be all you need as a chaperone for the short time the earl is courting you.'

This was indeed good news after so much bad. Being chaperoned by Aunt Harriet meant having no chaperone at all. All hope of freedom had not been entirely crushed.

'That is if the earl finds me acceptable,' she said, hoping and praying it would not be so.

'Your modesty becomes you, Lucinda, but of course he will find you acceptable. You are as good as married already.'

The bubble of pleasure provided by the thought of her father's departure popped.

'As good as married'. As good as buried back in the countryside. As good as dead.

'That is all I have to say. I'll leave you to digest this

fortuitous news. We will be leaving for the earl's estate this Friday.'

Friday. Three days away.

'Perhaps you could spend your time before we depart with that new lady's maid, organising what you will need to pack, gowns and what-not. Although if a father can be so bold as to make a recommendation on your clothing, you should select the most demure gowns, ones that will display your true personality to the earl.'

'Yes, Father,' Lucy said, trying not to sound as if she'd just been given notice of her execution.

'Good girl.' He turned back to his desk, uncapped his fountain pen, picked up a piece of paper and went back to his scribbling, letting Lucy know their discussion was at an end.

She lifted herself out of the chair and dragged herself out the door and up the stairs to her bedchamber, where she collapsed into an armchair.

Three days.

Three miserable days left, confined to this house, then off to the countryside to meet a dull earl who met with her father's approval. Then she'd be married, and all hopes for the Season would be dashed.

With a sigh that shuddered through her entire body she clambered across the room and pulled the servants' bell to summon her lady's maid, then stumbled back to her chair.

Dolly entered the bedchamber, smiling in her usually sunny manner, a smile that died as soon as she saw Lucy's expression.

'What is it, miss?' She hurried across the room, knelt in front of Lucy and took her hands.

'I'm to be married.'

'Um…is that not the point of the social season?'

'Yes. But I'm to be married right now. To some earl my father has chosen for me. It's a disaster.'

'Tell me all about it, miss.'

And she did. She told Dolly all that had happened in the study, in excruciating detail, from the ticking of the clock to her father imposing such a devastating fate upon her.

Her maid listened carefully, making the appropriate noises of indignation and sympathy.

It was so good to have Dolly to confide in, and it was Lucy's first experience of a lady's maid, such servants being deemed an unnecessary luxury back in Greyton. As was dressing in too much finery, wearing jewellery or having one's hair styled in the latest fashion. All such indulgences were deemed the height of vanity and lacking in the necessary humility expected of Reverend Everhart's daughter. But her uncle had insisted she have a lady's maid so she would not look out of place among the other debutantes and had hired Dolly from an employment agency for the duration of the Season.

Although Dolly came with excellent references, she had a mischievous spark that Lucy greatly appreciated, and the young women had quickly become more friends than servant and mistress. Having a friend her own age was another indulgence her father had deemed to be of no value and something Lucy had longed for as much as the fun and freedom of the Season.

When Lucy came to the end of her sorry tale, Dolly stood up, nodded slowly, a thoughtful crease between her eyebrows. 'But you do have three days left before your trip to the earl's estate,' she said.

'Yes, and the first ball of the Season will be on the very Friday when I am stuck out in the countryside.'

Dolly's lips curled slowly into a smile.

'You've got an idea, haven't you?' Lucy said, reflecting Dolly's smile.

'It's a bit naughty, but it would give you a chance to see some of, well, the more—shall we say—interesting side of London while you've still got the chance.'

Lucy clasped her hands together. 'Oh, yes, please. I have to. I just have to get out of this house and *interesting* is exactly what I'm after.'

'Then tomorrow night we'll sneak out after your aunt and your father retire for the night and I'll show you a bit of London's nightlife.'

It was indeed naughty; it was also risky, and her father would see it as the first step on the road to damnation, but it was exactly what Lucy needed.

She stood too, pulled Dolly towards her and encased her in a hug. 'Thank you, thank you. Oh, Dolly, you truly are a godsend.'

Chapter Two

When your family fortune was almost lost in a game of cards by your profligate grandmother, it's hardly surprising that you would develop an aversion to gambling. Such was the case with Sebastian Kingsley, the 10th Earl of Rothwell, which was why he rarely found himself in gaming houses.

That is to say, he rarely found himself in gaming houses except for the one owned by his half-brother, Nathanial Bowers.

Sebastian sipped his brandy and smiled in disbelief that the two men had become such good friends. He would never have expected such an outcome when he first discovered his half-brother had established a gambling den in London. At the time he had seen it as fitting that the issue from two scandalous parents would make his fortune from vice. What had surprised him was that he found Nathanial to be an amiable and pleasant fellow.

When Sebastian first visited The Royal Flush, it

was with the intention of confronting the man he was sure had returned from America with a scheme to fleece his wealthy, titled relation.

Now he often passed a pleasant evening, seated in Nathanial's office, sharing a convivial drink, while below them patrons happily squandered their money.

And that was where he found himself on this Wednesday night, although on this occasion it was because his half-brother had invited him to his place of business as he had something of great importance he wished to discuss with Sebastian.

They had already talked of recent events covered in the newspapers, given their opinions on various sporting fixtures, even exchanged a view or two on the latest bills before the House of Commons, but the important issue had not yet raised its head.

While Nathanial dealt with yet another problem brought to him by a staff member, Sebastian stood at the large windows providing a panoramic view of the gaming room and surveyed the scene below him. A band was playing in one corner, and several couples were dancing to its lively tune; groups were clustered around the bar, drinking, talking and laughing; but most patrons were surrounding the various gaming tables. Sebastian wondered how many children would go hungry, how many rents would not be paid, and how many valuables would be pawned as a result of the money lost at those tables.

He tried not to be judgemental of his half-brother

for making his living in such a dubious way. While Sebastian was the only son of an earl and had inherited a vast estate and fortune along with a title, his half-relative, as the son of a servant, had been forced to make his own way in the world.

And he quite obviously had done so with some success. Sebastian was yet to witness a slow evening at The Royal Flush, and the business was obviously thriving. That was no surprise. Where there was vice, there was always money to be made.

Sebastian took another sip of his brandy. The important issue Nathanial wished to discuss was unlikely to be a request for finance. Despite Sebastian's original suspicions, Nathanial had never asked anything of him except his friendship.

He looked over at his half-brother talking to a staff member and smiled again. It was so obvious they were related. Both had the same slightly untamed black hair and the same dark brown eyes. They were of matching height, at just over six feet, and even had the same dimple in the middle of their chins.

But in personality, they could not be more different. Sebastian gripped his brandy balloon tighter. Perhaps that could be put down to having different fathers, or perhaps it was because Nathanial had been raised by a mother. Sebastian's mother. While Sebastian had grown up without one.

His fingernails dug into his palm, and he slowly released their grip.

While he could reconcile himself to having a younger half-brother back in his life, Sebastian would never forgive nor forget the mother who had abandoned him to run off with her lover and start another family in America, leaving him behind with a cold, angry and bitter father. A father who dumped him at boarding school at the earliest opportunity, leaving Sebastian to bear the taunts and jeers from his fellow pupils who all knew the sordid details of his parents' divorce.

His jaw clenched in that familiar manner it always did when he thought of his absent mother and his distant father. And in that equally familiar manner, he pulled in a deep, measured breath and forced his jaw to release its tension as he exhaled.

'I'm sorry about that,' Nathanial said in his American drawl, pulling Sebastian's attention away from his unwanted introspections. 'It was a problem with one of our regular clients,' he continued. 'He was demanding credit, and I never extend anyone credit unless I'm sure they can pay. Gamblers have a terrible habit of borrowing so they can chase their losses, then losing that money and wanting to borrow even more. Too many men have ended up destitute that way, and I won't be responsible for doing that to anyone.'

'Very commendable, I'm sure.' Sebastian could only wish his grandmother's fellow gamblers had been equally as understanding.

'I'm afraid I'm going to have to talk to the man myself,' Nathanial said. 'He is quite irate.'

'I understand. Then, I will say goodnight.' Sebastian placed the now empty brandy balloon on the desk.

'No, don't go. There is still something I need to discuss with you.'

Sebastian waited. Nathanial looked increasingly awkward. Perhaps it was money he was after. That was often a source of embarrassment, and Sebastian did not want his sibling to feel uncomfortable asking.

'Your business appears to be prospering, so if it is a backer you are seeking, then I am more than happy to extend you—'

Nathanial waved both hands in front of his face. 'No, no, it's not that. I…um… I invited you here because…er… Mother is in London, and she wishes to meet with you.'

All air appeared to be sucked out of the room as Sebastian stared back at Nathanial.

'No,' he finally said, that one short, sharp word containing so much that he could not express.

Nathanial stepped towards him, his expression anguished. 'Sebastian, I beseech you. Please, think about it before you reject her out of hand. She's only in England for a short while, and she is so desperate to see you.'

He gave a snort of derision. Sebastian had been receiving letters from that woman since he inherited the earldom five years ago, letters he'd thrown straight in the fire. It was surely no coincidence that she had made contact just when he'd come into an enormous fortune. If he did not wish to read her excuses, lies or attempts to gain favour with the wealthy son she had turned her back on, he certainly did not wish to hear them from her duplicitous lips.

'I do not need to think it over. I will not be meeting with that woman.'

'But—'

'No. Not interested,' he said, picking up his gloves.

'I do wish you would reconsider. She really is a kind, loving woman and has so many regrets about what happened.'

Sebastian raised his eyebrows, and Nathanial had the decency to look embarrassed. If she was indeed *kind*, Sebastian would have no way of knowing, and as for *loving*, he doubted that. Was it the act of a loving woman to walk out on her firstborn son when he was a mere two years old?

'If that is the only reason you have invited me here this evening, then I will bid you goodnight,' Sebastian said moving towards the door.

'Please, don't go. Not yet.'

He turned to face his half-brother. 'Nathanial, I have no wish to fall out with you, but I do not want to meet that woman. I do not want to discuss her. I do not want to hear her name mentioned.'

'I'm sorry,' Nathanial said.

Sebastian could add that Nathanial had nothing to

be sorry about. None of this was his fault. All fault lay at the door of the woman who had walked out on him twenty-five years ago. But he wanted this conversation to come to an end, so he turned back to the door.

'Please stay,' Nathanial urged. 'I just have that problem with the patron to sort out, but then would you join me for another drink?'

Sebastian flicked his gloves against his palm. 'I'll stay, but only if there is no more talk about meeting up with that woman.'

Nathanial winced slightly but nodded. 'I did not mean to upset you.'

Sebastian wanted to say he was not upset but knew his lie would not be believed.

'Let me make it up to you.' Nathanial reached into the desk drawer, pulled out some coloured gambling chips and handed them to Sebastian. 'You look like you could do with a good time. Go and play a few rounds of roulette, poker or baccarat and enjoy the music and everything else The Royal Flush has to offer.'

Sebastian looked down at the chips in his hand, knowing that gambling could not possibly provide the distraction he now needed.

'And if that doesn't appeal, then I'm sure there will be plenty of pretty women in tonight just dying to make your acquaintance. Go on, enjoy yourself. We can talk later, and I promise I won't mention Mo— her name again.'

He had no desire to offend Nathanial, and while he also had no desire to gamble, right now Sebastian definitely needed to do something to divert his mind from all the unwanted thoughts and memories that were fighting for his attention.

And Nathanial was right. When a man needed to relax, there was no method more reliable than a flirtation with an attractive young woman. And if that flirtation led to an offer of further ways to unwind, then even better, especially as his time as a single man might soon be coming to an end.

He nodded to him and departed the office. When he reached the bottom of the stairs, he paused at the door that led to the gambling rooms and pulled in several long, deep breaths, shocked at how the mention of his mother could evoke all those emotions he had assumed were buried so deeply as to be all but crushed out of existence.

How dare she come back into his life and reawaken those feelings he had spent years extinguishing? He would not allow her to do so. He gripped the gambling chips so tightly they dug into the palm of his hand. He needed to exorcise that woman from his mind, and what better way to do so than with some flirtatious fun with a pretty, compliant young thing who was skilled at making a man forget all his troubles, especially as such diversions were something he would soon have to put aside. He'd delayed marriage for five years since inheriting the earldom. It was time he took a wife, did his duty and produced an heir.

He gripped the chips tighter. But unlike his father, and all the earls that had preceded him, he would carefully select a woman of upstanding, moral character. He would be the one to break the Rothwell curse and be the first to marry a woman who did not bring shame on the family.

He pulled open the door with more force than needed, stepped out onto the gambling floor and collided with a blonde woman, rushing past with undue haste.

'Oh no,' she squealed as her pile of chips flew into the air, along with his own. The colourful cascade clattered to the floor, landing at their feet. She looked down at them, consternation furrowing her brow, then gazed up at him.

Those pretty, red lips slowly moved into a smile.

'Oops,' she said, her big blue eyes sparking with mischief, that smile becoming delightfully flirtatious.

Sebastian smiled back at her. She was pretty, cheerful, playful. Exactly the sort of woman he needed to take his mind off any other unwanted thoughts.

'What a mess.' She looked back down at the myriad coloured chips surrounding her dainty feet. 'I don't know which ones are mine and which are yours.'

'You are most welcome to have them all,' he said with a gallant bow as he quickly scanned her body. Yes, she had all the requisite curves in all the right places—and in an abundance that was always his preference.

'I can't take your chips,' she said with a little pout of her lips. 'I'm sure that must be unlucky. And you wouldn't want to bring me bad luck, now, would you?'

'No, I most certainly would not.' Sebastian smiled back at this tempting beauty, taking in the thick blond hair piled in a loose bun on top of her head, the escaping tendrils giving her a sensual look that was decidedly inviting. He could only wonder what that hair looked like when it was set free and what those claret-red lips tasted like. Hopefully, by the end of this evening he would know the answer to both those questions.

'Then, I think we're just going to have to play together,' she said, tilting her head in an oh-so-coquettish manner that further illustrated the suggestiveness of her words.

This was getting better and better: a pretty blonde who wanted to play. She really was exactly what he needed, and already he was starting to forget the conversation he'd just had with Nathanial.

'That sounds like a very good idea indeed, and one I couldn't possibly refuse.'

'Right. Let's pick these up, then.' She bent down to retrieve the chips, and he joined her on the floor.

'I'm Lucy, by the way. I'm here with my friend, Dolly,' she said as she placed the chips into his open hands. 'We're both lady's maids,' she added somewhat unnecessarily.

'How do you do, Lucy?' he said as he helped her to her feet. 'I'm Sebastian, and I'm very pleased to have met you.'

This was greeted with a small giggle and a slight colouring of her cheeks. Tonight, Sebastian would put aside his aversion to gambling, so he could play an altogether different and more enjoyable game with pretty little Miss Lucy, the lady's maid.

Chapter Three

Lucy was finally having fun. Her first night out, away from the confines of her starchy father and their stifling home, and she was actually laughing and enjoying herself. This was exactly what she'd hoped for from her Season.

And on top of that, she had now met one of those elusive creatures. A rake.

It was obvious that was exactly what this man was. He had all the requisite qualities. His formal black evening suit, white shirt and tie marked him out as a gentleman, as did his accent and manners. He was a gambler. His presence at The Royal Flush confirmed that, and he frequented establishments in a less than salubrious part of town.

But the final defining quality that meant he was without a doubt a rake was his looks. He was handsome. Oh my, oh my, was he handsome. One could even say *devilishly handsome*, as all the best—or was it worst?—rakes were reputed to be.

Her smile grew wider as she stared into those brown eyes. Were they twinkling the way rakes' eyes were said to do? Yes, she was certain she spotted a twinkle or two in those dark depths.

His black hair was definitely behaving in a rakish manner, if hair was capable of doing such a thing. It was slightly long, swept back from his forehead... And those lips that were smiling at her—they had to be the lips that had kissed a multitude of young women.

Trying not to be too obvious, she quickly looked up and down his body. She swallowed down a lump in her throat as she took in the breadth of his shoulders, the slimness of his waist and those long, lean legs.

This really was the naughty fun Dolly had promised her, and surely she deserved it. If her father got his way, she'd soon be in a loveless marriage to a man he approved of and locked away back in the countryside.

This might be her last chance to enjoy herself, and as no one present tonight was ever likely to come into the orbit of her respectable father, she was surely safe to do so.

Her eyes returned to the rake, and she smiled. While she might not know much about men (how could she after a solitary life in the countryside?), it didn't take a great deal of insight to interpret the way he was looking at her.

He was assessing her, and to her delight, a look of approval crossed those handsome features.

All but floating with elation, she threaded her arm through his and led him towards the roulette table. Even if she lost every single one of her playing chips tonight and was short on pin money for the rest of the Season, it would be worth it for this one night of carefree rebellion.

Dolly was already standing beside the roulette table watching the little white ball spin around on the polished wooden wheel. She looked up as Lucy and Sebastian joined her, and Lucy sent her a quick wink in thanks.

'This is my friend, Dolly,' she said. 'We both work in the same house.'

'I'm pleased to meet you, Dolly,' the handsome Sebastian said, with a bow of his head.

Dolly raised her eyebrows slightly, questioning Lucy's claim, gave a quick curtsy and went back to watching the roulette wheel spin.

Her father would be outraged if he knew where she was, and Lucy had to admit she'd had her doubts at first when Dolly led her to an unassuming building in a back alley, but when the doors opened, she discovered another world. Music, laughter and excited chatter had greeted them, and she had stood at the entrance and smiled with pure pleasure. While the clientele could not be described as the cream of society, everyone was dressed in their finest clothes, and the décor had obviously been designed to mimic a grand house, with carpets in a deep burgundy, gilt mirrors on the walls and plush draperies blocking out the windows.

More men than women were present, and Lucy and Dolly had drawn a few curious glances when they entered, but everyone soon returned to their games of chance, more interested in the gambling than they were in them.

That was until she met Sebastian. His interest in her so far was deliciously obvious.

'Are you a regular at The Royal Flush?' he asked as she placed a few chips on a black square.

'No, this is my first time,' she said as she watched the croupier spin the wheel. 'I've only recently arrived in town.'

'So what brings you to London?'

'I'm here for the Season.' She bit her lip remembering that she should give nothing away of who she really was in case it somehow got back to her father. 'Or, should I say, my mistress is here for the Season. I have to help her with, you know, her clothes and that sort of thing.'

She looked over at Dolly, whose tight smile suggested she was suppressing a laugh.

'I'm surprised your mistress allows you out in the evenings, particularly to frequent gaming houses.'

This time Dolly did laugh, which infected Lucy who tried and failed to suppress a small giggle. 'Well, what they don't know can't hurt them.'

'And she appears to be either a wealthy mistress, a

generous one or both.' He looked down at her gown, and she knew what he was thinking. It was unusual to see a lady's maid in the latest fashion. Perhaps she should not have worn her pale lavender silk gown, with its tight bodice, nipped-in waist and neckline that left the shoulders bare. It was among the dresses her uncle had ordered for her and she had intended to wear it to her first ball. Thanks to her father, she would miss that ball but had not wanted to miss the opportunity to wear this beautiful silk creation.

'Yes, she's very kind. Isn't she, Dolly?'

'The kindest mistress I've ever had,' Dolly replied. 'Although she hasn't passed on any of her gowns to me yet.'

Lucy took a quick sideways glance. Was Dolly blackmailing her? She started to laugh, and a reassured Lucy joined in, much to the confusion of the rakish Sebastian.

'Well, you both look lovely,' he said.

The clattering wheel stopped spinning, and the little white ball clinked into a red pocket, and Lucy, along with several other gamblers, gave a groan of disappointment.

'It seems I'm not bringing you any luck after all.'

She sent him what she hoped was a flirtatious smile. 'I wouldn't say that.' And she was delighted that he smiled back at her.

'What about you? Do you come here often?' she asked.

'On occasion. I know the owner. I've not placed any bets here before, though.'

Lucy suspected his visits to The Royal Flush were more than on occasion. The croupier had nodded his acknowledgement of him when they joined the table, and numerous women had tried to catch his eye, presumably women who had kept him company during previous visits. And who but a regular would claim to know the owner?

Oh yes. This man was a rake, through and through.

She handed him some of the chips. 'It seems we're both innocents at this then. Here, you place the bet this time.'

His hand lightly touched hers, his skin warm, and the strangest, most thrilling sensation moved up her arm to her chest and throughout her body, filling it with a radiant glow.

'Not too innocent, I hope,' he said, his hand still touching hers and giving her a meaningful look. Her heart, already beating unnaturally fast, increased its tempo, and blood pounded through her body into places she was sure it had never pounded before.

She wanted to say something suggestive back, something that would show him she wasn't a naive young woman and this was not her first encounter with a man, but she could think of nothing.

How to flirt with a rake in a gambling house had not been part of the etiquette lessons her uncle had arranged for her in preparation for the Season, so she merely smiled back in what she hoped was a coquettish manner.

His hand moved from hers, and her mind suddenly cleared. What she could have said was *Perhaps you'd like to find out just how innocent I am?* Or *What I'm thinking could never be described as* innocent. Or even *I might be innocent, but I'm sure you can teach me a thing or two.*

That was what a heroine in one of those forbidden books might have said, but she knew she would never do so.

He placed the chips on a white square, and the croupier once again spun the wheel. Despite her fanciful imaginings, Lucy knew this encounter could go no further than a bit of harmless flirtation, but oh, she was enjoying herself.

The white ball dropped into a red square with the same number on which Sebastian had placed his bet. Lucy jumped for joy as the croupier pushed a large number of chips in his direction.

'See, you are lucky,' she said, smiling up at him.

'I certainly feel lucky tonight.'

They held each other's gaze, and she knew exactly what his words meant. He was referring to her, not the pile of chips stacked up in front of him. A little shiver of apprehension skittered through her. Was she playing with fire? Perhaps she should extinguish that flame before she got burnt. He was a rake, after all, and she knew nothing of men.

'Your turn,' he said, handing her a pile of chips.

She smiled at him, ignoring any pesky inner warnings.

His hand once again touched hers, and this time he lightly stroked her palm as he did so. Lucy's breath caught in her throat. That wave of heat once again enveloped her, burning hotter, leaving her almost gasping.

She really should stop this now, but as if under the control of a different Lucy, one who was sophisticated, even risqué, she continued to hold his gaze.

'Perhaps this time you should blow on the chips for luck,' she said, her husky voice hardly recognisable.

'My pleasure.' He took both her hands in his, lifted them up to his lips and blew lightly, those captivating brown eyes still staring into hers. His soft breath moved gently over her sensitive skin, and a sigh escaped her lips.

The croupier coughed. 'Miss, are you going to place a bet?'

'Oh, um, yes.' Lucy placed several of the chips on a square she randomly selected.

The croupier spun the wheel again. It whirled round and round, but Lucy was more conscious of the lingering sensation of Sebastian's breath on her skin than she was of anything happening on the table.

The ball fell into a slot, people at the table moaned while some gave shouts of pleasure, and the croupier pulled in the piles of chips, including her own.

'That didn't work after all,' he said with mock disappointment.

Oh, but it did, Lucy wanted to say. It worked marvellously.

'Do you intend to place another bet?' he asked, looking down at the pile of chips. 'Or do you want me to try and bring you some more good luck?'

'We need to go,' Dolly said, lightly tapping her on the arm. 'Now.'

'What?' Lucy frowned in confusion. Could she really leave now and miss the chance to feel his breath on her skin one more time?

'The servants will soon be going to bed, and if we don't go now the doors will be locked when we get home, and we'll never get inside the house,' Dolly said, a note of trepidation entering her voice.

'Just one more spin,' she begged her lady's maid. 'My luck has to change soon. Blowing on the chips didn't do any good.' *Apart from being the most glorious thing that has ever happened to me.* 'Perhaps this time you can kiss me for luck,' she added quickly before her nerve faltered.

It was such a bold thing to say she could hardly believe the words she had been thinking had actually come out of her mouth.

'More than happy to oblige,' he said, wrapping his arm around her, a roguish smile curling his lips.

That smile was the last thing Lucy saw before he tipped her back over his arm as if she was completely weightless. She had expected a quick peck, but when his lips met hers, the kiss was neither quick nor a peck.

With only his arm stopping her from falling to the floor, she was completely at his mercy as his lips pressed onto hers, and oh, it felt good. She surrendered herself to the sensation of his rough skin rubbing against her cheek and his musky masculine scent and taste filling her senses. When his tongue ran along her bottom lip, she gasped in pleasure and surprise and hoped this kiss would last forever.

His hands held her closer. Her body was pressed hard against his, her breasts squashed into his chest, and Lucy knew this was exactly where she wanted to be.

Then it was over. He lifted her up, and she was once again standing on her own two feet, although as the room appeared to be spinning like a roulette wheel, she was grateful for his arm still around the small of her back.

'Lucy, we have to go.' Dolly pulled on her arm just as Sebastian released her. 'We are in danger of getting caught.'

He gathered up all the chips, took Lucy's reticule from her wrist and placed the coloured discs inside.

'Goodbye, Lucy. I think you better go if you're not to get in trouble.'

She nodded, knowing that if anyone, especially her father, found out what she'd just done she would be in more trouble than she could possibly imagine.

'Enjoy your time in London, and hopefully I will see you here again sometime.'

He handed her back her reticule, and she gazed at him. She thought hard to find something to say, anything, preferably something witty and memorable, but no words came.

'Come on,' Dolly said urgently, and Lucy allowed herself to be dragged through the jostling crowd and out the doors at the front of the gaming house.

The doors closed behind them, and the cool night-time air hit her burning cheeks.

'Quickly, miss. We have to get home.' Dolly took her arm, and they ran down the alleyway. The moment they reached the busy road, Dolly signalled a hansom cab, gave the driver the address and bundled Lucy inside.

The cab clattered off down the busy cobbled streets and the two women looked at each other then burst into laughter.

'Was that the sort of fun you were after?' Dolly asked.

'Oh, Dolly, thank you so much. Tonight was wonderful.' She placed her fingers lightly on her still throbbing lips. 'My first kiss.'

'And what a kiss,' Dolly said still laughing and fanning herself as if she too had been overcome by the intensity of it. 'I wonder if the earl's kisses will be so passionate.'

The earl.

Lucy's high spirits evaporated. Tonight was an exciting escape from reality, but in two days she would be meeting the man her father expected her to marry, and her life was in danger of going back to being dull, tedious and predictable.

'Don't look so sad, miss,' Dolly said. 'Maybe the earl will be as attractive as Sebastian. Maybe his kisses will be just as delicious.'

Lucy could hear the disbelief in her voice, and her heart sank even further.

Tonight was supposed to make her feel better, but all it had done was increase her yearning for freedom, intensify her need to have laughter in her life and show her how much she wanted a man to look at her with desire in his eyes.

And that was not going to be found with a man her father had selected for her. Somehow she was going to have to make sure the Earl of Rothwell did not see her as the prim and proper wife he sought.

Once the ordeal of this weekend was over, she could have the Season she dreamt of. She could find the life she wanted with a man who made her feel the way Sebastian had tonight—a man who would not just desire her but who could give her something more meaningful than the kisses of a rake: a man who could love her.

Chapter Four

Dorset, two days later

If Sebastian needed any reminder as to why it was essential for him to marry a young woman of upstanding character, hearing of his mother's recent return to England would have provided it. But he did not need a reminder. It was impossible for him to forget the curse that had hung over his family since the 1st Earl of Rothwell had acquired the title back in the sixteenth century.

It was a curse that had moved down from generation to generation, but it would end with him. The shame of having countess after countess plunging the family into yet another scandal would not happen while he was Earl of Rothwell. His wife would be a paragon of virtue. His children would not be abandoned by a mother who would rather run off with her lover than take on her maternal responsibilities. His children would not be teased mercilessly at school because the gutter press had written about the family's troubles in excruciating detail. His children would not experience the anguish of feeling unloved and unwanted.

With that in mind he waited on the steps of his Dorset estate and watched the carriages roll up the long, tree-lined driveway. If Miss Everhart was half as respectable as his aunt had painted her, then by the end of this weekend he might be betrothed, and the ordeal of finding a wife who met all his requirements would be over before it had hardly begun.

He was not deluded enough to expect a love match. No one in his position did, but he was determined to do everything in his power to make his marriage one in which they would both be content.

To that end he was prepared to sacrifice his London lifestyle. The parties and clubs would become a thing of the past, and there would certainly be no more flirting with pretty lady's maids, even if that flirting had led to nothing more risqué than a kiss.

He smiled in remembrance of Little Lucy as he had affectionately come to think of her. She was a delightful bundle of energy, but if Miss Everhart proved to be what he was seeking, then there would be no more Little Lucies or any other women in his life.

Instead, he would settle down with this daughter of a clergyman, one who had acceptable family connections on both her mother's and her father's sides. As the third son of an earl, her father had done what was expected of him and joined the Church, but Sebastian's aunt claimed that unlike many third sons, the Reverend Everhart took his duties seriously. He was said to be a pious man who had instilled that piety into his only child.

The carriages finally crunched to a halt on the gravel driveway. The footman on the first jumped down, lowered the steps and opened the door, and a tall thin man, dressed entirely in black, apart from the distinctive white collar of a clergyman, stepped out.

'My lord,' he said with a low bow. 'It is an honour to meet you.'

'And you, Reverend Everhart,' Sebastian responded with a nod of his head, then looked up at the carriage door.

The reverend also turned to the carriage. 'May I present my daughter, Miss Lucinda Everhart.'

A young lady placed her small foot on the top step and climbed down, her head modestly lowered, her face hidden by a wide-brimmed hat.

She reached the bottom step and slowly lifted her head, her eyes still lowered.

Sebastian looked from daughter to father then back again.

What sort of jest was this? What was Lucy the lady's maid doing passing herself off as a clergyman's daughter?

He looked back to the clergyman for answers, but the man's serious expression was giving nothing away.

The impostor stepped forward and raised her eyes.

She stopped midstep. Her eyes grew enormous. Her mouth fell open.

Sebastian waited for an explanation as to what sort of game these people were playing.

'Come, Lucinda, now is not the time for shyness,' the reverend urged, waving her forward. He turned back to Sebastian while the daughter, the lady's maid or whoever the hell she was remained standing near the carriage as if incapable of moving.

'Lucinda has of course led a sheltered life. She has not long been out in Society and is not usually quite so reserved. Once you get to know her you will find she has a lively spirit.'

Was that a hidden message the man was sending him? Was that what this was all about? Did he know all about his daughter's *lively spirit* and he had been set up? Was that kiss she had extracted from him a means to ensnare him in marriage? Would he now be forced to continue the family curse and marry a woman of low moral character?

Well, if they planned to blackmail him into this marriage, they had made a fateful mistake. One they would come to regret.

He glared back at the daughter, intending to unsettle her, so she would realise her base scheming would not work on him.

Her eyes remained lowered, as if she were incapable of looking him in the eye. He turned back to the father. His impassive, rather dour expression suggested he was either a consummate actor or, more likely, the daughter was pulling the wool over his eyes just as surely as she had over Sebastian's.

'Come on, Lucinda,' the father coaxed. 'Come and be introduced to the earl.'

Miss Everhart shuffled forward, still staring down at the ground.

Sebastian was tempted to bundle her back into the carriage along with her poor, deluded father and send her on her way. But she had also aroused his curiosity. While she would be getting nothing from him, and certainly not a proposal of marriage, he was curious to know what her scam actually involved.

'Miss Everhart,' he said with a bow, keeping his eyes firmly on her to ascertain the extent of her subterfuge.

Her eyes still lowered she made a clumsy curtsy. 'My lord,' she said in a barely audible voice.

Oh, she was good. If he hadn't already met her, he would assume she had the right credentials and the right level of modesty he was seeking in the next Countess of Rothwell. She was even dressed in an appropriately demure manner.

Gone was the tempting hint of cleavage he had seen on the night they met. Gone were the naked shoulders covered only in diaphanous lace. Today she was shrouded from neck to foot in a muted shade of pale brown, a dark brown travelling cloak draped around her shoulders, the only concession to vanity being a small amount of white lace around her high neckline.

Nothing, however, could disguise those tempting lips. Nor did the modest dress completely conceal the luscious curves of her body, curves that he had felt when he'd held her in his arms.

Thank goodness he *had* met her before and seen her true character, or right now he might be falling for her abundant charms and would be in danger of continuing the Rothwell curse.

She looked up at him through lowered eyelashes. 'I am so pleased to make your acquaintance,' she mumbled. 'For the first time.'

Sebastian was tempted to scoff at her performance. It was clear she did not want her past behaviour revealed to her father, and yes, he would play along with her charade. For now. It was not up to him to inform the naive reverend of his daughter's true character. The man would no doubt find that out for himself eventually. But that was the only concession he would make to the untrustworthy Miss Everhart.

'Your estate is magnificent,' the reverend said, looking up at the three-storey façade of Rothwell Hall, as if there was nothing untoward about this situation.

'Thank you,' Sebastian said and wanted to add that despite what they may hope, his daughter would never be living here, and even though it was plain to see he was a wealthy man, she would not be extracting one penny of money from him or succeeding in any other nefarious plan she might have in mind.

'Please, come in,' he said instead, with as much politeness as he could summon. 'The housekeeper will show you to your rooms.'

The reverend took his daughter's arm and led her up the steps into the house.

Sebastian followed on behind, his eyes never leaving Miss Everhart. As soon as they were settled, he would find some excuse to get her alone so he could find out exactly what she was up to. Then he would let this scheming minx know in no uncertain terms that she had picked the wrong man on whom to play her tricks.

Numb. That was the only word Lucy could use to describe how she was feeling, should anyone ask. Or perhaps *dazed*, *shocked*, and *gripped* by a peculiar sensation that appeared to have taken her out of her reality and plunged her into a bizarre dream or nightmare.

Her Sebastian was also Sebastian Kingsley, the Earl of Rothwell. It simply could not be possible. And yet it was.

When she'd first looked up at him and seen his handsome face she had almost smiled, delighted that the man she had been thinking about constantly for the last two days was standing before her in all his marvellous glory. It was as if she had conjured him up in a wonderful act of magic.

She had been saved. Sebastian had saved her. Her father was not hoping to marry her off to a dull, boorish earl but to the most handsome, enticing man she had ever met, a man whose kiss had made her feel as if the earth was moving beneath her feet.

This was surely a dream come true. Then as quickly as that thought occurred to her, reality came crashing down. If it was her Sebastian she was standing in front of, then why was he scowling at her as if she was some lowlife that had deemed to appear in his exalted presence?

The answer to that was obvious. This Sebastian was expecting a pious clergyman's daughter. Despite being a rake who frequented gambling dens and kissed lady's maids, he wanted a wife who was above reproach, and that now excluded her.

Not only that, but his expression told her loud and clear that he judged her severely for her behaviour, even though she had done nothing he had not done himself.

It seemed as far as the earl was concerned, while she was good enough to kiss, she certainly was not good enough to be his wife. Despite being handsome, despite having rakish charm, it was obvious the Earl of Rothwell was a hypocrite.

From that moment it had been impossible to look at him. All she had wanted to do was climb back in the carriage and order the driver to take her as far away from Rothwell Estate as it was possible to travel.

But how could she explain her reaction to her father?

So instead, she had held her breath and prayed the earl would say nothing about their previous meeting. This man now had the power to destroy her, and from his contemptuous expression Lucy suspected nothing would give him more pleasure than to do so.

Fortunately, he had said nothing. Yet.

Her throat dry, her head spinning, she walked up the steps to his house, sure that this weekend would not end well for her.

Once inside, the friendly housekeeper appeared and took charge of the guests. She nattered away as she led Lucy up the wide wooden staircase and along the seemingly endless hallway to her bedchamber. Lucy nodded politely, not hearing a word she said and, the moment the woman left, staggered to the nearest armchair and collapsed into it.

There had been no mistaking the expression on the earl's face when he saw her. His surprise had quickly turned to barely contained outrage. But the question was, what was he going to do now? Was he merely biding his time before he exposed her? Was he going to stage some dramatic revelation so he could cause the most damage? One way or another, she knew she was going to be called to account for that one transgression.

The door opened, and Dolly burst in, her startled countenance mirroring Lucy's.

'Oh, miss! What are we going to do?' she asked before collapsing into the facing chair. 'If your father finds out, you'll be...and I'll be...we'll be... What are we going to do?'

Remembering herself, Dolly quickly stood up. 'Sorry, miss.'

Lucy signalled for her to take a seat. If Dolly's legs were as wobbly as Lucy's, then she, too, would need to sit before she collapsed.

'Thank you, miss,' Dolly said, sitting down with slightly more formality.

'I suppose we should take some solace in him not saying anything yet,' Lucy said. 'That gives us some time to think of something that will get us out of this situation.'

Dolly nodded and furrowed her brow. The furrow grew deeper. Despite her greater worldliness, her maid was struggling as hard as Lucy to concoct a plan.

'He did look right shocked to see you, miss,' Dolly finally said. 'I was watching from the other carriage, and he appeared about to burst into flames he was so hot and bothered. I suppose when you kiss a woman you think is a lady's maid, you don't expect her to turn up at your estate a few days later.'

'That's right,' Lucy said slowly, taking in what

Dolly had said. 'He thought I was a lady's maid. He kissed a maid.'

Dolly tilted her head in question.

'Don't you see?' Lucy sat up straighter in her chair. 'He has as much to worry about as we do. He's probably terrified that I'm going to expose him as a low-down rake who goes around seducing servants.'

Dolly's head remained tilted, and she gnawed on the edge of her lip, showing that she had not yet grasped what Lucy was saying.

'He probably thinks he can expose me, but I can tell him that if he does, I will let it be known that he kissed a servant.'

Dolly's furrow deepened. 'I'm not sure if that will work, miss. And, well, begging your pardon, but I'm also not sure if it matters much if men get such a reputation. Especially an earl, and one who is eligible and extremely wealthy.'

'Well, it should.'

'Yes, miss, it should, but…there might be another way out of this, where your father never discovers what you've been up to.'

Lucy waited while Dolly gnawed on her lip with more vigour.

'Usually if a gentleman kisses a debutante, he is expected to marry her,' she said quietly. 'You're here to see if the earl would make a suitable husband, and, well, you did enjoy his kiss.'

Memory of that kiss surged through Lucy. She

could almost feel his arms around her, his body pressed against hers, could all but taste that intoxicating masculinity. Then another more recent memory crashed in, driving away that heavenly image: the way he looked at her when he had seen her standing in front of the carriage. The disdain that had curled those lips, the haughty manner in which he'd glared down his nose at her, and her rapturous smile had turned to a frown.

'You did say his kisses made you giddy,' Dolly added unhelpfully. 'That it was as if you were floating up in the stars. As if you had been transported to paradise.'

'I was being overly poetic.'

'Even so, such a kiss does bode well for your wedding night.'

Her wedding night.

Warmth coursed through her body as she considered Dolly's idea. Marriage to the earl would surely not be a bad thing if she could once again experience his kisses? More than his kisses. And experience them night after night.

She shook her head lightly to drive out such foolishness.

The man she met in The Royal Flush was not the man she would be married to. While they superficially looked the same, just as handsome, just as superbly masculine, they also looked completely different.

Dressed in a light grey suit and blue-and-white

striped shirt, the earl looked a lot less rakish than he had in formal evening wear, although no less appealing. But that was where the similarity ended. Her Sebastian gave every appearance that he knew how to enjoy himself. This new Sebastian looked like a man who had never laughed in his life and was thoroughly disapproving and unforgiving, not to mention a hypocrite.

No, she could not marry the Earl of Rothwell. She knew exactly what her married life would be like. She'd be stuck away in the country, in this luxurious mausoleum, while he was off in London enjoying himself with women who frequented places like The Royal Flush.

That would never do, but Dolly had raised an important point.

'You're right,' she said. 'When a gentleman kisses a debutante, he *is* expected to do the right thing and make an offer of marriage.' She nodded slowly. 'The earl must be quaking in his highly polished boots at the prospect of having to marry me.'

She leant forward and took Dolly's hands. 'Don't you see? He does not have all the power after all.'

That dubious expression on her maid's face reappeared.

'He has made it clear he wants a respectable wife,' she added, feeling more confident with every word. 'If he hadn't met me in The Royal Flush, he might have assumed that was exactly what I was. A nice, obedient daughter of a clergyman who he could imprison in the countryside until she provided him with his heir.'

She moved slightly in her chair, trying not to think about what providing that heir would entail.

'While he goes off doing whatever he wants with any woman who takes his fancy,' she added with a scowl. 'This is all a blessing in disguise. He most certainly doesn't want to marry me. I don't want to marry him. We both have good reason for keeping our first meeting a secret.'

She sat back in her chair and smiled to herself. 'All I have to do is get the earl alone as soon as possible so I can clearly explain the situation to him before he ruins everything for both of us and says something he shouldn't to my father.'

Chapter Five

It was a different Lucinda Everhart entirely who strode into the drawing room an hour later. Sebastian noted that once again she was incongruously dressed, very demurely, in a plain grey skirt and white blouse, with a high white lace collar covering half her neck, but the gaze was no longer lowered in a pretence of modesty.

Those big blue eyes stared straight at him. That perky little nose was lifted in the air. It was an attitude that could best be described as *defiant*.

'There you are, my dear,' her father said. 'The earl was just telling me about his home. Do you know there has been a house on this very spot since the sixteenth century…since the time of the first Earl of Rothwell?'

'Fascinating,' she drawled, her manner suggesting she found his lineage an irrelevance.

'And the estate has twelve thousand acres,' her father added. 'Just imagine that…twelve thousand acres.'

'Yes, that's an awful lot of countryside,' she said in that same dismissive tone.

Sebastian suppressed his irritation. Once again, he had no idea what she was playing at, but the sooner he got this over and done with, the better. It was time to have that private talk. He turned towards the father. 'With your permission, I'd like to take your daughter for a stroll around some of that countryside and show her the estate.'

'Capital idea,' her father said. 'A stroll will be just the thing.'

'Yes, I'd love to see the estate,' Miss Everhart said, suddenly showing some enthusiasm. 'But Father, I'm sure you'll be wanting to rest after that long, tiring journey. Dolly can chaperone me. You should finish your tea…and didn't you say you wanted to add a little more to your next sermon? Something about the overstimulating effects of too much laughter?'

'Yes, you're quite right, my dear. My Lucinda is always thinking of others,' he said to Sebastian. 'You two go for a long, invigorating walk. It will give you a chance to get to know each other.'

Sebastian ordered some more tea for Reverend Everhart, and once the lady's maid arrived, they set off, out the house and into the garden, the wayward chaperone following at a discreet distance.

While they were still in sight of the house, Sebastian remained silent, and anyone watching would indeed think they were a couple meeting for the first time who were awkward in each other's company.

'What is your game?' he asked the moment they turned into the formal garden and several large topiaries meant they were no longer visible from the drawing room windows.

'My game? I'm not the one that plays games,' she said, her voice just as irate as his own.

'Before this charade continues a moment longer, I want to spell it out to you. Whatever trick you are trying to pull, you will not get away with it.'

She stopped walking and glared at him.

She glared at *him* as if she were the aggrieved party.

'I am playing no game. I am pulling no tricks. And you, of all people, have no right to take that tone with me.'

He stifled his anger, commenced walking and forced himself to remain calm. 'All right. Let's start at the beginning. Why did you lie to me?'

'I did not lie to you.'

'So you are Lucy, the lady's maid?'

'Oh, yes, that. Well, yes, I did lie about that, I suppose.' She gave a small laugh as if that made everything all right. 'But I had good reason. I wanted to—'

'Did you have me followed?' he interrupted, not wanting to listen to any further lies. 'Was that how you knew I'd be at The Royal Flush? Was that what you were up to? Were you intending to put me in a compromising position?'

'What? No?' She frowned at him. 'None of this is my fault. And if you didn't go around kissing servants, you wouldn't be in this position, would you?'

Sebastian's teeth clenched tightly together. 'I do not go around kissing servants,' he said seething, hardly able to believe she would accuse him of wrongdoing. 'And if you remember correctly, you asked me to kiss you.'

Colour tinged her cheeks, her expression revealing her discomfort.

'I demand an explanation,' he continued, refusing to be affected by her apparent embarrassment. 'What were you up to? Is it blackmail you intend? Are you after money? Or are you expecting a marriage proposal?'

She stopped walking and stared up at him. 'You think I did all this deliberately, don't you?'

There was no reason for him to answer that, so he didn't.

'I didn't know who you were when we met in The Royal Flush. I thought you were just some rake, out having a good time. I don't want your money, and I most certainly do not want to marry you.'

Sebastian stared down at her as he digested this claim. She continued to glare up at him, her chin lifted in challenge.

Her outrage appeared genuine, but she had already shown herself to be an accomplished liar.

'So what were you playing at? Why did you lie to me?'

She looked back at the house, then shrugged. That was all the answer he needed. She did not want her father to know she lived this double life, one where she was the devoted, obedient daughter of a clergyman, another where she went about giving herself freely to men in gaming houses.

'I know a debutante should not sneak out to gambling dens, nor should they, well, kiss anyone.' She shrugged again and lightly bit her lip. 'But it was just a bit of fun, and no one was supposed to find out.'

'Really?' he said in disbelief.

'Oh, don't sound so judgemental. I did nothing you didn't also do. You too were in a gaming house. You too were kissing a stranger, and worse than that, you kissed a servant when you're an earl. That's disgusting.'

'Again, I'll remind you that you asked me to kiss you.'

'Oh, all right. Yes, I asked you to kiss me.'

'And it was disgusting?'

Her cheeks flushed a deeper shade of red. 'Well, no, the kiss was not disgusting.' She blinked several times then lifted her head high. 'What was disgusting was that you would kiss a lady's maid. Especially,' she pointed a finger in his face, 'especially as you expect your future bride to be oh-so-respectable, when you're off frequenting dives and seducing servants.'

'I do not seduce servants,' he said slowly, enunciating each word and hoping to make her finally grasp that simple fact. 'I was at The Royal Flush visiting the owner. I was leaving his office when I collided with a young lady who insisted I join her at the roulette table.'

She continued to glower at him, although the way her eyebrows crinkled together in a frown suggested she was starting to remember the correct sequence of events.

'And I didn't seduce the so-called lady's maid. All that happened was a pretty young lady asked me to kiss her for luck, and I obliged.'

Those eyebrows crinkled further, and she resumed her rapid blinking, as if finally, *finally*, she was realising that she was the one in the wrong.

'Are we in agreement that I was not out seducing servants?'

'All right, I suppose so. But you don't deny you expect your bride to be held to a much higher standard than the ones by which you live?'

'On that point you will get no argument from me.'

'So you admit it. You are a hypocrite.' She placed her hands on her hips, and her expression became smug, as if she had tricked him into admitting something he had not meant to.

'I am an earl. It is my duty to marry and produce an heir, and I wish my wife to be a respectable woman who will not bring shame on the Rothwell name.' *Further shame* he could add, but he was not going to discuss his unfortunate family history with this irrational young woman.

'And while you leave some poor respectable woman trapped out here in the countryside, you'll be living it up in London with your mistresses and seducing every servant girl unfortunate enough to come your way.'

He resisted the temptation to repeat, yet again, that he did not seduce servant girls.

'Just to make things clear, I take it you are not expecting a proposal from me, despite our kiss,' he said instead.

'You?' she all but squawked. 'You think I would want a proposal from you? You think I want to marry you?'

'I take it that is a *no*.'

'You take it correctly.'

'Then, I suggest we get through this weekend as best we can and then go our separate ways.'

'Agreed.' She gave one definite nod, then lightly bit her bottom lip. 'Um…'

She paused. He waited, his eyes drawn to her lower lip, being tormented by those little white teeth. The memory of their kiss entered his mind. Damn. He did not want to think about that kiss. He did not want to remember what her lips tasted like, or how her soft breasts had felt, pressed against his chest, or what it was like to encircle her small waist.

'Um…what?' he said more sternly than he intended as he tried to drive out that image.

'Um... I would be grateful if you did not mention to my father where we met.'

'Of course I won't mention it.'

'Good. And I promise I won't tell anyone about you being a rake who seduces servant girls.'

'I am not a rake. I do not seduce servant girls,' he said, louder than he intended.

'Exactly, and that is what I'll say if anyone asks me,' she said with a teasing laugh.

'My God, do you try your hardest to be exasperating?'

'Of course not.'

'It comes naturally, does it?'

Her eyebrows once again crinkled. He hadn't noticed before, but her dark brown eyebrows were a striking contrast to her blond hair. Perhaps it was that dramatic contrast which elevated her above being merely pretty. Or was it the colour of her eyes, a deep blue that recalled a clear sky on a warm summer's day? Whatever it was, it mattered not, and now was certainly not the time to think about her appealing good looks.

'I am not exasperating at all,' she stated, those blue eyes sparkling.

'I believe that is a matter of opinion.'

She humphed out an inarticulate reply. 'Anyway, it would be cruel to say anything. I don't think my father's heart would be able to take the shock.'

'Perhaps you should have thought of that before you visited The Royal Flush.'

'And it would be terrible for Dolly,' she continued as if he hadn't spoken. 'She might lose her position if Father found out.'

'I can see your father is correct. You only ever think of others,' he said, his tone heavy with sarcasm. 'And if your father did find out about your maid's behaviour it would be no less than she deserved.' He looked over his shoulder towards where the girl should be and was not surprised to discover she had wandered off and left them alone.

'No.' She stopped walking. Her hand grabbed his arm, her eyes looked up at him, appealing. 'Please. You can punish me in any way you like, but please, don't punish Dolly. You must know what happens to servants who are dismissed from their position. They never get another job, and life for such a woman is, well it's—'

'I have no intention of causing any harm to your lady's maid, nor do I intend to punish you.'

She exhaled slowly and dropped her hand from his arm.

'You obviously think I'm a monster.' He waited for her to contradict this. She didn't. 'But even if I were the type of man who liked to punish young women, I am sure you are more than aware that it is also in my best interest to keep our meeting a secret. Your father would be well within his rights to insist that we wed, and neither of us wants that.'

She gave a mock shudder. 'No, that would be frightful.'

Despite his annoyance with her, he couldn't help but smile at her reaction.

She smiled back at him. That lovely, winsome smile that had first attracted him in The Royal Flush.

There was no denying she was appealing, but she was also exasperating, impetuous and far too unpredictable, and he wanted her out of his life as quickly and as quietly as possible so he could get back to his task of finding a suitable bride.

Lucy continued to smile. That had gone so much better than she had expected or hoped. She was now safe. Safe from her father finding out about her misdeeds, and safe from an unwanted marriage.

Her smile faltered. It might have been more flattering if he hadn't been quite so adamant that he did not want to marry her, but as she didn't want to marry him either, then she could hardly object. Could she?

No, of course she could not. She was now free to get on with enjoying the Season, and Sebastian could get on with finding a woman he did want to marry.

They continued to walk along in silence, and she fought to ignore the sudden gnawing sensation in the pit of her stomach. It could not be jealousy for the woman he would marry, a countess who did not yet exist, could it?

Of course it couldn't. Yes, she might envy the woman who was going to experience his kisses. After all, she knew from personal experience just how glorious they were, but the price would be too high. Wouldn't it? Yes, of course it would.

That woman might be lucky enough to marry the sublimely handsome Sebastian, but she would also be stuck out in the country for the rest of her life and expected to behave in a respectable manner at all times. Being held in his arms, kissed senseless and taken by an experienced rake would be no compensation for such a life. None whatsoever.

She just wished that throbbing sensation had not once again erupted deep inside her, the one that always consumed her whenever she remembered his kiss.

And even if the thought of his kiss did elicit such a reaction, that meant nothing. She was wholly incompatible with this judgemental man, and having a handsome husband who was a good kisser, make that a great…make that a *spectacular* kisser was not enough foundation for a happy marriage.

'Now that we have no more to discuss in private, shall we return to the house?' he said coming to a halt. He obviously now wanted rid of her.

'Yes, I suppose so,' she murmured, trying not to sound disappointed. 'So what are you going to say to my father?'

'I have already said I intend to tell him nothing of what happened at The Royal Flush.'

'Yes, I know, but what reason are you going to give him for deciding that I am far too repugnant for you to ever consider taking as your bride.'

'He would never believe that I find you repugnant.'

'No, I suppose not. He is my father after all and somewhat biased. You'll have to think of something else to tell him.'

'What do you suggest?'

'Do you want me to take an inventory of my faults?'

'Yes, and don't worry, we have plenty of time.'

She looked up at him and was pleased to see that a smile accompanied what would otherwise have been an insult. Although maybe it would be better if he didn't. That smile reminded her too much of the charming man she had seen in The Royal Flush, the man whose kisses had turned her body to jelly and made her feel woozy. She did not need to be thinking of that now, so she once again looked straight ahead and commenced walking.

'I suppose you could say you find me too immature. Father is always accusing me of that.'

'I wonder why.'

'It's because he confuses wanting to enjoy oneself with being immature. He thinks a mature young lady should be content to spend her time sitting still in church and listening to interminable sermons on the perils of vice and the rewards of a virtuous life, even though vice always sounds like so much more fun than virtue ever could.'

'All right, I'll tell him you are far too immature, and I suspect you would fidget in church.'

She laughed at what she assumed was a joke. 'You might need something a bit more objectionable than that.'

'Are there any other faults you are willing to admit to?'

'I never actually admitted to being immature. I just said Father thinks I am. And I don't think it really is a fault at all. Not if it means enjoying oneself and taking pleasure in all that life has to offer. That should not be reserved just for children.'

'If you say so.'

'For a rake you really are an old stick in the mud, aren't you?'

'I'm not a rake.'

She stopped walking and looked up at him. 'Oh, come. Of course you're a rake. You frequent gambling dens in the less salubrious parts of town. You kiss lady's maids. You're...' She was about to say dangerously good-looking but had no desire to flatter him and certainly did not want him to think she saw him as the sort of man who could have his way with a debutante, should he choose. Although, after what had happened between them at The Royal Flush, he probably already knew that.

'I've explained why I was at The Royal Flush and

why I kissed that particular lady's maid,' he said, once again sounding like the haughty Earl of Rothwell.

'Yes, and I'm sure most rakes are more than capable of explaining away their behaviour.'

He huffed out a loud breath. 'But it hardly matters. We are not discussing my faults. We are discussing yours and the reasons I can give your father for not marrying you.'

'Hmm, let's see. My faults? I'm afraid they are few and far between. In most respects I am close to perfection.'

'Perhaps I could say you lack sufficient humility.'

She laughed, assuming he had made another joke.

'Maybe you could tell him I'm far too serious, too studious and too pious.'

His black eyebrows rose. 'I suspect your father would believe that as readily as he would believe that I found you repugnant.'

'Yes, maybe, but if you said I was far too well-behaved, he might grant me a bit more freedom.'

'That's the last thing you need.'

'That's easy for you to say. You haven't spent the last twenty years locked away in a vicarage, expected to spend your time embroidering ever more samplers, with only the thought of a Sunday outing to church to look forward to.'

'In other words, you have had a very similar upbringing to most young ladies of your class.'

'Yes, unfortunately,' she said, shaking her head. 'A

rake like you could never understand just how horrid it is.'

'I am not a—'

She cut him off with a laugh before he could make that now familiar denial. 'If you're not going to say I'm too pious to be your countess, perhaps you could say I'm far too quiet and shy.'

Once again, those disbelieving eyebrows rose up his high forehead. 'Your father described you as having a *lively spirit*, so it is unlikely he would believe that.'

'Yes, you're right. This is all rather difficult, isn't it?'

'I should simply say we are incompatible. I'll tell your father that I have tried to find common ground with you and failed and would therefore like to continue in my search for the future countess.'

'Yes, good idea. Tell the truth. That's always the best way to go.'

Those criticising eyebrows rose again and she waited for another reminder of the necessary lie she had told him when they first met.

'Although, your father might find it surprising that I could come to such a conclusion after one short walk,' he thankfully said instead.

'Yes, I suppose so.' She smiled to herself as an appealing thought occurred to her. 'Perhaps I should stay the full weekend after all. That way you can really get to know me and discover just how ghastly I am.'

'Yes, that might be for the best,' he said then

laughed, which hopefully meant he didn't find her entirely ghastly.

She smiled up at him, and her heart seemed to swell. The prospect of spending the rest of the weekend with the earl was not entirely loathsome. In fact, now that they had come to an amicable agreement that they were not to wed, it was not objectionable in the least.

Chapter Six

Sebastian was certain he could easily inform Reverend Everhart there would be no marriage between him and Miss Everhart. However, now that it was clear she had no ulterior motives of marriage or blackmail, he had no objections to her staying for the rest of the weekend.

Her company was not entirely unpleasant, and if his decision regarding whom to marry was based purely on physical attributes, then Miss Everhart would certainly leave nothing to be desired. He could not remember when he had seen lips more enticing, and despite her demure dress there was no way she could hide that voluptuous, curvy body.

'I suppose this is what you'll do when you're seeking a woman who has the requisites to become a countess,' she said, breaking in on his thoughts at a most opportune time. Thinking about Miss Everhart's curves was not only unacceptable, it was foolhardy. He had succumbed to temptation once. To do so now he knew she was a debutante would be a very bad idea.

'What? Stroll around the estate?'

'Yes, show off to her all that might be hers if she plays her cards right.' She gave a little laugh, one that tinkled like the soft chiming of bells. 'Or perhaps not *play her cards*. We already know you don't want a gambler for a wife.'

He was grateful for the timely reminder of why she was wholly unsuitable. 'It is a good way for a couple to get to know each other, is it not?'

'And for you to impress the candidate with what she stands to gain.'

'I take it from your tone of voice you are not impressed.'

'No, I'm afraid not. I grew up in Cheshire surrounded by more pastoral landscapes than one can shake a stick at. Beautiful scenery, well laid-out gardens and tree-lined rivers are all very nice, but they're all a bit dull, aren't they?'

He looked around at his estate, which was considered to be one of the finest in the land, with its rolling manicured lawns that took teams of men to keep in trim, its herbaceous border that had burst into flower, with spring bulbs dotted among forget-me-nots and lobelia, and the woodlands full of trees planted centuries earlier, then over to the man-made lake with its fountains defying gravity and shooting plumes of water high into the sky.

His gardeners would be horrified to hear this described as *a bit dull*, as would the landscape designer who had worked so hard to achieve such beauty.

'I dare say it's all a matter of opinion,' he said.

'And I dare say that if you were facing the prospect of being stuck out here forever, with only yet more embroidery to keep you busy and the occasional visit to the local village to look forward to, you would also be of the opinion that it was dreadfully boring.'

'Is that what you assume I will be offering my future wife?'

'Isn't it?'

Sebastian thought for a moment, unsure how to answer, as it was not something he had given much consideration. 'Isn't that what most debutantes seek? A good marriage, preferably to a titled man, a home of their own, ideally one as extensive as Rothwell Hall?'

'Well, if it is, they have my sympathies.'

'So what do you seek, Miss Everhart?'

'I seek for you to call me Lucy, at least when we are alone. And as you have already introduced yourself as Sebastian, that is what I will call you.'

'As you wish, Lucy. So what is it you seek? Do you wish to make a good marriage, or do you intend to spend all your time in gambling dens?'

She shrugged her shoulder. 'Yes, I do expect to marry, but I want to have some fun before I do. To dance, to laugh, to be free to experience all of what

London has to offer.' She smiled with an exuberance he had to admit was rather delightful.

'And when I do marry, I hope to continue having fun with a man who also likes to enjoy himself and doesn't want to stick me away in the country to die of boredom.'

Tension gripped Sebastian's jaw. Fun, freedom, new experiences—weren't these the things that were sought by his mother? Hadn't every other woman who bore the title Countess of Rothwell put their own pleasure ahead of duty? And they, too, no doubt had delightful smiles that captivated men.

'And what of your responsibilities? Marriage is not all fun and games, you know.' Sebastian was aware he was sounding somewhat bombastic but could not rein in his annoyance that she was exactly the sort of woman who had brought so much shame on his family. 'A wife is expected to support her husband, not to go off gallivanting whenever the mood takes her. And what of your children? Would you be abandoning them so you could just enjoy yourself?'

'Of course not, but I will make sure my children enjoy their lives.'

'I believe there is more to motherhood than that.'

'Is there? Well, I believe the most important thing about being a mother is making sure your children are happy.'

'Hmm' was the only response he was prepared to give.

'So what was your mother like?' she asked. 'Was she terribly serious, and did she teach you that you had to marry a sensible, responsible woman who never wanted to have any fun?'

'I don't know. My mother left when I was two.' A familiar barb pierced his heart at the mention of that woman. That was why he chose not to mention her unless absolutely necessary, and he wished he had not done so now.

She stopped walking and placed her hand on his arm. 'I'm so sorry. My mother left me as well. I mean, she died in childbirth.'

She gave him a sad smile. 'Even though I never knew her, I still miss her terribly. Sometimes when I'm unhappy I can feel her hugging me.' She laughed lightly. 'It's a bit silly I suppose.'

'Not if the thought gave you comfort as a child,' he said. 'I too sometimes have a vague feeling, a memory perhaps, of the scent of violets and being enfolded in warm arms.'

'That sounds lovely,' she said quietly. 'I must admit even now, though I am no longer a child, I still often imagine my mother hugging me.'

She linked her arm through his, as if offering that elusive comfort, or taking some for herself, and they resumed walking.

Sebastian never revealed anything about his mother to anyone and had no idea why he had done so to Lucy, of all people. Perhaps it was simply that she, too, knew what it was like to be without a mother, but her mother had not chosen to leave.

'I sometimes wonder if my childhood might have been different if Mother had lived,' she said, as much to herself as to him. 'Maybe Father would not have been so stern. Maybe I would not have been kept so isolated from the so-called corrupt world.'

She looked up at him and smiled, that sad smile making him want to take her in his arms and ease her unhappiness.

'I know you think me silly and impetuous and that I only ever think about enjoying myself,' she said. 'But if you had been stuck out in the countryside for your entire life, not allowed to have friends because your father was certain they'd be a bad influence on you, would you not be seeking fun and laughter and the chance to enjoy yourself?'

'Perhaps,' he responded, conceding that for a bright, spirited young woman, such a life would be like a lonely jail sentence. 'I was sent off to school at seven, and while that was not exactly a pleasant experience, I did make good friends there, which made it tolerable.'

On both counts he was understating the truth. School had been torture, and his two closest friends, Thomas Hayward and Isaac Redcliff, had provided solace and a constant source of strength.

'I did on occasion sneak out to play with the local children,' she confided.

'Why does that not surprise me?' he said, and she playfully swatted his arm.

'But I always had to be careful Father never found out. That is why I intend to take full advantage of being out for the Season and enjoying all the sights of a great city.'

It was easy to imagine her on the dance floor, being whirled around by countless men wanting to enjoy her exuberant spirit. But he would not envy those men. She was pretty, she was captivating, and he could see there was more to her than he had first assumed, but she was not for him.

'So will you be attending the Season to search for your illusive countess?' she asked.

'Perhaps. I had been hoping to avoid doing so, but...'

'But I arrived on your doorstep, and you knew immediately the hunt would have to continue.' She gave another of those tinkling laughs. 'Whereas I was hoping I'd be nothing like the wife you wanted. I've been dreaming about having my Season since I was a little girl and was devastated by the thought that it might be snatched away from me before it had even started.' She looked up at him. 'Only one of us got our wish.'

'And for both of us the hunt, as you put it, continues.'

'Yes, I'll be on the hunt for someone who knows how to have fun, and you for someone who enjoys, shall we say, a life of quiet and solitude in the countryside.'

'Hmm,' Sebastian replied to her deliberate attempt to mock him. 'If you've had enough of this boring pastoral splendour, we should perhaps return to the house.'

'Yes, but when we get back, remember we have to act as if this were our first encounter and we don't particularly like each other. Although with regards to the second requirement, you shouldn't have too much trouble.'

'I never said—'

His words were cut off by her laughter, causing him to smile.

'Or, at least, that I have none of the attributes you are looking for in a wife.'

Sebastian thought it diplomatic to not reply to that.

'And I probably don't need to mention that we should forget all about that kiss and pretend it never happened,' she added, her cheeks colouring.

'Of course, that goes without saying.' Although he suspected that was the first lie he had told her. He would, of course, say nothing to disillusion the father that his daughter was pure and chaste as a debutante should be, but he could not guarantee he would be able to forget kissing her.

She had lied again. Lucy knew she would never be able to forget that kiss. Every time she looked at him, every time her eyes strayed to those divinely sculptured lips, a delightful flutter would stir within her, and her mind and body would be transported back to The Royal Flush, back into his arms.

It was such a shame he knew who she was. If they had not met again today, here, at his estate, she could have returned to The Royal Flush. Perhaps she could have arranged an assignation with him and encouraged him to kiss her once again.

That would not be happening now, and perhaps it was all for the best. Kissing was a bad enough transgression. His effect on her was so strong there was always the danger she would completely forget herself. That would never do.

They turned the corner into the formal garden, and the palatial Rothwell Hall came into view.

It looked like their walk had come to an end. That, too, was probably all for the best, even if it didn't feel that way.

'Remember, be serious,' she said as she released his arm and stepped away so there was a suitable gap between them.

He looked down at her, eyebrows arched. 'Perhaps you should take your own advice.'

'Right.' She frowned and squeezed her lips together so she would stop smiling like the ninny he must think her to be. 'And remember, we hardly know each other, but what you now know of me has convinced you that you don't particularly like me,' she said out the side of her mouth.

'Lucy, I—'

'You know what I mean,' she said, fighting to keep her expression serious.

They walked in silence towards the magnificent house, and Lucy could see why her father would be so keen to marry her off to Sebastian. The stone exterior had turned a soft honey colour, and the rows and rows of mullion windows on the house's three storeys glinted and sparkled in the late afternoon sun. If a woman wanted to be locked away in the countryside, this would make a luxurious prison.

Their boots crunched on the gravel driveway as they walked towards the grand entranceway. Their enforced silence continued as they walked up the stone stairs, worn down in the centre by the feet of generations of family members and years of countless visitors.

When they reached the imposing oak doors they paused, and he made a formal bow. If anyone was watching, Lucy was certain they would assume they were still all but strangers who had never lost that initial awkwardness in each other's company.

'I will see you at dinner, Miss Everhart,' he said, his voice even more starchy than usual.

Rather enjoying this play-acting Lucy made a low curtsy, her face solemn, but she said nothing.

They entered the house and walked off in different directions. Dolly appeared from somewhere and followed Lucy up the stairs to her bedchamber, her anxious expression making it clear she was desperate to hear what had happened.

'We've nothing to worry about,' she reassured her the moment the door closed behind them. 'He will say nothing about meeting me at The Royal Flush or the kiss. He doesn't want to marry me, and he'll think of some excuse to give Father that doesn't make me look too bad. Then we can go our separate ways.'

Dolly's tense face relaxed. 'A lucky escape, miss.'

'Yes.' Lucy supposed that it was.

'So did you threaten to expose him as a rake who kisses servant girls?'

'Well, yes and no, but he explained that. He said he doesn't usually kiss servants, and he's not a rake.'

Dolly met this reply with a sceptical look, much to Lucy's chagrin.

'He reminded me that I was the one who invited him to the roulette table and I was the one to ask him to kiss me,' Lucy said, a note of defensiveness creeping into her voice.

'I see,' Dolly said slowly, then crossed the room, removed Lucy's dinner gown from the wardrobe and began checking it carefully. It was obvious she did not see at all.

'Honestly, I really believe he is not a rake,' Lucy tried to explain as she watched Dolly vigorously brush down the gown. 'I just made that assumption because he was in a gambling den and he's so devilishly handsome, but he's not like that at all. Not really.'

'So what is he like?' Dolly asked, pausing in her task.

'He's quite different from the man I met at The Royal Flush. Well, obviously he's just as handsome, but he's much more serious. I can't imagine this Sebastian tipping me over and kissing me.'

That was not entirely true. She certainly could imagine it and had done so more times than she could count during their walk. She just doubted it would ever happen.

'And which one do you prefer?'

'Oh, the kissing one, definitely,' she said with a little laugh.

'Except he only kisses servants, never debutantes.'

'No, yes...well, I've explained that.'

'You're very kind to not judge him harshly. I assume he has been equally fair-minded with you.'

'Well, he said he won't tell anyone, so that means my reputation is safe.'

'And his.'

'Yes.'

'And was he as keen not to marry you as you suspected? Was he quaking in his well-polished boots?'

Lucy chewed the edge of her lip. 'Yes, I suppose he was. Seeing me in a gambling den and asking him to kiss me has ruled me out as a potential wife, because I'm no longer seen as respectable enough.'

Dolly once again raised her eyebrows in question, then went back to vigorously brushing.

Lucy had to agree with her maid's unspoken opinion. 'It's all rather unfair, isn't it?'

'Yes, miss,' Dolly said, not looking up from her task.

'He kisses me, and that's why he won't marry me. He kissed me and then assumed it was some sort of trick to force him to marry me against his will, when it was no such thing.'

'Yes, miss,' Dolly repeated as she removed the undergarments Lucy would wear that night from the chest of drawers.

'He kisses a lady's maid and knows he can get away with it because he thinks I'm just a powerless servant.'

Dolly made no response.

'He kisses me, and if he'd known I was a debutante, he would have had to marry me, but well, he got off scot-free. I've let him get off scot-free.'

She looked to Dolly for her agreement, but she was busy doing something or other with Lucy's corset.

'Instead of judging me he should be expressing his gratitude to me for not holding him to account and making him marry me.' She could feel her indignation rising with every word.

'Except you do not wish to marry him, miss.'

'I know, but that's beside the point.' Lucy wasn't entirely sure what the point was, but she knew she felt aggrieved. 'He must be feeling so full of himself that he got to kiss a debutante or servant girl or whatever with absolutely no consequences.'

The anxious expression returned to Dolly's face. 'Do be careful, miss. You've escaped a difficult situation. You don't want to create another one for yourself.'

'Don't worry, I won't,' Lucy reassured her. Her maid was correct, but somehow she still wanted to make sure Sebastian-Judgemental-Kingsley did not think he had got everything his own way.

Chapter Seven

Sebastian braced himself for a dinner which he was certain would be a trial. He had to give the impression there was no common ground between himself and Lucy so her father would not be surprised when he made no offer to court her.

But if he were to use the excuse that they were incompatible, he would have to ensure he did not talk companionably with her this evening or laugh at any of the things she said. In other words, he would have to act as if a woman whose company he rather enjoyed, whom he found decidedly attractive, left him indifferent.

What he needed to remember at all times was that despite possessing a physical beauty he found captivating, and even though she was amusing and entertaining, her rebellious nature meant she could never be the next Countess of Rothwell. Too many of the countesses had possessed that dangerous quality, and that had always resulted in scandalous behaviour. The Rothwell name did not need further scandals.

Perhaps the situation in which he now found himself was exactly what had happened to past earls. His forebears might also have met women they wished to bed, but instead of being rational and resisting those desires, they had married those inappropriate women. He would not be so weak or imprudent to let any lustful urges get in the way of selecting a woman who would make a good, trustworthy countess, one who would not besmirch the name of Rothwell.

Lucy entered the room for pre-dinner drinks which, out of respect for the reverend's opinion on the demon drink, were all fruit cordials.

Once again, she was modestly dressed, tonight in a cream gown bedecked with layers of pale brown lace that covered her shoulders and the lower half of her neck and tumbled down her chest. The voluminous sleeves and skirt appeared to be doing their best to disguise her curvaceous figure but were failing. He could still see her cinched waist and knew that under all that fabric were temptingly rounded hips and full breasts.

Sebastian coughed lightly, bowed his head in greeting and forced his eyes not to linger.

She gave a low curtsy, and when she looked up at him her expression appeared decidedly vexed. Was she playing a part for the sake of her father, or was this yet more proof that she was not just impetuous but of a mercurial disposition? If it was the latter, then that, too, was something that ruled her out as his countess. He needed a wife who was steadfast, level-headed and dependable.

'There you are, my dear,' the reverend said. 'Did you have an enjoyable walk?'

'Yes, Father,' she responded like a dutiful daughter.

She walked across the room, the silk fabric shimmering in the candlelight, sometimes appearing cream, at other times gold. He pulled his eyes away from her gown. Why on earth was he noticing something as ridiculous as the fabric of a woman's dress?

With much rustling, she took her seat, and Sebastian was certain he also heard the soft whisper of silk stockings moving against each other. He shook his head slightly to drive out that erotically charged image. The last thing he needed to be thinking about right now was her stockings, her garter belts or the soft pale skin of her inner thighs.

'What did you see?' her father said, and it took Sebastian a moment to grasp what he was asking.

'We walked through the formal garden, along the herbaceous border and across the grasslands to the woodlands,' he said, glad of the distraction from the thought of Lucy's naked thighs. 'Miss Everhart expressed her interest in seeing the grove of oaks that were planted in my great grandfather's time and are said to be among the finest specimens in the county.'

Lucy raised her eyes briefly and sent him a questioning look. He shrugged his shoulders quickly in reply as if to say *I had to give him some reason why we were away for so long.*

'Splendid,' the father declared. 'Yes, Lucinda's love of nature rivals only my own. There's nothing she enjoys better than tending her garden bed. Isn't that right, Lucinda?'

'Yes, Father.' She continued to hold Sebastian's gaze, a challenge in her eyes, but also kept her head angled in what she presumably saw as an appropriately demure manner for the sake of her watching father. 'And what of you, my lord? I imagine you spend a lot of time in flower-beds?'

She took a sip of her lemonade, that defiant gleam still in her eyes.

Sebastian flicked a quick look at the reverend to see if he was aware of the double meaning of her words. Her father was merely looking at Sebastian with a serious expression as if it were a genuine question and he were waiting for the answer.

'Not as often as some people might think,' he responded.

'I'm sure if you marry a young woman who enjoys gardening as much as my Lucinda, she'll be able to tempt you into joining her in the flower-beds,' the clergyman said, causing Lucy to almost choke on her drink.

'I'm sure the earl has plenty of servants to perform those tasks,' she said, once she had finished coughing.

'When I marry, the woman I choose will be welcome to tend the beds if they are interested,' Sebastian declared, becoming increasingly irritated by the absurd direction of this conversation. 'And even while I remain single it is not an endeavour in which I involve any servants.'

'Is it something you prefer to do for yourself?' the reverend asked in complete innocence.

'When need demands,' he said, not making eye contact with Lucy in case she laughed.

'That is quite commendable, isn't it, Lucinda?'

Before she could answer, the footman entered, much to Sebastian's relief, and announced that dinner was served.

As politeness demanded, he offered his arm to Lucy, but also sent her a warning look to inform her she was testing his patience. She responded with a fake smile, while her eyes continued to glare at him as if he were in some way at fault.

He fought to keep his irritation in check. Despite his best efforts to convince her otherwise, she still believed him to be a rake who seduced servant girls. If she wanted to cling to that falsehood, then so be it. By tomorrow she would be gone, out of his life, and what Miss Lucinda Everhart thought of him would not matter one iota.

They entered the dining room, and Lucy stood behind a chair. Before the footman could pull it out for her, Sebastian stepped forward to do the honours. She moved past him, and momentarily forgetting himself, he breathed in her delicate scent of lavender and rose water. It was an innocent perfume, befitting a debutante, but Sebastian was sure that beneath that artificial aroma of modesty was a womanly scent that was enticingly sensual. He held his breath as she took her seat, determined to not let any more inappropriately erotic images enter his mind.

As she sat, her arm lightly moved against his. Was that a mistake or a flirtatious gesture? It had to be the former. It was in no one's interest for the reverend to think there was any attraction between himself and Lucy. And, more to the point, it was not in his own interest for such an attraction to exist. She was a debutante. She was out-of-bounds unless he wanted to marry her, and he most certainly did not want to do that.

Along with the reverend, Sebastian took his seat, then watched as Lucy removed her napkin from its silver ring, placed it on her lap and undid the buttons of her gloves. Was she deliberately being provocative by slowly releasing each button, exposing the delicate white skin on the inside of her wrists, inch by inch?

When the small pearl buttons were all finally released she pulled at each finger with the same torturous deliberateness. Once her elegant hands were fully exposed, she placed the gloves beside her plate and looked over at him.

Did that slight curl of her lips show that she knew

what affect she was having on him? And furthermore, why on earth *was* she having this effect on him? Had he been too long without a woman in his life? Was that the problem? He had no mistress at present, preferring not to be bedding one woman while seeking another as his wife. That was possibly a mistake if it was turning him into something akin to a lustful adolescent boy aroused by the sight of a woman performing the innocent task of removing her gloves.

While the footmen brought in the soup terrines, Sebastian turned to the reverend. 'Did you have a chance to write your sermon?' he asked, making polite conversation.

'Yes. When I return to the parish I intend to instruct my flock on the virtue of austerity and stoicism.'

'Worthy topics, I'm sure,' Sebastian said.

'Yes.' The vicar looked down at his empty soup bowl, appearing even more doleful than usual. 'I thought they were topics about which I, too, needed a reminder.'

The footman served the lobster bisque, and Sebastian wondered if his guest was about to push it away in an act of stoicism and austerity, but he began spooning it into his mouth and even took some bread rolls and smothered them with butter.

'I'm afraid I'm soon going to have to practise what I preach,' the reverend said, pausing between mouthfuls. 'While I know selfishness is also a sin, I would be bearing false witness if I did not admit that I will miss Lucinda when she marries and will be forced to show some stoicism. She is such a help to me in the parish and always has wise insights that I can use in my sermons.'

Sebastian's soup spoon paused momentarily on its way to his mouth. 'Really?' he finally asked, that one word holding a wealth of disbelief.

'Yes, indeed,' the gentleman said, nodding solemnly. 'She was particularly helpful on the sermon I gave before departing for London on the dangers faced by young ladies in this wicked world of ours.'

Sebastian was tempted to ask if Lucy provided a model for all the things a young lady should not do if she was to stay safe in this wicked world of ours. Such as go out in London alone at night, with only a negligent lady's maid for company, frequent gambling dens and, worst of all, kiss complete strangers. Any one of those acts could have found her in a great deal of danger.

'I'm sure her behaviour is quite the inspiration,' he said instead.

The father nodded his head in acknowledgement while Lucy sent him a wide-eyed look as if to say *Do not say anything else on this subject*.

He smiled to himself, pleased he had got some revenge for her comment about him finding himself in various beds.

'Father is perhaps overstating my contribution,' Lucy said, which Sebastian did not doubt in the slightest. 'My help is generally confined to copying out his sermons so he can send them to the *Church Times* for publication. He is the only one, apart from myself, who can read his writing.'

'Yes, my Lucinda has a lovely hand.'

Sebastian looked down at those lovely hands, at the long tapering fingers, the dainty pink fingernails and the faint blue veins, like delicate threads of lace under the soft, creamy skin.

'Indeed,' Sebastian said, knowing he had no idea how legible Lucy's handwriting was, but admitting she did indeed have lovely hands.

He looked over at her father. 'And have you had many sermons published in the *Church Times*?'

'Alas, no.' The father then began to discuss the various topics of his sermons, and Sebastian was happy to let him talk. Although, perhaps *happy* was not the right word, as the reverend mentioned some of the rejected sermons, including ones on the demon that is overindulgence, the evilness of lustful thoughts and how idle amusements are the devil's temptation.

With every word Sebastian's sympathy for Lucy grew, and he could see why a young woman subjected to such constant moralising might become rebellious and yearn for freedom.

'I'm sure the earl agrees with every word you've said, Father,' Lucy said when he finally came to a halt. 'Don't you, my lord?' she added. 'Although, Father, you did not allude to one of your favourite topics, how women are the moral guardians of society and it is their job to keep men on the righteous path.' She placed her chin in her hand, teasing eyes intent on him. 'I believe that is a belief that is dear to your heart, is it not, my lord?'

Sebastian forced himself not to scowl at her. Yes, he wanted a wife who was moral and upstanding, but he was surely not as sanctimonious as her father.

The father was also watching him, apparently waiting for his opinion on the matter. 'A moral woman has a lot to recommend her,' he finally said.

'Yes, you are so right,' the reverend said, raising his hands as if preaching to a congregation. 'And few women are more moral and virtuous than my daughter, Lucinda.'

Sebastian was tempted to roll his eyes at the man's delusions.

'Perhaps you can provide me with some guidance on the matter of morality,' Lucy said to him, those eyes still mocking but her words polite, and Sebastian readied himself for what was sure to be an underhand insult. 'Is it not also important for the husband to set a high standard in all things moral and righteous as an example for his wife to follow?'

The reverend nodded. 'That is an excellent question.' He turned to Sebastian. 'If I may answer this?'

Sebastian waved his hand to say *Yes, please do*.

'You are right, my dear. The husband is the one to

instruct the wife in all things moral. She must defer to him, and he should be her guiding light.'

Lucy nodded slowly as if trying to understand this principle. 'So she should use his behaviour as an instruction on how she should live her own life?'

'Exactly,' her father said.

She sent Sebastian a sweet smile. 'I assume you agree with that, my lord, that your wife should follow your exemplary example and live her life accordingly.'

Sebastian sighed. He was not going to debate morality with her. Nor was he going to defend his position on wanting a wife who was the epitome of respectability. Lucy knew nothing of his past, nothing of the shame his family name had been subjected to by generations of duplicitous women. He was determined to be the Rothwell who broke the curse, and he would not let this little minx question his resolve.

'Do not question the earl,' her father said sternly, misinterpreting Sebastian's sigh.

'I apologise, my lord. This is all my fault,' the reverend added as the footmen served the next course. 'I'm afraid I have been derelict in my duty as a father and allowed my daughter to receive too much education. I should never have allowed her to learn Latin and Greek or read the works of many scholars of divinity.'

Latin? Greek? Divinity? That was not what he'd expect from a young woman who claimed all she wanted to do is dance, laugh and have fun.

'*Ita vero. Yes indeed*, in Latin,' she said with a smile.

The reverend continued, his expression mournful. 'While those skills have helped me immensely in my work, it has also meant that sometimes she likes to think for herself and forgets that a woman should always defer to a man's wisdom and not ask so many questions.'

The man lowered his head as if in shame while Lucy rolled her eyes. Then he looked up at Sebastian with an expression of appeal. 'But I'm sure the right husband would be able to correct this one fault, and in all other ways my Lucinda would make any man an exemplary wife.'

Sebastian nodded diplomatically, not wishing to say that speaking her own mind was hardly a fault, and especially not compared to all the other shortcomings that had already ruled her out as the exemplary wife.

Lucy lifted one small scallop to her lips and smiled, enjoying the thought she was disconcerting Sebastian. He deserved to be disconcerted. He had everything his own way, and Lucy could see no good reason why that should be. Her father's old-fashioned ways would never change, so it would be a waste of breath trying to point out how wrong he was, but Sebastian needed to see the error of his behaviour and his attitudes towards women.

If she could make him feel even a little bit uncomfortable for being so two-faced, then this weekend would be well worth it. Then he might think twice before he consigned the chosen wife to the countryside against her will while he continued to live his life however he liked. He might get a glimmer of what life married to him would be like from the wife's point of view.

Lucy doubted she would ever meet the next Countess of Rothwell, so the woman would not be able to thank her in person, but as her father would say, virtue is its own reward, and in this case, making a man see what a hypocrite he was and how his lofty expectations for his wife were beneath contempt would be its own reward.

'But Lucinda also learnt all the womanly skills as well,' her father continued, still trying to do the impossible and convince Sebastian she had the qualities he sought in a wife.

'Her watercolours are sublime.'

Lucy almost choked on her scallop. 'I believe you exaggerate somewhat, Father,' she said once she had cleared her throat.

'Your modesty is commendable,' her father said. 'And her embroidery is perfection itself. One can tell that each stitch has been made with the love and devotion of a young woman who is never more content than when staying at home and dedicating herself to feminine activities.'

Lucy was tempted to point out to her father that *Thou shalt not bear false witness* was one of the Ten Commandments and in his desire to marry off his daughter to an earl he was surely telling outrageous lies. Or was it because her father had never actually looked at the blobs and streaks of paint that were her paintings or the embroidery samplers that always ended up as tangled knots of threads that got thrown in the fire?

Sometimes she suspected her father did not know her in the slightest. He had an ideal in his mind of what a clergyman's daughter should be like and convinced himself that she personified it. Sometimes that was to her advantage, but at other times it would be nice to be loved for who she really was and not who she was expected to be.

'And she plays the piano with a heavenly touch, and her singing is so sweet it could make the angels cry.'

A groan of disbelief escaped Lucy's lips before she could cover her mouth. Her father had heard her sing and play the piano, but this time he was breaking no commandments. As a man who was completely tone-deaf he had no idea just how lacking in musical talent she was. If any angels really did cry when she was singing, it was because of the pain she was inflicting on their ears.

'Then, she must perform for us after dinner,' Sebastian said, his lips curling into a wry smile.

Drat it all, he had seen her hesitance and was now getting his own back for her mocking behaviour.

'A delightful idea, my lord,' her father added. 'Then

you'll be able to see just what an accomplished young lady she is.'

'I'm sure the earl is just being polite,' Lucy said, her words coming out in a desperate rush. 'He doesn't really want to hear me play.'

'Nonsense. I would be delighted,' Sebastian said, sending her a taunting smile.

She screwed up her face to say *You rotter*.

'Modesty is one of the many virtues Lucinda possesses,' her father continued. 'It is so difficult to get her to perform in front of my guests, but tonight I believe you must put your modesty aside and let the earl see your God-given talents.'

'I would love to play.' Lucy shook her head and frowned with feigned sadness. 'But I'm afraid I have not brought any sheet music with me.'

'But that should not be a problem, my dear. I've heard you play many a song without the use of sheet music.' He turned to the earl. 'She's so talented.'

'And I believe you'll find plenty of sheet music on the piano,' Sebastian said, his expression becoming decidedly smug.

Lucy gave a sigh of resignation. There was no escaping this persecution.

Throughout the rest of the dinner, she sat in silence, trying to gather her courage for the humiliation to come.

She'd performed in front of some of her father's friends when he'd insisted, finding it funny that her father was oblivious to just how terrible she was, and amused at the way the guests sat politely as if her playing and singing were not an assault on their ears. But she did not find anything funny about revealing her ineptitude in front of Sebastian.

Far too soon, the meal was finished, and they walked through to the music room. Lucy sent a quick look at the dreaded grand piano in the corner. It was such a beautiful instrument, with its polished black cabinet, its lid lifted in expectation, it would be cruel to subject it to her playing, and even crueller to subject Lucy to this embarrassment.

She moved swiftly to a seat as far removed from the piano as possible and hoped against hope that her father and Sebastian had forgotten about their threat.

'Now, now, my dear,' her father said, his hand coaxing her in the direction of the piano, 'don't be shy. We want to hear your lovely voice and your musical expertise.'

With her shoulders slumped Lucy walked to the piano. If she played really quickly, perhaps the mortification would also be over as soon as possible. She sat on the embroidered piano stool, laced her fingers and stretched them, not that it would make much difference if her fingers were limber or not.

Her hands plunked down on the ivory keys, which made a discordant sound. 'Oh dear, the piano appears to be untuned.'

'It was tuned last week,' the merciless Sebastian said, with a taunting smile.

All right, you asked for it, she wanted to say. *If you want to suffer, then so be it. I did try to warn you.*

'As I have no sheet music with me, I will have to play a simple tune a local lady taught me.'

Lucy smiled to herself. *Lady* was perhaps stretching things. Before their maid-of-all-work was employed at the Greyton rectory, she'd made a living playing piano at a public house. Lucy adored Dolly. She was such fun. Not only had she provided Lucy with that forbidden book containing lurid tales of rakes, highwaymen and damsels in distress but she'd also consented to give Lucy some much-needed additional piano lessons. The tunes they played together were so much livelier and enjoyable than those the piano instructor had tried to drum into her, and Lucy was almost able to master them. Almost.

She launched into her discordant version of 'What Shall We Do with a Drunken Sailor?' which her father attempted to tap his foot to, even though he consistently missed the beats.

As expected, Sebastian's eyebrows rose, hopefully in disapproval. If he knew the song, then it meant he, too, had been frequenting low bars or the musical theatre. She was confident he would not mention the nature of the tune, but if he did, she was prepared to act shocked and contrite at such a revelation.

When she came to the end, possibly quite a bit faster

than the song required, her father clapped enthusiastically as if he had just been entertained by the finest pianist to grace the stage at the Royal Albert Hall.

'Marvellous, simply marvellous,' her father exclaimed still clapping.

'Yes, it was unlike any performance I've heard in this music room,' Sebastian said, then that wry smile returned. 'But we haven't heard your divine singing voice yet.'

Lucy sent him her most venomous scowl, which only caused those lips to curl more.

'Yes, my dear,' her father gushed. 'Play another tune, something you can sing to.'

Something she could sing to? Lucy knew all the words to 'A Drunken Sailor' but as much as she wanted to horrify Sebastian, she did not want to give her father palpitations of the heart.

She thought through all the songs she knew, ones she was almost capable of playing without sheet music. Unfortunately, they were all ones with dubious lyrics taught to her by the delightful maid.

'The Lambeth Walk'? No, the line 'everything free and easy, do as you darn well pleasy' would horrify her father, especially the curse word. 'Champagne Charlie'? No, too many references to the demon drink. 'Ta-ra-ra Boom-de-ay'? No, that mentioned a girl with a roguish smile and was decidedly suggestive. She would have to play it safe and opt for 'Greensleeves.'

Once again, her hands clunked down on the keys,

and the moment she started massacring the introduction she realised what a big mistake she had made. While the lyrics to the song were not going to offend, it required the ability to hit the occasional high notes, something she most certainly did not possess.

Cringing, her clumsy fingers continued to move over the keys. She got to the part where she was supposed to begin singing.

She didn't.

Instead, she replayed the introduction. That dreaded part where she was expected to launch into song came around again. She repeated the introduction, yet again. When she got there for the fourth time she knew she could put it off no longer or they would spend the entire night listening to that one section.

Her voice sounding distinctively like a cat being strangled, she squawked out 'Alas, my love, you do me wrong...' keeping her eyes fixed firmly on the piano keys, not wanting to look up and see the pleasure Sebastian would be taking in her mortification.

With as much forbearance as she could gather, she stumbled on.

'To cast me off discourteously...'

When she reached 'For I have loved you well' a man's voice joined in, a lovely baritone, that fortunately drowned out her squeaks and squawks. Lucy's voice grew quieter with each line of the song until she was merely mouthing the words, but there was nothing she could do about her appalling playing.

When her fingers finally plonked to the end of the song, her father gave them an unexpected standing ovation.

'Wonderful, simply wonderful,' he declared, wiping away a tear from his eye. 'Your voices complement each other perfectly, as if you were made to be together.'

Lucy and Sebastian exchanged matching looks of disbelief, then they both smiled. His smile was probably one of amusement, but Lucy's was of gratitude. She had handed him the perfect opportunity to tease and embarrass her, and he had graciously chosen not to do so.

Perhaps she had judged him slightly more harshly than he deserved.

'We simply must have another,' her father said, still clapping.

'Maybe this time the earl might like to play,' Lucy said, sending him a beseeching look.

'Or maybe we could play together,' he responded, causing Lucy to suppress a giggle at hearing the words she had said to him when they first met.

She shuffled over on the piano stool, and he sat beside her. His thigh almost touched hers, and Lucy was sorely tempted to inch a little bit closer but was certain such a move would not be welcome. Not by him, and certainly not by her watching father.

He began playing the melody to 'The Celebrated Chop Waltz' or 'Chopsticks' as it was more commonly called. Lucy laughed. It was the piece she was first expected to learn, but she had been unable to master even that simple tune. Fortunately, all that was required of her was to play a few basic chords in accompaniment. Even that was perhaps stretching her level of skill, but as the piece went on, it didn't really matter anymore. This was rather fun, and Sebastian was more than accomplished enough to cover up her mistakes.

By the time they reached the end, both were laughing, while her father applauded with enthusiasm as if they had just performed Beethoven's fifth symphony or some other complicated piece that Lucy would never attempt to butcher.

They turned to face each other, still laughing. Lucy's laughter settled down into a happy smile. Her smile then slowly melted. Her eyes held his. The laughter crinkling the edges of his eyes smoothed. The gaze became more intense, more intimate. Her breath caught in her throat as sparks seemingly skittered across her skin. She leant in closer, remembering the touch of his lips on hers, the feel of his rough skin against her cheek, his strong arms encircling her.

'I demand an encore,' her father said. Lucy sprang back as if caught doing something wildly inappropriate. And she was. Or at least, she was thinking of doing something wildly inappropriate.

Or was she?

The only thing inappropriate was her father's presence. She had already kissed Sebastian. The damage to her reputation in his eyes had already been done. She had nothing more to lose by kissing him again. And he'd already promised to tell no one.

She smiled to herself, her heart skittering, warmth flooding her body. She still did not want to marry him, and he had made it clear he had no interest in marriage to her, but there was absolutely no reason on earth why she could not kiss him again, as long as it remained their secret.

Such an act would be even more daring and reckless than sneaking out to The Royal Flush, but would it really do any harm if before she left his estate she demanded her own encore?

Chapter Eight

Sebastian woke the next morning with a renewed determination. Last night he had forgotten himself. When he'd played the piano with Lucy he'd got so caught up in the pleasure of her company that his true mission and the reason for this weekend had slipped from his mind.

To find a suitable bride.

And that was not and never could be Miss Lucinda Everhart. Nor could there be anything else between them. He'd made the mistake once before in kissing a debutante. That time he had ignorance as his excuse. No such excuse existed now.

What he needed was a reminder of why he had to resist being enchanted by Lucy's melodic laughter and her vivacious spirit and, more importantly, why he could not be tempted by those treacherously sweet lips.

To that end, after breakfast he asked Lucy if she would like to accompany him on another walk.

Father and daughter both looked delighted at this prospect. The father was probably under the illusion that he was soon to ask for Lucy's hand. Why Lucy looked so pleased he chose not to dwell upon.

'You are most welcome to join us,' he said to the reverend. As they no longer had to discuss their past encounter he could see no reason for them to be alone, and if he was being honest, he would prefer to be chaperoned by the reverend than the feckless lady's maid.

'No, no, you young people go off together. I'm happy to stay here and read the newspapers. Not that there's much in them these days,' he said with a huff, flicking open *The Times*.

Sebastian couldn't help but feel sorry for the man. He thought his daughter was pious, sensible and steadfast and about to become a married woman. It was a pity, because if she did possess even a modicum of those qualities, then he would indeed be asking for her hand.

'Another walk in the garden?' she asked, rising from her chair. 'I'll ask Dolly to fetch my cloak.'

'While I am well aware of your love of nature, I thought you might like to take a walk through the family portrait gallery.'

'Looking at pictures of your illustrious ancestors, how fascinating.' The edges of her lips curled downwards in a mock frown, letting him know that yet again she was making fun of him.

The father tucked his newspaper under his arm,

saying he could be found in the drawing room should anyone need him. Then with a meaningful look at Sebastian, he left the room. Sebastian took Lucy's arm and led her down the long corridor towards the gallery, the hapless maid following well behind.

He opened the door, allowing her to enter first, and his gaze swept across the paintings of his ancestors lining the walls, their faces a solemn reminder of the gravity of his undertaking.

'They look like a riotous crowd,' she said, looking from one serious portrait to another. 'Sorry,' she added, not sounding the slightest bit regretful. 'They're your family, and I'm sure they're all lovely people.'

Lovely was not the word he would use to describe them, but it mattered not. He was not here to impress her with his family lineage, or their personalities, lovely or otherwise, but to remind himself of his purpose in life.

Many a time his father had led him into this room, made him stand in front of each painting as he listed the sins and transgressions of each Countess of Rothwell, until Sebastian could recite them by heart.

At the end of each tour his father always said the same thing. 'Take the utmost care when you select a wife. Assess all her qualities carefully, and be absolutely certain that there is nothing about her that will bring further shame on this family, or you will be in danger of continuing the Rothwell curse.'

It was a lesson he thought he had learnt well, but now he needed a timely reminder.

He led her to two head-and-shoulder portraits hanging side by side, depicting the 1st Earl of Rothwell and his wife. 'The first earl was granted his title by Henry VIII,' he informed her. 'Prior to becoming an earl, he was a knight.'

'He must have pleased the king to be given such a title.' She looked from one portrait to another. 'His wife is very pretty.'

'Yes, she was reputed to be quite the beauty, and rumour had it she was the one to please the king, not her husband, and that is why the family's social position was elevated and they were granted extensive lands here in Dorset.'

Her gloved hand covered her mouth to suppress a little giggle. 'You mean she was…' She looked back at the portrait and scrutinised it with sudden glee.

'Yes, it was said she was one of Henry VIII's many mistresses and the earl was granted his title in exchange for his wife's favours.'

'Oh my.'

'Yes. *Oh my* indeed.'

They both looked at the portrait of the first countess who, despite the need to remain serious in such a portrait, still had a flirtatious glint in her eye and a coquettish pout to her full lips.

'The first earl eventually sent her to a nunnery, so

shamed was he by the gossip surrounding her prowess in the bedroom.'

Lucy frowned. 'Oh no, the poor woman.'

'Hmm,' he responded to such unwarranted pity. 'Shall we move on?'

They stopped in front of a pen-and-ink sketch of a man wearing a large stiff white lace collar and bejewelled velvet hat.

'This is the fourth Earl of Rothwell.'

She looked around the room. 'What happened to the second and third?'

'Nothing much is known of the second earl and countess, but the third Countess of Rothwell shot her husband then attempted to burn down the estate. Most documents were lost in the fire, along with any portraits that might have existed of the second and third earls. The paintings of the first earl and countess were among the few things salvaged from the destruction.'

'Oh my,' she repeated, and he was pleased she was starting to get an idea of the Rothwell curse, but he had only just begun. They moved onto the next portrait.

That depicted a pretty blonde woman dressed in an elaborate silk gown in a rich shade of burgundy. The tightly fitted bodice was intricately embroidered in gold thread, and a string of pearls adorned her slim neck, matching her earrings and the pearls woven into her hair. Standing beside her was a proud, dark-haired man dressed in blue velvet doublet and hose, also adorned with gold embroidery, and with a layered ruff of white lace around his neck. A wide-brimmed felt hat adorned with pearls sat proudly on his head.

'Well, these two look happy enough.' She turned to face him. 'You're not going to tell me she shot her husband as well, are you? Or did he send her off to a nunnery before she got the chance?'

'No, this countess shot no one, as far as I am aware.'

'Good.' She turned back to looking at the portrait. 'However...'

She made a small groan.

'During the Civil War, the countess reputedly had affairs with commanding officers on both sides. When the two men found out, it nearly caused her to lose her head, literally. It was only the intervention of her husband and her ability to convince the winning side that it was all subterfuge and she was working as a spy that saved her head. Along with her husband surrendering a large amount of the family fortune to Cromwell's government.'

She made no comment but moved on to the next portrait. 'So what did this one do wrong? She looks far too joyless to have taken lovers.'

They stood in front of a portrait depicting a woman seated on a straight-backed chair, wearing a severe black gown buttoned up to the neck and her hair tucked under a black bonnet, with only a small bit of white lace around her neck for decoration. The man standing behind, his hand firmly placed on her shoulder as if holding her in place, looked equally dour in his Puritan clothing of black doublet and breeches, his hair hanging lank to his shoulders, his face clean-shaven.

'Appearances can be deceptive,' he said. 'Her husband died mysteriously not long after this portrait was painted. Some suspected poisoning, others talked of witchcraft.'

'Witchcraft?' she exclaimed. 'Oh, surely not.'

'That was the rumour, but somehow she managed to save herself from the gallows for murder or burning for witchcraft. The records do not show how, but given the family history and past countess behaviour…' He shrugged in explanation.

They moved on to the next painting of his ancestors dressed in the elaborate finery of the Restoration period. Lucy turned towards him with a questioning expression.

'Adultery, again. She was also suspected of embezzlement. Not proven.'

They moved passed a painting of a woman in Georgian clothing. 'It is believed this young woman liked to drink. Rather a lot.'

They passed the painting of his grandparents, dressed in the simple clothes of the Regency period.

'Oh, she's pretty, and he's certainly handsome.' She looked at him. 'Yes, I can see the family resemblance.'

He looked at the couple but could not see it himself. The woman that he remembered as a miserable old lady looked young and pretty in this portrait, with a sweet, innocent expression on her face. Blond ringlets surrounded a heart-shaped face, and she was dressed in a plain cream muslin gown with a short blue-and-white striped jacket. Her husband, dressed in a dark grey tail-coat, cream breeches and a white cravat lifting his head high in the air, looked delighted to be standing next to such a lovely, young wife.

'Gambler,' he said.

'Well, many people gambled in those days,' she said defensively. 'It was just a bit of fun.'

'That *bit of fun* nearly cost the family its entire fortune. The only reason we still have the Rothwell estate was due to her being a favourite of the Prince of Wales. He had a word with her debtors, and they were forced to drop their claims, thus the family was saved from ruin.'

She looked up the hallway at the rogues' gallery. 'And what of the men? You've told me nothing about them. I bet...' her lips pulled into a little moue, and she wrinkled her nose at him '... I mean, I would not be surprised if some of them committed adultery, or gambled, or were underhand on occasion. What of them?'

'I have no idea. All I can say is that the only scandal surrounding them concerns being cuckolded by their wives or having to fight to save the estate because of their wife's misdeeds.'

'And this is why you want an oh-so-respectable

wife, because of all of these women?' She waved her arms in the air to take in the whole line-up of countesses.

He saw no need to answer.

'You selected me because you thought if you married a clergyman's daughter you would get a demure wife who would behave herself.'

Again, he saw no need to answer self-evident statements.

She looked slowly up and down the gallery. 'So which sins do you think I'm capable of? Gambling away the family estate? Committing adultery with multiple men? Or do you think I might put arsenic in my husband's morning coffee or blow his head off with my shotgun?'

She turned towards him, her chin lifted, her hands on her hips. It was hard to tell whether she was teasing or angry with him. But neither response mattered. The walk through the gallery had served its purpose. It had reminded Sebastian why it was essential he be the one to break the family curse.

'Well?' she prompted, her voice losing any hint of teasing.

'We did meet in a gambling den…'

Those blue eyes grew bigger in consternation as she audibly inhaled.

'I do not see why you are getting so het up,' he said. 'That is merely a statement of fact.'

'Well, you were there as well.' She looked back at

the portraits and threw her hands in the air. 'How do you know your grandfather didn't gamble as well?'

'I don't, but it hardly matters. My grandmother was the one who nearly lost the estate.'

She huffed out her annoyance. 'And I suppose you think I will cuckold my husband as well.'

He shrugged. 'I have no idea what you will do.'

'You think just because I kissed you,' she said her voice rising. She took in a deep breath, her lips tight. 'You think just because I kissed you, I am the sort of woman to commit adultery,' she said in a quieter, strained voice.

'Again, I have no idea.'

'You do think that, don't you?' she spat. 'That's why you brought me here. To show me that you think I'm just as bad as all these women.'

'I do not think that. I merely—'

'Yes, you do. You wanted to show me that you disapprove of me as much as you disapprove of these women.'

Sebastian did not know how to answer. He had brought her here to remind himself why he could never marry Lucy Everhart. He wanted to remind himself of the folly of letting one's heart—or an even less trustworthy organ—decide whom to wed rather than one's head.

'As if I could possibly think of marrying a man with such an attitude to women. My father has these antiquated ideas, but he has the excuse of being old and in a profession that unfortunately advocates such views. But you,' she said and pointed a finger at him, 'you have no excuse.'

'And I offer no excuses nor see any reason why I should defend myself,' Sebastian said, pushing down his anger at her irrationality.

'At least my father lives by his values, misguided as they may be. He doesn't have one set of rules for himself and another for other people,' she continued, her voice once again rising. 'And to think you were arrogant enough to think I might want to marry you so much that I would trick you into it.'

Sebastian breathed in deeply and released the muscles of his jaw on an exhalation. 'That was a misunderstanding that has already been settled,' he said, determined to not let her emotional state affect him.

'And to think I wanted you to…' She came to a halt and glared at him.

'Wanted me to what?'

'Never you mind,' she said, her chin lifted defiantly. 'Well, thank you for letting me know exactly what you think of me.'

Sebastian was certain he had done no such thing, but given her agitated state he felt it circumspect to not contradict her.

'Now, let me return the favour and tell you exactly what I think of you,' she said, seething. 'I think you are the most judgemental, sanctimonious, arrogant man one could ever have the misfortune to meet.'

Before Sebastian had a chance to respond she turned and strode out the gallery.

He stared at the door she had slammed behind her. That was not how he had expected this walk to go, and her anger was surely excessive. He had accused her of nothing and certainly never suggested she was someone who might poison or shoot her husband.

Gamble? Yes. Murder, no. As for adultery, he had no idea, but it was a risk he would not take, and as she had pointed out herself, she had kissed a stranger she met in a gambling house.

And as for being judgemental, sanctimonious and arrogant, it was surely his right to be so. In selecting his wife he would of course be judging her to make sure she had exactly the qualities he was looking for. If he were sanctimonious, that, too, was his right. Given his family history he had every reason to hold his wife to a high moral standard. As for arrogant, no one ever expected humility in an earl, and after a lifetime of living under the shame of continued scandals, he knew better than to let his guard down and show any vulnerability. He'd been taught that lesson the moment he arrived at boarding school and had been the target of every child who had heard the salacious details of his parents' divorce.

That was what he would focus on, not that irrational woman's overreaction. No child of his would suffer the loneliness of being cast aside by a mother who preferred her lover over her son. His children would not be weighed down by the shame of the name Rothwell. Standing in this very room he had promised his father and himself that he would be the one to break the curse, and he would be.

He looked from the door to the empty space at the end of the gallery. That was where the portrait of his parents had once hung. It had been painted just after they were married, and at some stage had been removed and placed in the attic.

It was a tangible reminder of the gap she had left in his life. His angry father often glared at that empty space as he listed all the sins his former wife had committed.

Despite knowing what she was like, as a child he had often visited the attic to gaze at his mother's face, wishing she would return to them, until it ceased to give him any comfort and merely made him as angry as his father.

That woman had abandoned them both, leaving behind a bitter husband and a lonely child. He would never risk such a fate for himself. The woman he married would not be the type to run off with her lover, nor would she be someone he let himself love so intensely she had the power to inflict that level of pain on him.

He would marry a sensible woman with whom he could have a calm, untroubled and unemotional life.

He looked at the door once again. That was why he

needed a wife who did not kiss strangers and did not sneak out at night to gambling dens. Nor did he need a wife who was overly emotional, quick to anger and prone to histrionics.

Lucy Everhart was wrong for him, and if she thought him judgemental, sanctimonious and arrogant simply because he wanted a wife who knew how to act with propriety, then so be it.

'You are such an imbecile, Lucinda Everhart,' Lucy muttered to herself as she strode down the corridor.

When he'd asked to spend time with her, she'd had a ridiculous fantasy that he might kiss her again, but all he wanted to do was show her those portraits, and let her know, yet again, why she was lacking any attributes that would put her in contention for what he considered to be the oh-so-grand prize of Countess of Rothwell.

The man was insufferable.

She reached the drawing room, paused and tried to bring her breathing under control and swallow down her anger. She gripped the door-handle tightly, then with as much composure as possible slowly turned it and resisted the temptation to fling open the door.

Her father looked up from his newspaper with a questioning expression.

'I would like to leave now,' she said, trying with all her might to keep her voice level.

'Lucinda, whatever is the matter?' he said rising

from his chair. 'What happened?' His eyes narrowed. 'What did that man do? Where is Dolly? Is she not chaperoning you?'

'What? No, yes. I've sent her up to her room,' she said, not knowing where Dolly had got to, but knowing the chaperone's whereabouts was not the issue. 'And no, the earl did nothing untoward, but I'd like to leave.'

'But you are obviously upset, my dear. If that man has made improper suggestions or—'

'No, no, it's nothing like that.' An improper suggestion would be far preferable to his moralistic attitude to women and harsh judgement of her. 'It's merely that I am disappointed to realise that the earl is not the man I wish to marry.'

'But surely—'

'Please, Father. I wish to leave.'

Her father continued to stare at her, the newspaper clutched in his hands as he waited for a further explanation. But what could she say? She certainly could not repeat the details of her conversation with Sebastian. Her father would never understand her wrath. He would surely agree with Sebastian and probably launch into another sermon about the value of a virtuous woman and the evils of vice.

'As you wish, my dear,' he finally said much to Lucy's relief. 'I'll arrange for a carriage while you tell your lady's maid to pack our things.'

'Thank you, Father,' she said and raced out of the

room and up to her bedchamber, where she found Dolly. After a quick explanation, the two women began throwing piles of clothing into her trunk.

Lucy remained in her room until the carriage arrived outside the front door then all but ran down the stairs, entered the carriage and waited for her father to say his goodbyes to Sebastian.

She had no idea what her father would say regarding their early departure and cared even less. All she wanted was to be away from that despicable man.

Time passed, and still there was no sign of her father.

Eventually she pulled aside the small curtain and peeked out the carriage window to see Sebastian and her father deep in conversation. Her father's expression was stern as he listened to whatever it was Sebastian was saying. She wished the carriage was parked closer so she could overhear the conversation and hoped there was no mention of adultery, gambling or poisonings.

Her father finally climbed into the carriage and signalled to the driver. 'I am so sorry, my dear. I can see why you are so upset,' he said as the carriage moved up the long driveway.

Lucy looked warily at her father. 'You can?'

'I was certain he was the right man for you and you would make him a suitable wife.' Her father continued as the carriage turned onto the country lane. 'Last night when you were playing the piano together, I even had a rather amusing thought.'

Lucy frowned slightly. When had her father ever had an amusing thought?

'Really?' she asked tentatively.

'I thought how much in harmony you were. Do you see what I mean? Playing the piano? In harmony?'

'Hmm.'

'I'd even considered writing a sermon on it, how a good marriage is like a duet on the piano.'

Lucy could point out that she was constantly off-key and her playing out of tune, but that would suggest she was the one at fault, and she knew she'd been pushed into playing piano in the first place. By her father and Sebastian.

'It is such a shame he feels the two of you are incompatible and have no common ground on which to build a foundation for a solid marriage,' he said as he shook his head slowly.

'And that is what the earl said to you?'

'Yes.'

Relief surged through her. Sebastian had stuck to what they had arranged. She had to at least give him credit for that. He could have got her into a great deal of trouble but chose not to.

'He said while you are a pleasant enough young woman, you do not possess the qualities he is looking for in a wife.'

Relief was pushed aside as annoyance once again

bubbled up inside her. *Do not possess the qualities he is looking for* indeed. Well, thank goodness for that. What were they? Being boring? Being obedient? Being dull as ditch-water? Well, nor did he possess any of the qualities she was seeking in a husband. The sanctimonious prig.

'I blame myself,' her father continued. 'I should never have mentioned the extent of your education.'

Lucy chose not to counter her father. If he thought it was her command of Latin that was at fault, then who was she to contradict him?

'You must be so disappointed you are not to wed and will have to endure the Season.'

She nodded sadly then realised what she was doing. Of course she was not disappointed. She'd got exactly what she'd hoped for when this weekend began. She did not want to marry so early in the Season. She wanted to enjoy balls and parties. She wanted to laugh, dance and flirt the Season away. Now she could. She had no reason to be angry.

Her father reached over and lightly patted her knee. 'But I am confident there will be plenty of other men looking for wives who will realise what a splendid wife you would make them.'

'Thank you, Father.' For once her father was correct.

She would put all thoughts of priggish Sebastian Kingsley behind her, and by the end of the Season she would be married to a man who knew how to enjoy himself, one who appreciated her for who she was and did not think she was going to turn into a gambling, licentious felon the moment he put a ring on her finger.

Chapter Nine

After his first disastrous attempt to find a wife, Sebastian was in no hurry to jump back into the fray. Eventually he was going to have to marry and sire an heir, but fortunately he was under no real pressure to do so immediately. He had wanted to get it over and done with so the succession would be secure, but his father had been in his late forties when he'd married. In that regard, if in no other, Sebastian was now more than happy to follow his father's example.

That gave him thirteen years to find the right woman. Surely that was more than enough time. Unfortunately, relying on his aunt to do this for him had proven a disappointment, so at some stage he was going to have to partake in the London social season. He had managed to stay well away from that so-called genteel marriage mart so far and intended to do so for as long as possible. However, there was one event on this year's social calendar he could not avoid. Nor did he want to.

His valet helped him into his evening jacket and brushed it down one more time in case a piece of lint had the temerity to land upon it since the spotless item had been removed from the wardrobe.

Tonight, one of his closest friends, Isaac Redcliff, now the Duke of Hartfield, and his wife Adelaide, were hosting a ball following their recent return to England after an extended honeymoon tour of Europe.

It was a bold move by the couple. While away, they had been the subject of a great deal of gossip surrounding their marriage, and Sebastian wanted to be in attendance tonight to show his support for his friend and his new wife as they re-entered Society.

He'd met Isaac, along with his other closest friend, Thomas Hayward, on his first day of school, twenty years ago. It had immediately become apparent that the three were outcasts, when they were shunned by the other pupils and even looked down on by some of the masters. Thomas was seen as socially beneath everyone else at the school because he was the son of a wealthy industrialist. The school was happy to take fees from his father but never let Thomas forget for a moment that he was from 'new' money, unlike all the other boys at the school who could trace their lineage back countless generations. Isaac's father had been a duke, but his mother an actress. That too was something the other boys took great delight in taunting him about. As for Sebastian, the entire school was aware of the Rothwell's shameful history, and how his mother had run off with a man who was little more than a servant, and the other pupils saw it as their duty to never let a day go by without reminding him of that fact.

The three boys had become firm friends from that first day and had remained so ever since. Each knew that if they ever needed help, the other two could always be relied on to provide it.

And in a small way, that was what he would do tonight. Nothing, other than helping a friend, would have got him to a ball so early in the Season. The hunt would still be fierce to find a husband, and every debutante and her mama would see an unmarried earl as a prime catch.

It was not a prospect he relished.

He stood in front of the full-length looking glass and tied his white bow-tie. It was likely Lucy would also be in attendance tonight. Unlike him, she would be under pressure to find a marriage partner as quickly as possible. The social season was expensive, especially for the parents of a debutante. He doubted Reverend Everhart's finances stretched to more than one Season, making her choices stark: either find a husband this Season or return to Cheshire as the spinster daughter of the local clergyman.

But that was her problem. He would waste no more time considering her prospects. Nor would he allow his thoughts to stray to memories of her pretty face, her smile or her teasing manner. Some other man would hopefully marry her, and that would be that, and he would never have to think of her again.

Sebastian arrived early at the ball and was greeted enthusiastically by Isaac and Adelaide. Despite their obvious nerves about hosting this event, they both looked radiant. There was no other word to describe them. It was hard to believe that a man who previously had had a stream of actresses in and out of his bed could be so content with one woman, but marriage obviously suited his friend.

He greeted Thomas and his wife Grace, who also possessed that inner glow, as if they had somehow discovered the answer to all life's questions.

Before he had time to ponder the perplexity of his friends' transformations, the room started to fill up with guests, including the very cream of society. It looked like the scandal surrounding Isaac's unexpected elevation to the peerage and his marriage to Adelaide had been put to one side. But their scandal did not go back generations, as his did, so was more easily remedied.

He looked around at the pretty debutantes, all dressed in pink, blue or cream silk, as befitting demure young ladies. They all appeared so sweet and innocent, but as he had so recently learned, appearances could be deceptive. How many would remain as virtuous after they had bagged themselves a husband?

As if drawn by a magnet, his gaze moved to the entranceway where Lucy was standing, her arm linked with an elderly lady, whose baffled expression suggested she'd much rather be at home tucked up in bed than entering this packed ballroom.

Sebastian shook his head in disbelief. Her father had sent her out into the world with only that old biddy as her chaperone? That was simply asking for trouble. There were plenty of men here tonight who would be more than happy to put a young debutante in a compromising position, and they would not all be as discreet as him.

She needed to be warned.

He crossed the room and bowed in front of her. 'Miss Everhart.'

She performed the low curtsy expected of a debutante, but her gaze remained as defiant as it had been the last time he had seen her. 'Aunt Harriet, may I present Sebastian Kingsley, the Earl of Rothwell. My lord, Lady Harriet, my father's sister.'

Lady Harriet attempted a wobbly curtsy, and Sebastian hoped and prayed she did not topple over.

'If you don't mind, sweetie, I think I'll join the other chaperones,' Lady Harriet said to Lucy. 'There are too many people here tonight, too much noise—and why do they need to have the lights so bright?'

Sebastian looked up at the row of crystal chandeliers hanging in a line down the middle of the ballroom, the candles casting a soft warm glow over the assembled guests.

'May I escort you across the room?' he said to the aunt, offering her his arm.

She gave him a delighted smile, and he got a glimpse of the young woman she must have once been before her face became lined with age.

'Thank you, young man,' she said, taking his arm. 'And then you can dance with my niece. I'm afraid we don't know many people here tonight, and dear Lucy can be a bit shy at times.'

Shy? Lucy?

'It would be my pleasure,' he said with a bow of his head. He then slowly led the aunt around the edges of the ballroom towards the seats in one corner, where the chaperones had established a strategic position that enabled them to gossip while keeping an eagle eye on their charges.

When he returned to Lucy she was chatting with Baron Windale.

What was that man up to? He needed a wife with a substantial dowry far in excess of what marriage to Lucy would likely provide. There was only one reason a man such as Windale would be interested in a debutante who was not from a wealthy family. Whether she knew it or not, Lucy needed his protection.

'Excuse me, Windale,' Sebastian said. 'Miss Everhart has promised me the first dance.'

Before Windale could protest or ask her for the following dance, Sebastian linked his arm through Lucy's and led her to the middle of the dance floor.

'I see it didn't take long for you to overcome your alleged shyness,' he said.

'Isn't that what I'm supposed to do? Talk to as many men as possible, dance with all that ask, laugh and flirt until one falls hopelessly in love with me and asks for my hand in marriage?'

Sebastian chose to say nothing as he took her hand in his and placed the other on her slim waist for a waltz.

'That's what the Season is all about,' she continued. 'You can hardly condemn me for doing what every other deb in this room is doing.'

The music started, and they moved off together. Sebastian was pleased to note that while she had no sense of timing when playing the piano, she was a graceful dancer, and they had no difficulty matching each other's rhythm.

'So have you set your sights on Baron Windale?' he asked, hoping she would say no and this conversation could come to an end before a warning was necessary.

'I haven't set my sights on anyone. Not yet.'

'I feel it is my duty to inform you that Windale is a degenerate gambler. His estate is said to be almost bankrupt as a result.'

The slight rise of her eyebrows was the only change in her expression. 'Then, I had better set my sights on someone else, as I need to marry a man with enormous wealth, so I can flutter it away at the card table.'

Sebastian could point out he had never said she

would gamble away anyone's estate, merely that his grandmother had almost done so. But at least he had informed her of Windale's true character, and hopefully she would give that rascal no encouragement.

'And what of you?' she said. 'Have you set your sights on some pure, innocent and virtuous young woman whom you deem worthy of being your wife?'

He resisted sighing with exasperation. 'I have not.'

'No,' she said and shook her head in mock pity. 'It must be so difficult when you demand a standard so high, one that even you are incapable of reaching.'

'And have you lined up some suitably reprehensible rake that you wish to charm?' he responded, annoyed at himself for letting her goad him.

'I thought I had already met a reprehensible rake.'

'Believe me, there are plenty of men here tonight whose reputations more than match the low opinion you have of me.'

She looked around at the dancing couples. 'What? Is the room full of hypocrites?'

His teeth clenched together. She really was the most infuriating woman he had ever met. He was not a hypocrite. There was nothing wrong with a man expecting his wife to be a respectable woman, and he had more right to make that demand than most.

'I'm afraid, Miss Everhart, if you are hoping to find a man who extends the same liberties to his future wife as he does to himself, then you will have a difficult task ahead of you.'

'Oh, I believe I am up for the challenge.'

He swung her around, determined not to respond.

'So what is it you expect of this man, this paragon you would deem suitable as a potential husband?' he asked, his determination failing immediately.

She shrugged one shoulder, drawing his eye to the naked skin beneath the gossamer thin lace at the top of her gown. The pale pink dress was cut lower than the high-neck ones she had worn during her visit to Rothwell Hall, revealing a tempting hint of soft cleavage. The sheer fabric that covered her shoulders created the illusion that the gown was suspended in air and could easily float down, exposing her beautiful body to his gaze.

He quickly looked back at her eyes, which were staring boldly into his.

'I don't expect much, just honesty. Honesty with me and honesty with himself.'

Damn, she knew what he was thinking. If she needed further confirmation that he was a hypocrite, the lustful look he had just given her would have provided it.

'I expect him to appreciate me for the woman I am,' she continued. 'Not the woman he expects me to be. I expect him to want me to be true to myself, and,' she said and lowered her eyes briefly then looked up at him, her gaze once again bold, 'and I expect him to love me.'

He gave a snort of disbelief. 'When it comes to your

last requirement, I suspect you are going to be sadly disappointed. Members of our class rarely marry for love.'

As if taunting him she once again shrugged a shoulder. He fought not to let his eyes wander. He would not let that gesture draw his gaze back to her barely covered skin. He would not let his mind speculate on what the rest of her naked skin would look like, feel like, taste like.

'Didn't the hosts of tonight's ball marry for love? That is what everyone is saying. It's rumoured that they were the unlikeliest of couples, who married under unusual circumstances and, horror of horrors, caused quite the scandal in doing so.'

It was his turn to shrug. Yes, that was true, but Isaac's situation was completely different from his own and that of most of the men present tonight.

'And I believe they are not the only couple here tonight who have married for love.'

His friends Thomas and Grace waltzed past, staring adoringly into each other's eyes as if they were the only couple on the dance floor. Yes, perhaps they too had married for love, but once again, they were the exception, not the rule.

And while his friends had no restrictions surrounding who they could marry, Sebastian did not have that luxury. His ancestors had married the wrong women for the wrong reasons. He would not repeat their mistakes.

'So how are you to find this man with whom you can fall in love with and have your fairy-tale ending?'

'Oh, I don't know, maybe I'm going to have to kiss lots of frogs before I find my prince.'

Sebastian came to a halt in the middle of the dance floor. 'Do not be so thoughtless,' he said, as several couples nearly crashed into them. 'You will get a reputation as a—' he lowered his voice '—as a woman of easy virtue. Men talk, you know. Once your reputation has been tarnished, there will be no getting it back.'

'I think you are in danger of causing a scene, my lord,' she said, a taunting note in her voice. 'That would never do. It might put off the mothers of all those upstanding debutantes, and then where would you find your virtuous wife?'

He looked around and saw that several nearby couples were staring at them, so he recommenced dancing.

'Do not concern yourself with my reputation,' he said. 'You are the one who is in danger of ruining your chances of marriage before they have even begun.'

'And I think you are in danger of being accused of having no sense of humour. Of course I don't intend to go round kissing all and sundry.'

'And yet you kissed me, a man you had only just met, and in a somewhat dubious place for a debutante to frequent.'

She gave no answer, just another shrug of her shoulders.

They continued to dance in silence, irrational anger

still coursing through his veins. If she did decide to risk her reputation by kissing other men, it was surely no concern of his. He had warned her about Windale. He had tried to warn her against doing anything that might set tongues wagging. That was even more than he was expected to do. He would do no more for Miss Everhart.

The waltz came to an end, and Sebastian led her off the dance floor. Lucy had expected Baron Windale to be waiting for her. She looked around, hoping to irritate Sebastian further by dancing with the baron. Windale was across the room, flirting with another young lady who, like Lucy, was not being guarded by a vigilant chaperone.

Sebastian's expression said it all, and Lucy stifled her annoyance that he had been proven right.

Lord Coldridge bowed in front of her. 'May I have the honour of the next dance, Miss Everhart?' he said.

'Indeed, you may.' She gave him her sweetest smile for Sebastian's benefit and hoped this man, too, was someone he would disapprove of. 'I would be delighted.'

Sebastian made a terse bow to them both, strode off across the room and was absorbed by the crowd of milling guests.

That, she supposed, was that. She was unlikely to see any more of him tonight. He probably would not have danced that one waltz with her if it hadn't been for Aunt Harriet's insistence.

Well, who cared? Not her. She would concentrate on enjoying herself, away from his judgemental looks and criticisms.

'Shall we?' Lord Coldridge said, offering her his arm.

Hoping Sebastian was watching, she fluttered her eyelashes, took his arm and allowed him to lead her to the centre of the ballroom, where they took their places for a polka.

The music started, and they danced off to the jaunty tune. Lucy kept a smile fixed on her face while her gaze flitted around the room to see where Sebastian had gone and whether he was dancing with anyone. He was nowhere in sight. Good.

Lord Coldridge placed both hands on her waist and lifted her up, as did every man in the room with their partner. She attempted to giggle along with the other debutantes, but it was hard to do so when she was busy scanning the room from her elevated position.

Her partner lowered her to the ground, and they bounced off in tune to the music. Lord Coldridge was such an eminently suitable man, but despite what Sebastian thought, she had no intention of kissing any of the men present tonight.

She gave a small, unintentional huff of annoyance. How could Sebastian not know she was joking when she said she'd have to kiss a lot of frogs? Did he think her so much of a trollop that she would go round kissing men hither and thither?

Probably. He did have a rather low opinion of her. All because she had visited one gambling den and asked one man to kiss her. And it wasn't as if she wanted to kiss any other man.

Only him.

Drat it even more. It would have been so much better if she had not met him. If she had not kissed him, then she would not be wasting time thinking about a man who did not want her. She would not be remembering a kiss that had made her giddy, which continued to make her giddy every time she thought of it.

'A penny for your thoughts,' Lord Coldridge said, snapping Lucy out of her reverie.

Heat warmed her cheeks. 'Oh, I was just thinking how wonderful tonight is and how much I'm enjoying this dance,' she stammered.

Lord Coldridge smiled at her. 'And I, too, am enjoying dancing with you,' he said, presumably misinterpreting her blushes.

She smiled back at him. He was a rather nice man, and she suspected he might even be fun. He was not quite as handsome as Sebastian, but then, what man was? And that hardly mattered. It was a man's character, his personality that were important, not the fact that Sebastian's thick black hair was threaded with attractive shades of copper. Nor did it matter if his brown eyes reminded her of chocolate or rich toffee and gave her a warm, delicious sensation every time he looked at her.

No, none of that mattered, and she refused to dwell on Sebastian's appearance. He was a hypocrite, and marriage to him would be an absolute nightmare.

Although, as Dolly pointed out, the wedding night was bound to be blissful. She nearly tripped over her dance slippers and only the quick action of Lord Coldridge stopped her from falling and making an exhibition of herself.

'Sorry, that was clumsy of me,' she said.

'Not at all. My fault entirely.'

That was so gracious of him. He was everything she should be looking for in a husband. If that dratted Sebastian had not come along she might indeed be setting her sights on Lord Coldridge. He spun her around, and she took the opportunity to once again quickly scan the room.

Sebastian was over in the corner, talking to another man. Did that mean he was not going to dance with any other women tonight? Did no one reach his exacting standards? Maybe the young ladies present all looked dangerously as if they might like to enjoy themselves on the odd occasion.

A young woman joined Sebastian, and he kissed her on the cheek. Lucy's heart sank to her stomach. The woman turned her head to look at the dancing couples. It was the hostess. A married woman. Her heart soared back up to where it belonged and pounded in the middle of her chest.

The dance finally came to an end, and Lord Coldridge led her off the floor, making the requisite small talk, to which she responded with appropriate smiles and nods when needed. Across the room Sebastian was still talking to the hostess, who had now been joined by the host.

'May I have the honour of this dance?' she heard a man's voice beside her.

'Hmm,' she murmured, still looking in Sebastian's direction.

'Miss Everhart?'

She turned and saw a man smiling at her.

'Oh, yes, I'd be delighted,' she said to Mr Montclair. While Lord Coldridge was the third son of an earl, Mr Montclair was the second son of a second son. He was still a highly suitable husband for a young lady with no title and a dowry provided by her uncle that could never be described as generous. Once again, he was exactly the sort of man she should, as Sebastian said, set her sights on.

He led her out onto the dance floor, and she tried to focus on her partner, but it was hard not to take yet another peek and see what Sebastian was up to and with whom he was dancing. He continued chatting to his friends.

Good. Not that it mattered, not really.

They lined up for a quadrille. Excellent. It was her

favourite dance and would give her the opportunity to flirt with four men all at once. That was exactly what a debutante was supposed to do in such circumstances, and if Sebastian saw her do so, then all the better. It would show him what little regard she held him in and how his rejection of her meant nothing to her.

The orchestra struck the first note, and the dancers moved forward. As she passed from one man to the other, she took the opportunity to chat and laugh with each in turn, thoroughly enjoying herself, just as she intended to do. And her sense of pleasure was increased by the sight of Sebastian watching her from the edge of the room.

She lifted her head higher and smiled brighter, and her feet became light as air as she skittered from partner to partner, letting him know just how easily she had forgotten all about him.

Lady Priscilla and her chaperone joined Sebastian's group and began chatting to the host and hostess. Lucy's sense of self-satisfaction died a sudden death. Lady Priscilla looked suitably modest, despite the shy glances she was giving Sebastian, and Lucy could easily imagine her stuck out in the country with only her embroidery for entertainment.

Not that it mattered to Lucy. Not one bit. And if her stomach had suddenly clenched up into a tight little knot, it had to be because she had pity for Lady Priscilla. She was most certainly not jealous of her or the life she would live as Sebastian's imprisoned wife.

Another chaperone joined Sebastian, this one with two young ladies trailing behind her. Sebastian now had his pick of three debutantes, each as pretty and demure as the next.

She gave a yelp of dismay as in her distracted state she nearly missed the hand of her next partner. This would not do. Lucy tried to focus on the dance so she didn't make any more missteps, but couldn't help but keep a discreet eye on Sebastian and his coterie of admirers.

When a fourth young lady joined the group she nearly stumbled in astonishment. He was now surrounded by a swirl of pastel silk and lace. Only his dark hair was visible above the ornate feminine hairstyles.

Drat. Was he to have his pick of all that was on offer? That was not surprising, she reluctantly supposed. An unmarried earl who was reputed to be in search of a wife would be like the proverbial honey to the bee for every debutante in the room.

He must be feeling so pleased with himself. He'd be able to judge them to his heart's content, weigh up their faults and flaws and dismiss any that did not meet the exacting standard he had set for the next countess. Well, good luck to him. She cared not one little bit.

As one, the group of women curtsied, and above their heads she watched Sebastian perform a bow. Then the group parted.

The quadrille required Lucy to move around the outside of the couples, blocking her view of Sebastian and his harem. If she wanted to see what he was up to, she would have to make a spectacle of herself and jump up to look over her dance partners' shoulders.

It was tempting, but she resisted the temptation.

When she'd finished the circuit and came back to her place, she spotted his retreating back disappearing out the French doors that led to the terrace.

A wave of relief washed over her.

He was merely taking some air. Alone.

She skipped through the remaining dance-steps and even exchanged a few words with each man in the quadrille. When the music came to an end, Mr Montclair led her off the floor, bowed and departed, not even bothering with the requisite small talk.

Instead of trying to look nonchalant while she waited for another man to ask her to dance, Lucy crossed the floor to where the chaperones were clustered, their heads close together in conversation.

Lucy had to cough several times, each time getting louder, until finally she managed to draw her aunt's attention.

'There you are, sweetie,' her aunt said, as if surprised to see her. 'Are you having a nice time?'

'Yes, thank you, but it is getting rather warm in here.' She rapidly fluttered her fan in front of her face to emphasise her point. 'I thought I might step out for a moment to take some air.'

'Well, don't catch a chill, will you?' her aunt said, as if that were the worst fate that could befall an unchaperoned young lady.

'I'll come back inside the moment I cool down.'

'Good girl,' her aunt said and went back to whatever riveting conversation she was having with the other chaperones.

Every debutante should have a chaperone like Aunt Harriet, Lucy thought, smiling to herself as she skirted around the dance floor and headed towards the French doors.

Chapter Ten

Sebastian could breathe again. He knew an eligible earl would be seen as a prize to be fought over but had not expected to find himself so quickly at the centre of a feminine scrum. His ears were still ringing from so much giggling and twittering as each young woman had tried to drown out the other, and he had never seen so much fluttering of eyelashes.

At some stage he would have to partake in that game, but not tonight.

His hands on the railing, he took a moment to enjoy the cool air and looked out at the black outlines of shrubs and trees, lit only by the moonlight. As tempting as it was to remain here, it would not do to spend the rest of the ball hiding out on the terrace, if for no other reason than his friends would wonder what had happened to him.

With a sigh of resignation, he turned toward the French doors and halted immediately. Lucy was standing silhouetted in the doorway, the warm light from the ballroom framing her body and playing on her blond hair, turning it into a golden halo.

'Oh, you're out here,' she said, stepping forward. 'I didn't realise. It's so hot in the ballroom I thought I'd just take a moment to get some air.' Even in the subdued light he could see that her cheeks were indeed flushed.

He took a step towards the door. 'I'll leave you to collect yourself, then.'

'No, there's no need to leave.'

Sebastian hesitated, then stepped back to the railing. It was highly inappropriate for a debutante to be alone with a man, but then, it was Miss Lucinda Everhart, a young woman whose behaviour tended towards the inappropriate.

She joined him at the railing, and they both looked out at the dark garden. They were now standing in semi-darkness, out of reach of the light spilling from the ballroom, with only the moon providing any illumination.

'Is the ball all you hoped it would be?' he asked, making the required small talk.

'Oh yes. It's wonderful. The dancing, the music, the laughing.'

'The flirting. I see you've managed to make a few conquests already this evening. Lord Coldridge gave every impression he was smitten with you, and Mr Montclair couldn't stop staring at you throughout the quadrille.'

She turned towards him, her head angled slightly in question. He silently cursed himself. It would not do for her to think he had paid any heed to whom she danced with. But wasn't that another reason he had retreated to the terrace? Watching Lucy being feted by two such eligible and entirely respectable men had affected him far more than it should.

'And I noticed you did not join in any further dances yourself,' she said. 'I would have expected you to take this opportunity to assess all the available debutantes.'

'That is not why I am here. I'm here because my friends, the Duke and Duchess of Hartfield, are hosting this ball.'

'But surely there are plenty of respectable young ladies here tonight who have piqued your interest. Lady Priscilla, for example.'

'Who is Lady Priscilla?'

'She was one of the young women who joined you when you were talking to the Duke and Duchess of Hartfield.'

Had she, too, been watching him? He had assumed she was too busy flirting with each of the four men who made up the quadrille.

'I'm not here tonight to have my interest piqued or to assess debutantes,' he said, cursing himself silently. Why did he always sound so pompous when in her company? 'And what of you, Miss Everhart? Have you had your interest piqued?'

'Oh, for goodness' sake. Call me Lucy. There is no one present to overhear us.'

He looked over his shoulder, through the open doors to the ballroom, where couples swirled around the floor, oblivious to their presence. She was right. There was no one to overhear them, nor could anyone see them shrouded in the dark.

'And no, my interest is yet to be piqued, but it's still early in the Season,' she continued. 'Thank goodness. I wouldn't want to be taken out of the marriage mart so early, before I've had a chance to have some fun and do my own assessing.'

Sebastian sent her a sceptical look.

'The men don't do all the choosing, you know,' she stated. 'The debutantes like to check over what's available as well. You'd be shocked if you heard some of the discussions that take place in the ladies' retiring room.'

Sebastian chose not to point out to her they could assess away to their hearts' content, but in the end it always came down to the man deciding which young lady best served his purpose, whether it was through the dowry she brought to the marriage or her family's connections.

In some cases a man might be dazzled by a young lady's beauty, and if he were in a position to need neither connections nor money, then he might make an offer of marriage. But that was rare indeed.

Lucy might not have a substantial dowry, but she

did possess beauty in abundance. That was a blessing and a curse. It would draw men to her but not necessarily the right type. She was exactly the sort of woman unscrupulous men would choose to dabble with.

'Don't raise your eyebrows like that, as if I'm talking nonsense,' she said, swotting his arm with her fan, a gesture that from any other woman would be seen as flirtatious, but from Lucy was more like a challenge. 'I know you think you can have any debutante you want because you're an earl, but I'm sure I'm not the only young lady present who wants more from a marriage than just a title.' She gave a light laugh. 'Although, perhaps I'm wrong. Judging by tonight's antics I *am* possibly the only young lady who has not been swept away by the desire to become a countess. I thought you were about to drown in a sea of satin and tulle.'

'Yes,' he said on a long exhalation.

'I almost felt sorry for you,' she said, her smile contradicting any claim of pity.

'I take it Lord Coldridge and Mr Montclair have been assessed and dismissed,' he said, as much to change the subject from himself as out of curiosity.

'Not necessarily. I'm yet to find out how good they are at kissing.'

'Lucy—'

'Don't worry, I'm just teasing.'

'Lucy, I beseech you, do not take your teasing too far. Do not kiss another man just to thwart me.'

She made a small, dismissive huff. 'You do have a high opinion of yourself, don't you? Do you really think I'm going to throw myself into the arms of some other man just to prove our kiss meant nothing to me?'

'I have no idea of what you are capable, I merely entreat you towards caution. No one knows of our kiss. Your reputation remains unblemished. I advise you to keep it that way if you wish to find a suitable husband.'

'And what of your reputation?' She gazed up at him, her eyes glinting in the moonlight. In the soft silver light, her skin appeared almost translucent, the shadows emphasising the curve of her high cheekbones and the lushness of her mouth. Any man seeing her as she looked tonight could surely be forgiven for wanting to kiss those ripe red lips, and she needed to know just how vulnerable she was.

'It is not my reputation that is in danger,' he said.

'No. You're lucky, aren't you? No one knows you kiss lady's maids or indeed innocent debutantes.' She fluttered her eyelashes in a parody of coquettish behaviour. 'If it became known that you kissed me, I'm sure you're aware what would happen, aren't you? Society would disapprove of you chasing after respectable women rather than marrying the tarnished one.'

She pointed one finger hard into the middle of her chest, drawing his eyes to her full breasts. 'Me.'

'Are you blackmailing me, Lucy?' he asked quietly, his gaze returning to her flashing eyes.

'Yes, that's exactly what I'm doing. If you don't stop

lecturing me on what I should and shouldn't do, I'll let the cat out of the bag and we'll be rushed up the aisle sooner than you can say *But she's the last woman in the world I want to marry.*' Her voice had adopted a pompous tone he was sure sounded nothing like him.

'You are not the last woman in the world I want to marry.'

She raised those exquisitely arched eyebrows.

'All right, you're one of the last, just not *the* last.'

She laughed as he'd hoped she would, breaking the tension between them and hopefully distracting his mind from straying to inappropriate thoughts, such as her lips or her breasts.

'And you have no need to lecture me,' she added in a calmer voice. 'I have no intention of kissing anyone else. I know the rules society imposes on young ladies. I'm not entirely gormless, nor as reckless as you suppose me to be.'

It was his turn to raise his eyebrows.

'Oh, all right. I know I kissed you, and yes, perhaps to do so was reckless and maybe a tad gormless, but I didn't think we would see each other again. I thought it was just a bit of fun to kiss a handsome stranger.'

'Handsome?'

She nudged him slightly with her elbow. 'Don't be so coy. You know you're handsome.'

'Just as you know you are beautiful.'

'Beautiful?' she gasped out as if she knew no such thing.

'Whose being coy now? Why else would I allow a young lady to lure me to a gambling table when I am so opposed to such games of chance?'

Her lips curled into a smile. 'Ooh, I tempted you and led you into sin, did I?'

He laughed at her playful retort. 'That's what beautiful women do.'

'So it's all my fault, is it?'

He looked down at her. She was still smiling, and he had every intent of continuing with this light-hearted exchange, but his gaze was drawn to those smiling lips and all thoughts fled his mind. His gaze lingered on her full bottom lip, then moved to the curve of her top lip. Even in the dim light they appeared red, lush and inviting.

'It's not your fault you're so beautiful, but I wish you weren't,' he murmured.

Hardly aware of what he was doing, he lifted the stray lock of hair that was artfully draped down the side of her cheek and curled it around his finger. Her lips parted. The smile became a sensual pout. He lightly stroked his finger down the side of her neck. She gasped in a series of rapid breaths, causing her breasts to rise and fall.

He had not lied when he had called her beautiful. While other debutantes had been listed as the most desirable available this Season, in Sebastian's eyes, Lucy's beauty far exceeded them all.

And, like a forbidden fruit, he wanted her, craved

her. He had to taste her intoxicating sweetness once again.

His hand slid to the back of her neck, his fingers threading into her hair, pulling her towards him. He should not do this. His mind still demanding that he stop, his lips covered hers. Unlike their first playful kiss, this time he did not hold back, could not hold back. Like a starving man presented with a magnificent banquet, he kissed her with a hunger that was all-consuming.

Her body crushed against his, her breasts hard against his chest, sending erotic heat surging straight to his groin. His tongue ran along her lips, forcing them apart, and he entered her mouth, tasting, exploring, probing.

A small part of his brain still capable of reasoned thought hoped she would push him away, protest, do something to stop the madness over which he appeared to have no control.

She did not push him away, did not protest. Instead, she kissed him back with a passion as fierce as his own. With her arms wrapped tightly around his neck, she pressed her body closer to his, her thighs rubbing against him, driving out any thoughts of stopping.

Still kissing her, he released a low groan of desire. God, he wanted her, wanted to explore every inch of her beautiful body.

Doing what he knew he must not, his hand cupped her breast, wishing he could rip away the silk fabric and feast his eyes, his hands, his tongue on those soft mounds. His lips left hers, and he kissed a line down her neck, loving the taste of her soft skin.

She gasped in pleasure and tilted back her head, her breasts arching towards him. She was ready for him. She wanted this as much as he did. And by God, he wanted her. What he wouldn't give to take her, here and now.

That was what he should do. He should lift her up, wrap her legs around his waist, bury himself deep inside her and relieve his pounding need for her.

Compromise her, a voice deep inside him urged. *Make her yours.*

His lips left her neck. His hands dropped to his sides. He all but jumped back.

What on earth was he doing? This was unforgivable.

'I am so, so sorry,' he said, his thick voice unrecognisable.

She opened her eyes, but they remained hooded. Her swollen lips parted, drawing in small, ragged breaths, her cheeks and neck flushed a warm pink.

'That was unforgivable,' he continued, still hardly able to believe he had done such a thing, and that he had wanted to do so much more, and with a debutante, for God's sake.

Her hand covered her heart, and she inhaled deeply and slowly.

What he had done *was* unforgivable, but what was

worse, he still wanted her. He wanted to feel her lips against his, her body pressed into his. It would take so little for him to give in to his raging desire and once again have her in his arms, to kiss and caress her until she surrendered herself to him and he could take what he so desperately wanted.

'I should never have done that,' he said as much to himself as to her. 'I should never have succumbed to temptation.'

She took a small step backwards, blinked several times then her hooded eyes opened wider, her parted lips pressed tightly together as she drew in a shuddering breath.

'And I suppose you will not be able to forgive me for that either,' she said, circling her hand in the air as if to encompass what they had just exchanged. 'You'll once again see it as all my fault and further proof that I am reckless and shameless.'

'No, I...' Sebastian didn't know what he wanted to say and found himself lost for words.

'Well, you've done what you set out to do, haven't you? You've proved that I'm nothing but a little trollop who gives away her kisses freely.'

With that she turned and fled back into the ballroom, leaving Sebastian staring at the door, trying to make sense of the multitude of unfamiliar emotions waging war within him.

Chapter Eleven

Lucy was hardly aware of what she was doing as she fled from the terrace. She stopped on the other side of the French doors, leant against the wall and looked around. No one was looking in her direction. The musicians were still playing, couples were still dancing, groups were still clustered together on the edges of the room, chatting and laughing. It was as if the encounter between herself and Sebastian had never taken place.

Except her heart was still pounding so hard as if trying to escape her chest, her body was burning as if she'd just undertaken vigorous exercise, and her lips were tingling along with other parts of her body best not thought about if she were to try to regain any sense of composure.

She willed herself to calm down, to breathe slowly and deeply, then with as much dignity as possible she walked over to the refreshment table. With shaking hands, she picked up a ladle and served herself a glass of punch. In one long gulp she drank it down, poured herself another and in a most unladylike manner drank that just as quickly.

It did little to cool the heat raging inside her, and she doubted if more punch would help. She returned the ladle to the side of the bowl and looked around.

Her heart jumped in her chest. Sebastian was striding across the ballroom and straight towards her.

Remain calm, she ordered her body. Do not let him think that kiss meant anything to you. Do not let him think that you feel as if you've been caught up in a whirlwind and don't know which way is up or down.

She cast a glance at the punchbowl, her mouth once again dry, then looked around at the assembled men and gave what she hoped was a welcoming smile, as if waiting for her next dance partner.

'Lucy,' he said as he reached her, his voice tense. 'We need to discuss what just happened.'

'What? Oh, that?' She pointed towards the French doors that led to the terrace. 'Yes, that was very nice… very nice indeed.' She forced a little laugh. 'You've set a rather high standard for my other paramours to match.'

'This is no joking matter,' he said, his body rigid.

She forced a small laugh as if to say for her it was all just a bit of fun.

Another gentleman joined them and made a low bow. 'Miss Everhart, may I have the honour of this dance?'

Lucy stared at him, wondering who he was, where he came from and what he was asking of her.

'Miss Everhart has promised this dance to me,' Sebastian said, gripping her upper arm firmly.

Before she was able to gather her thoughts and counter this claim, he was leading her onto the dance floor.

'That was a bit rude, wasn't it? Poor Mr Barrington.'

'Forget Barrington. We have more important things to discuss.'

'No, not really,' she said as dismissively as possible. 'We didn't do anything we hadn't done already. Nothing has changed between us. Nothing needs to be discussed.'

His hand slipped around her waist and she bit back a sigh. Why did it have to be another waltz?

Do not react, she commanded her body, as she placed one hand in his and the other on his broad shoulder.

'What just happened was a great deal more than what occurred at The Royal Flush,' he said as they moved off together to the rhythm of the music.

On that he would get no argument from her. She had thought the kiss at The Royal Flush was divine, but it was nothing more than a brush of the lips compared to the passion of their encounter on the terrace.

She clenched her teeth as her body reacted to the memory of that kiss. She fought to ignore the ache in her breasts at the memory of his touch and the pounding tension gripping deep in her core.

'Yes, I suppose it was,' she said keeping her voice as light as possible. 'We both managed to prove the other right, didn't we?'

His dark eyebrows knitted together.

'You had been lecturing me on not being so, shall we say, free and easy with my kisses. I'd been denying that I was. You managed to prove me wrong.'

'I was not—'

'And I had accused you of being a rake who kisses women he shouldn't, such as lady's maids. I proved my point tonight when you kissed a known debutante.'

'That was not—'

'Let's just call it a draw, shall we? We both won our argument, or lost our argument, depending on how you look at it.'

'But you have every right to demand—'

'I have every right to insist that you never lecture me again on what I should or shouldn't do,' she interrupted before he could make an embarrassing and reluctant proposal.

She laughed as if this was all a jolly jest. 'If I choose to frequent places such as The Royal Flush, if I choose to kiss other men, you will have no right to judge or question what I do.'

'Lucy, I beseech you—'

'Tut, tut, tut,' she said, removing her hand from his shoulder and wagging her finger in front of his face.

'No lectures, remember.' She returned her hand to his shoulder. 'We've established we are as bad as each other, haven't we?'

'If that is what you wish,' he said through clenched teeth.

They continued dancing in silence, and Lucy slowly released a held breath, feeling rather proud of herself. She had just saved her dignity and talked her way out of what was a decidedly awkward situation. If women were allowed to be politicians or lawyers, she was certain she would make an excellent one.

The dance came to an end, and he led her to the edge of the dance floor, where Mr Barrington was waiting. Instead of doing as she expected him to do, bowing and departing, he kept hold of her arm and continued walking, down the length of the ballroom.

'You really are being rather rude to poor Mr Barrington, aren't you?' she said as he kept walking towards the doors. 'I believe he was about to ask me for the next dance.'

'I'm sure he's more than capable of coping with a bit of rudeness,' he said, as he came to a stop beside the stairs that led out of the ballroom. 'I will abide by what you say and not lecture you on your behaviour.'

She all but rolled her eyes, suspecting this was going to lead into the type of lecture he was promising not to give.

'What happened between us should not have happened, and for that I am deeply sorry.'

She shrugged. 'Don't be sorry. Just be grateful you kissed the one debutante in the room who will not be demanding an immediate proposal.'

'As is your right,' he said. 'But I do entreat you, be careful.'

'Maybe I don't want to be careful,' she said, squaring her shoulders and staring into his eyes with as much defiance as she could muster.

'Lucy, for God's sake,' he said, his expression strained.

'And maybe I don't want you interfering in my life. Maybe I want you to leave me alone.'

He continued to glare down at her, muscles bulging in his jawline, his eyes fierce. She would not back down, so she glared back at him with equal intensity.

'Is that what you wish?'

'It is. I want you to leave me alone so I can do whatever I want with whomever I want.'

'Then, I shall abide by your wishes,' he said with a bow. 'Goodbye, Lucy.'

With that he turned and walked up the stairs and out through the doors that took him from the ballroom.

'Miss Everhart, I believe you promised me the next dance.' Mr Barrington had somehow appeared at her side once again.

'I'm sorry, I'm rather tired,' she said, not looking at him, but still staring up at the doors through which Sebastian had departed. 'I think it might be time for me to go home.'

'Then, I hope you reserve the first dance at the next ball for me,' he said with a bow before he, too, departed and went in pursuit of some other debutante.

Lucy had not lied to Mr Barrington. Suddenly she did feel tired and no longer had the energy for this game. She crossed the room and joined her aunt, who was chatting happily with the other chaperones, completely oblivious to anything that had taken place in the ballroom.

'I'm a bit weary, Aunt Harriet,' she said, when she'd finally drawn her aunt's attention. 'Do you mind if we leave?'

Her aunt looked at bit surprised, as one would expect. When had Lucy ever been one to want to retire early?

After much rustling of skirts, a search for her aunt's missing shawl and reticule and repeated goodbyes to her new friends, the two women walked around the perimeter of the dance floor, up the stairs and through the same doors through which Sebastian had departed so abruptly.

'Did you have fun tonight?' her aunt asked as servants helped them into their cloaks.

'Yes, indeed.'

Although, Lucy knew she could not really describe tonight as *fun*. That was far too tame a word for what she had experienced. When he'd taken her in his arms, she had completely lost control. It was like riding a wild, unbridled horse—both terrifying and exhilarating—and now she was left reeling.

Lucy had said she wanted him to leave her alone. She knew that if she were to stop her emotions from running rampant again, avoiding him was the safest and possibly the only option.

Chapter Twelve

Sebastian had no difficulty abiding by Lucy's command. All that was required for him to never see her again was to avoid all Society events, something he was more than happy to do. He still visited The Royal Flush on occasion, and as casually as possible at some time during the evening he would ask Nathanial whether Miss Everhart had been seen in the gaming house. Nathanial's response was always the same. He'd send Sebastian a questioning look, which he would choose to ignore, and reply that he had seen nothing of the lady in question.

Despite not seeing her, that did not mean she was not constantly in his thoughts, but that was surely to be expected and nothing for him to be unduly concerned about. What had happened between them was not something that could be easily dismissed. Only a complete cad would kiss a debutante and then immediately forget all about her. He had transgressed, and that troubled him deeply. Although, if he were being honest with himself, it was not so much guilt or regret over his lack of self-control that haunted him but thoughts of her lips, that kiss and the feel of her body against his.

But that would surely pass. Any day now he expected to read in the newspaper an announcement of her betrothal to some suitable man. Then it would definitely be all over. Even he was not so debased as to lust after another man's wife.

And such an announcement could not come soon enough. While he waited, he tried to distract his mind by indulging in all that London's night life had to offer, and for a man seeking diverting feminine company, he was spoilt for choice. Every night the city was alive with boisterous parties and clubs, and he had attempted to throw himself into such entertainment with abandon. Unfortunately, none of the young ladies who had made their availability clear attracted his attention, and he was starting to tire of so much forced carousing. It was hard to ignore the irony of his situation. Lucy had accused him of being a rake, something he had vehemently denied. She had even said that kissing a debutante proved he was a rake, again something he would say was completely out of character. Now that he was trying to indulge in the lifestyle of a rake to get thoughts of her out of his mind, he was failing dismally. It would be amusing if it weren't so damn frustrating.

He was tempted to return to his estate in Dorset, but

before he did so, he had been invited to meet Thomas and Isaac at their club, The Eldridge, as Thomas had something he wished to discuss with them.

His friends arrived looking as buoyant as usual and joined him in the bar, and all three ordered brandies. They exchanged conversation on Thomas's business activities and the goings-on in the theatres that Isaac managed before conversation turned to Isaac and Adelaide's ball.

'I take it the ball achieved its intended aim,' Sebastian said. 'And the two of you have been accepted into Society, and all scandal has been put behind you.'

Isaac laughed. 'Yes, I've been fully rehabilitated, just as Adelaide said I would be, and all scandals have been buried in the past.'

'Speaking of scandals,' Thomas added, 'you and Lucinda Everhart, eh?'

'Nothing happened,' Sebastian fired back faster than he had intended, which caused both friends to pause, brandy balloons halfway to their mouths.

'All right, I'm attracted to her,' he admitted. 'But that is all. She will never be my countess.'

Thomas and Isaac exchanged knowing looks. Those two had become decidedly self-satisfied since they had become happily married men.

'And the reason she won't become your countess is…?' Thomas prompted.

'Let's just say I have certain expectations for the

next Countess of Rothwell, and Lucy Everhart does not meet them.' It was the only answer he was prepared to give. He had no intention of discussing their kiss or, rather, their kisses.

'So you'd rather marry someone you weren't attracted to?' Isaac asked with a confused frown.

The answer to that was a decided *yes*. He wanted a woman whom he wasn't lusting after with such an intensity it was addling his brain. He wanted a woman he wasn't so desperate to bed that he could almost be arrested for the images that ran through his mind every time he thought of her.

Nor did he want a woman who elicited such strength of feeling from him. They had both acknowledged they were completely unsuitable for each other. To marry a woman like Lucy, one who was hell-bent on having fun, was to court disaster. How long would it be before she too came to the realisation that such fun could be found elsewhere and, like his mother, would leave her husband in search of a good time?

If he felt this way after being told to stay away following a few kisses, a few dances, a few conversations, how would he feel if she became his wife and then deserted him? It did not bear thinking about. He knew the pain of abandonment, had suffered it as a child, and knew how hard it was to crush that pain. He also knew he never wanted to experience that again.

'I need a woman who will make a suitable countess, and whether I'm attracted to her or not is of no relevance,' he stated emphatically.

He looked at his two friends. Were they now smirking?

'You both know the scandals that surround my family,' he added. It was surely something of which they did not need reminding.

He waited, and both men finally nodded.

'I need a wife who knows how to behave herself, one who doesn't...' He did not wish to discuss what Lucy had or hadn't done.

'One who doesn't go out onto a terrace alone with a man and remain there for some time,' Isaac said.

'Exactly,' he nodded. Then the intent of his friend's words hit him. 'Were we seen? Has Lucy's reputation been ruined?' he asked, desperation in his voice.

'You have nothing to worry about,' Isaac added. 'Adelaide and I were taking quite the interest in the two of you during the ball, but I suspect no one else saw.'

'Good, good.'

'My wife informs me that having two dances with an earl at her first ball increased Miss Everhart's status considerably,' Thomas said. 'And at the next ball she was greatly sought after. So what you may or may not have done on the terrace did no harm to her reputation.'

Sebastian should have felt relieved, but the tension gripping his chest on this news did not feel like relief.

'That is good to hear,' he said, forcing his clenched jaw to relax. 'Anyway, I'm pleased your ball was a success, Isaac,' Sebastian said, hoping to change the topic. 'Adelaide must be so pleased that you can now focus on your future and stop worrying about the past.'

'Yes,' he said and smiled, like a decidedly contented cat. 'We are both very happy.'

'Speaking of making our wives happy,' Thomas added, 'Grace has recently become involved in a charity raising money for a children's hospital in the East End.'

'Very commendable,' Sebastian said, hoping that the subject of Lucy Everhart was now done and dusted.

'She has come up with a fundraising idea, and I need your help, Sebastian.'

'Mine? Yes, of course. If she wants a donation, I'm more than happy to make one.'

'Good, very generous of you, but that's not what I mean. She wants to host a card evening.'

'And I'll be happy to attend and lose as much money as she requires.'

'Also good,' Thomas said. 'But she wants to make it a bit more, shall we say, risqué—albeit risqué in a safe environment so the ladies can think they're being a bit devilish without anyone's reputation suffering. As Grace says, that will add to the fun, and if people are having fun they're happier to part with their money.'

'And you want me to provide the risqué element

without making any ladies suffer,' Sebastian asked, confused over how he was supposed to achieve this.

'Well, no, not you. Your half-brother, Nathanial. If you could arrange with him to set up his gaming house in our ballroom, then the ladies can play games they're not usually allowed to, such as having a spin on the roulette wheel, playing baccarat, vingt-et-un, hazard, that sort of thing.'

'I'm sure Nathanial will be happy to oblige.'

'Excellent. And as the house always wins, the children's hospital should also win, and those that do end up with some money left in their pocket at the end of the night will hopefully feel obliged to donate it to the charity anyway,' Thomas said.

'So Grace wants to completely fleece all the punters?' Isaac asked.

'Exactly,' Thomas said. 'My wife is acquiring quite the head for business since she married into my family.'

Once again, his friends exchanged those contented smiles and went on to discussing the joys of married life and their seemingly flawless wives.

Lucy was not usually one for regrets, but she was coming to regret telling Sebastian to leave her alone, or rather, she was regretting that he had done as she told him.

For weeks, every time her body remembered that kiss, she would force herself to also remember his sanctimonious lectures. Self-righteous indignation would bubble up inside her, pushing out all other thoughts, and she'd enjoy thinking of everything she wished she'd said to him before they parted.

At her next ball, she had waited eagerly for his appearance so she could show him just how much she did not need him telling her how she should live her life and showing him how she was more than capable of looking after herself.

He had not made an appearance.

She told herself not to worry and hoped gossip of all the men she had danced with would reach him. She imagined him becoming enraged at her being imprudent with her kisses—even though she had kissed no one else. That would bring him running to the next event on the social calendar, full of recriminations and demands that she explain herself. She had even practised possible responses that would put him firmly in his place.

He was not at the next ball either. Nor was he at the one after that.

With nowhere to go, all her indignation had eventually deflated, and all she was left with was the memory of his kiss. As if it were imprinted indelibly on her lips, it would not leave her alone. Nor was she capable of forgetting the feel of his arms around her or his hand caressing her in such an intimate manner.

But it seemed he had been able to forget all about her.

With resignation she sat across the breakfast table

with her aunt, as they discussed yet another ball at which Sebastian was not in attendance.

'Last night was rather marvellous, wasn't it?' Aunt Harriet said, as she had said about every other ball they had attended. Despite her initial reluctance, her aunt now appeared to be enjoying the social season even more than Lucy. The same group of chaperones gathered at each event, gossiping away, and making all these new friends was putting quite a glow in her aunt's cheeks.

'Yes, a delight,' Lucy responded with as much enthusiasm as she could summon.

'It's a shame there are still no offers of marriage,' her aunt said with a sad shake of her head. 'But I suppose it is still early in the Season.'

'Hmm,' Lucy said, as she buttered her toast.

The lack of requests to court her was something of which Lucy was all too aware. She was never short of dance partners, but none came to call the next day. No flowers or cards were sent. No invitations to more private events such as walks in the park or visits to country estates were extended.

Lucy was obviously doing something wrong, and drat it all, she had her suspicions of what it might be. It was hard to do the requisite flirting, to show the required interest in what her dance partners were saying, to provide the expected level of flattery when you were constantly thinking about another man.

That had to change, and as her aunt said, it was

early in the Season, even if announcements had already been made regarding the forthcoming marriages of several debutantes. None of which involved the Earl of Rothwell, she was pleased to note. Even when at her most vexed over his moral outrage concerning her behaviour, she had to admit that hearing he was to marry another would be crushing.

The footman entered with the day's first post on a silver tray and placed the letters beside Aunt Harriet. She slit each one open while sipping her tea. 'You're still receiving plenty of invitations, though,' she said and smiled at Lucy.

Then she frowned, looking down at a card in her hand. 'No, I don't think your father would approve of that one.' She placed the invitation to the side of her plate and opened up the next letter.

Lucy reached over and picked up the discarded invitation. If her father disapproved, then it was sure to be more interesting than yet another ball.

It was an invitation from Thomas and Grace Hayward for a gaming evening at their London residence. Thomas Hayward was one of Sebastian's closest friends. It was an event he was sure to attend, even if it did involve the sinful act of gambling.

She re-read the crisp white card embossed in gold lettering.

'This gaming evening is to raise money,' she said to her aunt.

'Raise money?' Her aunt frowned in confusion. 'At a social event. For whom?'

'For a charity, a children's hospital.'

Her aunt looked unconvinced.

'Father would so approve of that. In fact, I think he would approve so strongly that he would see it as remiss if we did not attend.'

'But gambling, sweetie?'

'It's just a bit of fun and a way of giving money to a worthy cause. Not gambling at all, really.'

'I suppose,' her aunt said doubtfully.

'It's for a children's hospital, Auntie,' she repeated, appealing to her relative's better nature. 'We cannot deny the poor children, can we?'

'You are such a kind girl, always thinking of others.'

Lucy kept smiling. She would not feel ashamed of her ulterior motive. The children *would* benefit, even if that was not the only reason she wanted to attend this event.

'You are right, Lucy. We will attend for the sake of the children, and for one night put aside our abhorrence of gambling.'

'Good. I'll let Mrs Hayward know that we will be delighted to attend and will try and lose as much money as we can, all for a good cause.'

She all but ran out the room and into the study, picked up pen and paper and dashed off an acceptance before her aunt had a chance to change her mind.

Chapter Thirteen

Lucy's nerves were fizzing as she entered the Hayward ballroom on the arm of her aunt. That was to be expected. She was to see Sebastian again for the first time in more than a month. What she hadn't expected was her reaction when she saw him, standing beside his half-brother Nathanial at the roulette table.

Air left her lungs. Her heart clenched in her chest, and her stomach did strange summersaults. Had he always been so handsome, so tall, so masculine?

And this magnificent man had kissed her. Twice.

He turned from talking to his half-brother and looked at her, which did nothing to assuage her rampaging heartbeat. No wonder she was reacting this way. Everything about him was perfection.

'Lucy?' her aunt said, her voice coming out of a fog. 'Sweetie, are you all right?'

'Oh yes, absolutely,' she said, smiling at her aunt. This was impossible. There wasn't a trace left of the indignation she had felt for Sebastian in the past. Now there was only a powerful attraction for an undeniably handsome man.

What on earth was happening to her? Why was she feeling like this? Why was every inch of her body suddenly tingling, and why was her entire focus on that one man? She gasped as a devastating thought hit her like a giant wave crashing against a rocky shore. She couldn't be falling in love with him, could she?

Heaven help her if she was. Sebastian desired her, of that she was certain, but was he capable of loving her? Unlikely. As for wanting to marry her? Definitely not.

This was beyond hopeless, beyond anything she had experienced before or had ever expected to experience. She had wanted to fall in love but had assumed it would be something gentle and sweet, involving lots of flowers and affectionate words, not something akin to being caught up in a thunderstorm and torn between embracing the excitement of the tempest and running for cover.

If she were falling in love, and she hoped and prayed she was not, then this was something about which she could not let Sebastian know. It would be devastating if the man who had so firmly rejected her thought she had fallen so hopelessly under his spell.

'Perhaps we should move from the doorway, sweetie,' her aunt said, indicating the line of people behind them. 'We're blocking the entrance.'

'Oh, yes, sorry.'

On her aunt's arm she strolled around the room,

observing all the gambling tables as if seeing such things for the first time and trying not to look in Sebastian's direction.

The ballroom had been set up in a similar manner to The Royal Flush, with tables for roulette, poker, baccarat and vingt-et-un. A band was playing in the corner of the room and an area had been set aside for dancing. In another corner was a bar, just as you'd find in a gambling den, rather than the usual refreshment table found at a ball. The dealers she recognised from The Royal Flush were standing at each table, looking smart in their red frock coats, many of whom were explaining the games to giggling ladies.

The only difference was the clientele, which consisted of the upper echelons of Society, all dressed in elaborate ball gowns and formal suits, and there were as many women as men present. The women all wore identical expressions, as if they were doing something delightfully naughty, and it was obvious that none had ever stepped into such a gaming establishment in their lives.

Their circling of the room took them to the roulette table, where Sebastian was waiting. Lucy's already rapidly beating heart immediately accelerated.

Stay calm. He does not know how you feel.

'Why, my lord, how lovely to see you again,' she said with as much feigned nonchalance as she could muster.

'Miss Everhart, Lady Harriet,' he said with a bow. 'Would you like me to explain how this game works?'

'Oh, no, no,' Aunt Harriet said before Lucy could answer. 'I don't believe I should gamble, even for a good cause. Explain how this contraption works to Lucy,' she added, pointing to the roulette wheel. 'I shall be with the other chaperones at the whist table.'

With another exchange of curtsies and bows, Aunt Harriet raced off at a surprisingly fast pace, eager to join her new friends seated around several tables at the end of the room, all staring at their cards as intently as the most ardent poker players.

Lucy smiled at Sebastian and hoped her quivering lips did not betray her nerves. 'Thank you for that. Aunt Harriet would be mortified if she thought I knew how to play roulette.'

He nodded his head slightly. 'I wonder if your luck will be in tonight.'

Lucy pursed her lips and blew out a held breath. That was exactly what she had been thinking.

'I haven't seen you at any of the other social events,' she said, stating something they both knew to be so.

'No, but that surely pleases you. The last time we spoke you said you wanted me to leave you alone.'

Lucy bit her bottom lip wanting to add that while at the time she thought that was what she wanted, deep down she hadn't expected him to do as she asked.

'Perhaps you would prefer if I abided by your wish now.'

He moved away from the table, and Lucy placed her hand on his arm. 'No.'

He turned and looked down at her, his eyebrows knitted together in question.

'You promised to show me how to play roulette.'

The eyebrows pressed even closer together.

'For appearances' sake and all that,' she said and gave a little laugh, feeling somewhat ridiculous. Why was she so uncomfortable in his company? Why couldn't she go back to making fun of him or admonishing him or anything other than acting like a ninny? She knew the answer to that, and if she were to keep any semblance of composure, it was something best not dwelt upon.

'As you wish.'

He commenced explaining about the red and white squares and the numbers and how each was weighted to provide a different amount of winnings, according to the odds of how likely the spinning white ball would land on that number and colour.

'Thank you,' she said when he had finished. 'So which square shall I pick?' she quickly added so he would not race off.

'First I believe you need to buy some chips.'

'Oh, yes, of course,' she said, fumbling into her reticule for her pin money.

'Allow me.' He handed some coins to the croupier then offered her the pile of chips.

She looked at the coloured discs, smiled and looked up into his eyes. Like her, was he remembering the first time they met? Had an image of the rainbow of chips falling on them when they collided at The Royal Flush also entered his mind? She still had the chips he had placed in her bag that night, foolishly keeping them as a memento of their first kiss.

She reached out her hand. He cupped it with one hand and placed the chips in it with the other. He held her eyes for a moment then looked back at the roulette table.

'You didn't say which square I should pick,' she repeated lest he take the opportunity to race off.

He took a few chips from her hand and placed them on the nearest square.

'Have you been enjoying the Season?' he asked, not looking at her but watching the ball spinning around the roulette wheel.

'Yes, thank you,' she responded, wishing she could shake off this sudden shyness in his company. She was never shy. But then, she had never felt this way before, as if the floor was unsteady under her feet and everything she did and said was of monumental importance.

'And, well, if you're staying away from balls and such because of what I said, well, I am sorry,' she added.

He looked down at her, with a questioning frown.

'You know...when I told you to leave me alone,' she said.

'I see.'

'If you wanted to attend balls and things, I wouldn't object.'

Just stop talking. You're starting to sound desperate.

'Thank you. I shall keep that in mind,' he said, giving away nothing of how he was feeling about her.

The croupier reached out across the table with a small rake and drew in their chips along with those of most of the people at the table.

'Oh, well, unlucky for us, but lucky for the children's hospital,' she said and attempted to give a light laugh to prove she was not feeling increasingly uncomfortable.

She looked up at him and smiled and wondered if she should make some light-hearted reference to how he had tried to bring her luck the last time they had gambled together, but the words wouldn't come. She was incapable of teasing, incapable of such light-heartedness.

'Now that you have learnt the intricacies of roulette, will you excuse me?'

'Oh, but I might want to play one of the other games. I'll need to have them explained as well,' she said, horrified that her words tumbled out in a garbled flurry.

'I believe that is what the croupiers are for, and at every table there appears to be plenty of men more than happy to show off their skills to the assembled ladies.'

But the only one I want showing off his skills is you, Lucy would have said if she were capable of flirting.

Instead she merely nodded her head. 'I thank you for your assistance, my lord.'

He nodded in response and walked off.

Tightness gripped her body, and her heart seemingly splintered within her chest as she watched him walking away from her.

You're a fool, Lucinda Everhart, a complete fool.

Her hand trembling slightly, she pushed a few chips onto a square, then attempted to give the other patrons a delighted smile.

'Isn't this fun,' she said, determined to hold on to her dignity. She would continue playing, continue looking as if she were enjoying herself and hope that Sebastian had no idea of the depth of her unreciprocated feelings for him.

Sebastian had to get away. Being in such proximity to Lucy was torture.

He walked over to the bar and asked the man for a large brandy. As he drank the amber liquid he looked over to the roulette table. She was so beautiful it was almost painful to watch her. Like many of the other debutantes present tonight, she was dressed in a pale cream gown, adorned with lace and ruffles and heaven knows what else, but she still stood out from the rest.

Her hair was piled on top of her head, with a cascade of ringlets flowing down the back of her naked neck. It was impossible not to imagine lifting those locks of hair and kissing the pale skin beneath.

He downed the rest of the brandy in one swallow.

Leave, he told himself. Now.

There was no reason that he had to remain for the duration of the event and suffer any further. He had already made a generous donation to the charity so no one could blame him if he did so.

He looked over at the hosts, Thomas and Grace, chatting with Isaac and Adelaide. All four looked in his direction and sent him matching smiles. If he didn't know better, he would think there was some conspiracy afoot and they had concocted this entire evening to put him and Lucy in the same room together.

No, that was ludicrous. He had already told his friends he had no interest in her. Although that, of course, was a lie. While he had no interest in marrying her, he had far too much interest in her as a woman he was damnably attracted to.

His attention turned back to the roulette table where several men were talking to Lucy, explaining the intricacies of a game she was more than capable of understanding without their assistance. Bile burned up his throat as he glared at her companions. But surely that was what he wanted. The sooner she captured some man's heart, was married off, out of his life and out of his thoughts, the sooner he could start focusing on finding a bride for himself.

'Is she the one you've put your money on?' the man standing beside him said.

'What are you talking about?' Sebastian turned to

him. Baron Hughes had a whisky glass to his mouth and was looking in Lucy's direction.

'Don't you know about the book that Lord Smythe is running? He does it every year. The man would bet on anything,' Hughes added with a laugh.

'What sort of bet?' Sebastian asked, not liking the sound of this.

'It's on which debutante is married off next. You should place a bet on Miss Everhart. The odds on her keep getting better and better. If you get in now while Smythe is paying out ten to one, you could make a killing if she's the next one to bag herself a husband.'

Sebastian stared at the man with a mixture of horror and contempt.

'Oh, come on. You must know that if an earl pays a girl attention she instantly becomes of interest to all the men in search of a wife. It's like she's been given a seal of approval. That's what happened to that little chit.' He angled his glass in Lucy's direction. 'When you danced with her twice at the Hartfield ball, it drew the attention of other men, particularly those not in need of a large dowry. At that stage she was running at two to one as everyone was sure Montclair or Coldridge would ask for her hand before you had a chance. Then you disappeared, and with each ball the odds went up. Men still dance with her, I suppose because she's a pretty little thing and rather light on her feet, but none have expressed any interest in courting her.'

Hughes took a sip of his whisky. 'What you need

to do is place a bet now, then act as if you're interested. That will increase her perceived value. Once some other man swoops in and asks for her hand, then you'll make a tidy sum of money.'

He raised his glass to Sebastian. 'And if I make a healthy return as well, then where's the harm?' He downed his drink and winked at Sebastian.

The entire enterprise was obscene, but Hughes was right. He was an earl. Sebastian was wealthy, and he was eligible. Any young lady who caught his eye was sure to also catch the eye of men seeking a desirable and sought-after wife.

If he wanted Lucy married and out of his life, the best thing he could do was pay her as much attention as possible.

He ordered another drink from the barman and rolled the brandy balloon round in his hand as he contemplated the absurdity of this situation. Lucy had told him to leave her alone. For his own reasons, he had vowed to do exactly that, but he would be breaking that vow for the best of reasons. There was no denying it was somewhat underhand, but what harm would it really do? Lucy would find a good husband, and he could finally put all that had happened between them behind him and continue with life as if they had never met.

That at least was what he told himself as he approached the roulette table.

'Miss Everhart, would you do me the honour of a dance?'

'What?' she all but yelped. 'Oh. Yes.'

He took her arm and led her across the room to the corner where a few couples were dancing to the same band that played at The Royal Flush. He placed his hand on her waist and hoped that every man in the room had taken note of what was happening.

'I hope you don't mind,' he said as they moved off to dance the lively polka.

'Mind? Why would I mind?'

'You did ask me to leave you alone.'

'Oh, yes, that. What I meant was I wished you to stop lecturing me.'

'Then, I promise I will never lecture you again.'

She looked up at him, her head inclined, as if trying to work out what was going on. Should he tell her about Smythe's gambling book? Or about Hughes's conversation? That was probably an unwise idea. She was of such a contrary nature, if she knew what he was up to she was just as likely to stomp off the dance floor and ruin any chance she had of increasing her marriage prospects.

'Are you sure you're going to be able to control yourself?' she asked.

He stared at her in shock. 'I assure you, I am more than capable of doing so.' He may have broken one vow, but he would not break his other vow to never kiss her again. He was on a mission to marry her off. Once that happened such temptation would be removed, and he would be safe from even thinking of doing such a thing.

'Well, you've succumbed before.'

Was he never going to be allowed to forget that he had kissed her?

'And I believe you will succumb again,' she added.

This was a mistake. She was right. With her in his arms it was impossible to forget kissing and caressing her. Only a dullard tries to avoid temptation by putting temptation in his own way.

'I do not believe for one moment you are going to avoid the pleasure of lecturing me, at least a little bit,' she said, her smile whimsical.

He released the inhaled breath and laughed in relief. 'Perhaps you are right. Have you done anything lately you feel deserves a lecture?'

'That would be telling, would it not?'

She smiled up at him as he continued to spin her around the floor. How he'd missed that lovely smile.

'And what of you? Have you done anything that deserves a lecture?' she asked.

Apart from lusting after a woman I should not, no.

'You can rest assured, I have been living a life even your father would approve of,' he said in all honesty, although it was not for lack of trying. Lucy had accused him of being a rake, and it was true he often kept a mistress, but since meeting Lucy he had not even indulged in that one rakish behaviour. As for attending wild parties, they held even less appeal.

She inched slightly closer to him. His hand slid further round her waist.

'Then, it appears we have both become paragons of virtue,' she said.

With her breasts almost touching his chest, his hand caressing her waist and his thoughts moving to places they should not, he would hardly describe himself as virtuous, but having her in his arms was all in a good cause, he reminded himself yet again.

'And I hear you have not been visiting The Royal Flush,' he said, wishing to distract his mind and body from places it should not wander.

'There's no need. I crept out that night because I thought my time as a debutante was about to come to an end before it had even begun and I was going to be stuck out in the country, married off to some boring earl my father approved of.' She sent him a playful smile that caused him to smile in return. 'But I was saved from that fate.'

He had to admit he missed her teasing, and that warm smile that somehow melted away his resistance.

'And I believe we have the owner of The Royal Flush to thank for tonight's entertainment,' she continued then raised one of those finely arched eyebrows. 'Who I have been informed is your half-brother.'

'Yes. On both counts you are correct.'

'It must be lovely to have a brother.'

Sebastian pulled her in slightly closer, knowing that her loneliness as a child might have been eased somewhat if she'd had a sibling.

'Yes. I'm pleased Nathanial and I have made contact and only wish we had known each other growing up.' He swallowed down his ire towards his mother who had deprived him of that brotherly relationship. But he would not let thoughts of that woman undermine his enjoyment of having Lucy back in his arms.

And he *was* enjoying himself. He might have ulterior reasons for dancing with her, but he was actually doing what she put so much stock in—having fun—something he had to admit rarely happened and never happened at society events.

'But you had close friends,' she added. 'That too must have been wonderful. When I first started sneaking out to play with the village children they were wary of me because I was the clergyman's daughter. So I had to prove to them that I was not the little Goody Two-shoes they thought I was.'

He laughed at that image. 'Something I doubt you had difficulty doing.'

'No. Fortunately, it is one of my skills.'

The others including the ability to light up a room with one smile and amuse even a hardened cynic like myself.

It was difficult to believe that she'd had no proposals, but then the marriage mart was rarely about finding the most attractive, most delightful, most charming young lady to marry but about making the most advantageous match. Or, as he was hoping after tonight, winning the young lady whose status has risen due to the competition.

The happiness he had been feeling was replaced by a gripping sensation in his stomach. Yes, he was jealous of the man who would eventually have her as his wife, but it could not be him. When he did marry it would be to a woman who he knew would break the Rothwell curse, and that could only happen if he used his head and not his heart to select his future wife.

Heart?

He pushed that thought away. He would not and could not have any such feelings for Lucy that would lead him down a path he refused to go.

Before he could spend too much time analysing these dangerous emotions, the music came to an end, and he led her off the dance floor, where Montclair was waiting.

'Miss Everhart, may I have the next dance?' Montclair said with a bow.

Sebastian's ruse was working, but Montclair had paid her attention before, only to withdraw it when he thought Sebastian was no longer interested. This was going to demand a higher level of subterfuge.

'Miss Everhart, I would be greatly honoured if you would accompany me for a walk in Hyde Park tomorrow afternoon,' he said loudly enough so that Montclair was not the only man to hear.

'What? Where?' she said, her eyes growing large.

'Hyde Park. It's a large grassed in area in central London where people often promenade when the weather is pleasant,' he said, amusement in his voice.

'Oh, yes, that sounds delightful,' she said, with a note of uncertainty.

'I shall make the arrangements with your aunt and call for you tomorrow,' he added with a bow to Lucy and a nod to Montclair.

This was all working out splendidly, and hopefully one walk would be all that was necessary for the expressions of interest in courting Lucy to come flooding in, and he would not have to test himself further by spending any additional time in her company.

Chapter Fourteen

Lucy hardly got a wink of sleep but woke the next morning with excitement pushing away any tiredness. She'd lain awake for much of the night trying to work out Sebastian's change in behaviour. He had dismissed her as a potential bride, kissed her, lectured her, ignored her, and now he wished to promenade with her in a public place for all of Society to see.

Her hoped-for answer to his sudden change of heart might be wishful thinking, but perhaps—just perhaps—his opinion of her was softening. Maybe he was starting to see that she *could* be his bride. Was there a possibility he was coming to the realisation that *he* was starting to fall in love with *her*, just as she realised she was now falling for him?

If he was having such thoughts, then it was up to her to nudge him further in that direction. And that was exactly what she planned to do. She wasn't sure how, but surely something would occur to her.

With Dolly's help, she spent the morning trying on

one day dress after the other. She needed something that showed herself off to her very best, without looking as if she had gone to too much trouble. Something that would present her as a desirable young woman but still demure enough to be a respectable future countess. In the end she selected a cream skirt and jacket with a lacy white blouse. The jacket was tailored so it pulled across the chest, highlighting her breasts, nipped in at her waist to give her the required curves and flared out over her hips.

The high neckline suggested modesty, although the lace was sheer so the skin beneath could be seen.

Carefully inspecting her appearance, she turned slowly in front of the full-length looking glass, observing herself from every angle, and finally declared the outfit to be exactly as she hoped: one that showed off her feminine attributes to the best advantage without appearing to do so.

'A good choice, miss,' Dolly agreed.

Dolly then spent a considerable amount of time carefully styling her hair, so it had the carefree, effortless look of a loose bun at the back of her neck, but with a few feminine curls framing her face, as if they had escaped of their own volition. Several hairpins were then used to attach a feathered hat at what they both declared to be a jaunty angle.

'What do you think?' Lucy asked, as she performed a few more twirls in front of the looking glass.

'You look like a countess,' Dolly said as she handed Lucy her gloves and lace parasol.

Lucy smiled at her maid, and with her nerves fizzing, the two young women walked down the stairs to the drawing room, where Sebastian was waiting for her.

She bit down a smile when she entered and found him taking tea with Aunt Harriet, who was smiling and simpering under his attention like a flirtatious young debutante.

He stood up as she entered and placed his undrunk cup of tea on a small side table. Was that a look of admiration that crossed his features? She hoped so. She'd hate to think all the trouble she had gone to in dressing was wasted on him.

'I hope you and the Earl of Rothwell have a lovely time,' Aunt Harriet said. 'But I'm afraid Dolly will have to chaperone as my walking days are sadly over.'

Lucy leant over and kissed her aunt on the cheek. 'I'm sure we will have a delightful time, Auntie, and Dolly will no doubt also enjoy a walk in the park.'

'Don't catch a chill, will you?' her aunt added with concern.

'I promise you I won't,' Lucy said.

And if I do get cold, I'm sure Sebastian will be able to warm me up, she was tempted to add.

Sebastian bowed farewell to Aunt Harriet and escorted Lucy out to his waiting open-topped carriage.

Lucy could hardly contain her excitement as they

rode through the sunny streets. The man she could not stop thinking about, the man who had kissed her until she hardly knew which way was up or down, was taking her for a walk in Hyde Park. The man who considered her lacking in the correct level of modesty and decorum to ever be worthy of being his wife was all but courting her. And if he was courting her, surely that would mean there was no reason why he could not kiss her again.

As they drove through the ironwork gates at the entrance to the park, her excitement mounted, and she wondered whether there were any secret places where they could hide away. She gave a little giggle at the thought of hiding away in Hyde Park. Perhaps that was where it got its name.

The carriage came to a halt, and he helped her down then offered his hand to Dolly.

'Right, let's promenade,' he said, taking her arm. They joined the line-up of people walking almost in formation along the pathways. She scanned the well-spaced trees and the open, grassed areas. It looked like they would not be finding any secret places to hide away.

But perhaps it mattered not. This was lovely, walking in the sunshine with a handsome man on her arm. Several of the young ladies she had met at various balls glanced in her direction with a look of envy in their eye. She didn't blame them. She, too, would be envious of a woman walking with a man such as Sebastian.

'We seem to be drawing rather a lot of attention,' she said.

'I believe that is one of the main reasons for promenading in Hyde Park. To see and be seen.'

'Oh, silly me, and I thought it was to enjoy the scenery and get some exercise and fresh air.'

He smiled at her, and what a wonderful smile it was, all the more precious because of its rarity. 'I would have thought by now you had learnt that in Society everything has more than one reason.'

'Yes, the Season gives the appearance of being about having fun, but really it all comes down to the juggle for position and advancement,' she said. 'Only the lucky few actually marry for love.' She looked up to see how he reacted to this. He made a small huffing noise as if she was making an ironic joke. She wasn't.

'So you've finally worked that out, have you?'

'Hmm,' she responded, her heart deflating inside her chest. That did not sound like the response of a man who was falling in love. So what was he up to? Why had he invited her on this walk? Why was he so keen to be seen in public with her? There was so much about this man that was impossible to decipher.

They walked along in silence while she contemplated this conundrum. Then with a concerted effort she pushed all questions aside. She was strolling in the sunshine with the man she adored. That is what she would focus on, that and looking as pretty as possible, being as agreeable as she was able and convincing this man that, even if he didn't yet know it, he was starting to have strong feelings for her. And while other people might not marry for love, that did not mean they should not do so.

This was even more of a success than Sebastian had hoped. Men were looking at Lucy, including eligible men. Courtship and marriage from one of those eligible men would surely soon follow.

In the meantime, he could just enjoy the company of a delightful, enchanting and beautiful young woman, albeit one who would make a disastrous Countess of Rothwell.

'I think everyone in Society must be here this afternoon,' she said looking around. 'I can't believe how crowded this park is.'

'This is de rigueur for a young lady during the Season. I'm surprised your father or Aunt Harriet hasn't insisted that you and your lady's maid take the air in Hyde Park on a regular basis.' He looked over his shoulder for Dolly who, as expected, was walking well behind her charge.

'Well, Aunt Harriet's coming out was a long time ago, and anything she did or didn't do has probably been lost in the mists of time. My parents married before the start of the Season, so I doubt Father even knows what's expected.' She shrugged one shoulder.

'But you appear to know. Is that what your mother did to attract the attention of your father, or was their marriage arranged the way my parents' was?'

'I have no idea,' he said, not wishing to talk about his father and that woman.

She stopped walking and turned to face him, with a look of curiosity. 'You've told me about your ancestors, but you rarely mention your parents.'

'Do you not know about my family situation?'

She shook her head slowly.

'Then, you must be one of the few people in Society who doesn't.'

'In case you've forgotten, I've been stuck away in the Cheshire countryside for the last twenty years. I could write a book about all the things I don't know, if such a thing were possible.'

He gave a small laugh at this ridiculous comment. She was such a delight, and he did love the way she could make him laugh.

'Well?' she probed.

'My mother had an affair with the estate manager and ran off with him when I was but two years old,' he said, staring straight ahead, surprised at himself for revealing so much. 'My father divorced her for adultery, and she disappeared to America with her lover and started another family. It was quite a scandal at the time.'

'That must have been awful for you,' she said quietly, placing her hand lightly on his arm.

'I was young at the time. I knew nothing of what was taking place.'

'When did you find out what had happened?'

'When I was sent off to boarding school at the age of seven, and it became obvious that all the pupils and masters knew about the divorce. They took great delight in telling me all the sordid details.'

'That's awful. You must have been so unhappy.'

He lifted his shoulders, as if to shrug off the memory.

Her hand still held his arm in a gentle grip. 'Have you spoken to your mother since? Do you know what it was like for her? Have you found out why she did it?'

'No, I have not spoken to her, and I never will,' he said with more force than he intended. 'She made her choices twenty-five years ago, and there is no going back.'

'Does that mean she has tried to make contact with you?'

'Yes. Nathanial has informed me she is presently in England and wishes us to meet before she returns to America, but that will not be happening.'

She looked up at him, those big blue eyes swimming with tears, as if she were pleading the case of his mother. 'That is a shame. I wish I had a chance to speak to my mother, just once.'

He stopped walking and took hold of her arms. 'Oh, Lucy, I am so sorry. It must be hard for you to have grown up without a mother.'

'We both grew up without mothers,' she said.

They stared at each other for a moment, and he was so tempted to take her in his arms and comfort her.

'Oh, the world can be so unfair at times, can't it?' she said as they resumed their walk. 'You have a mother you never want to see, and I would give anything to be able to spend even a few moments with mine.'

He lightly patted her hand. 'Has your father or your aunt Harriet told you much about what your mother was like?'

'They say I look like her and we are similar in temperament.'

'Then, she must have been very beautiful and a delightful lady. I'm sure she would have been proud to have taken you on her arm and seen you presented to the queen.'

Lucy gave one of those tinkling laughs which somehow caused the tightness in his jaw to release the tension always triggered by talk of his mother.

'I doubt that. My presentation was, shall we say, a little unconventional.'

'I think that claim needs some explanation,' he said with a smile, looking forward to what he was sure would be an entertaining and diverting story.

'I had expected my presentation to be a magical experience, but…well, it was a bit ridiculous.'

'*Ridiculous*? I've never heard it described like that.'

'Well, you've never had to stand in line for simply

ages, along with countless other young women, all dressed in white gowns with these enormous white ostrich feathers sticking up from your hair. We looked like a flock of rather anaemic birds. Everyone was excited to begin with, but as the day dragged on and on and on, we all started to wane. I could see this line of feathers in front of me slowly starting to droop.'

Sebastian laughed at this image.

'When my name was finally read out, I walked down the middle of the throne room and stood in front of the queen.'

She dropped her hand from his arm, stood up straight, her head held high, but her eyes modestly lowered, as if about to be presented to the monarch.

'It was my big moment, something I'd spent months and months training for. I took a quick peek up, to get a glance of Her Majesty, and realised the old queen was sound asleep. I suppose no one felt they had the authority to wake her up. So I performed my elegant curtsy in front of someone whose eyes were closed and whose head had dropped down to her chest.'

'Most unfortunate,' he said, amused by her tale.

'That wasn't the worst of it. When I had lowered myself almost to the ground she made a snorting noise in her sleep.'

'Even more unfortunate,' he said, trying not to laugh.

'It gets worse. Then she started to snore. Loudly. And I couldn't help myself. I got the giggles, which made it rather difficult to get up from my curtsy. I tried really, really hard to control myself, but the harder I tried the funnier it got. Then the queen made a really loud snort, and I lost any sense of composure completely and was almost doubled up with laughter.'

Sebastian couldn't help but laugh at the ludicrous nature of this scene.

'I finally got back up to my feet, and when I turned around I saw this long row of debutantes and their mothers all looking at me with horror, which of course made the whole thing even funnier, especially as their outrage was causing all those ostrich feathers to quiver, like a flock of scandalised birds.'

She joined in his laughter.

'Fortunately, Aunt Harriet is a bit hard of hearing and didn't hear the queen snoring or my giggling and assumed I was merely overtaken with the excitement of the occasion, and my father heard nothing of my unconventional presentation.'

'But everyone else in Society would have known about it.'

'Perhaps, although no one told you, otherwise you would never have seen me as a potential countess and invited me to your estate. My bad reputation would have preceded me.' She took his arm again, still laughing. 'You most certainly would not want to be stuck with a wife who giggles in front of the queen.'

Sebastian chose to ignore that particular piece of teasing.

'So have you had any other requests, men wanting to court you, offers for your hand?' That was what he wanted, wasn't it? So why had he braced himself before asking that question, and why was he now uncertain about what he wanted to hear?

'I'm still getting lots of invitations to social events, and I dance the night away at every ball, so I'm not entirely left on the shelf yet.'

'I believe that after today, when all of Society has seen you on the arm of an unmarried earl, interest in you will rise immediately.'

She came to a stop and looked up at him, a frown creasing her forehead. 'Is that why you asked me to accompany you today? So other men will become interested?'

'No,' he said vehemently.

She continued to stare up at him, her lips turned down.

'All right. I mean *yes*. You have to find a husband, Lucy. You have to settle down. You must not attend places like The Royal Flush. You have to save your kisses for the man you marry.'

'If you're not interested in me, then why should you care who I marry?' she asked, still frowning.

What could he tell her? That he needed her married so she would stop tempting him with her luscious lips, so that he would stop constantly thinking about her curvaceous body?

'And as for my supposedly bad behaviour, I've already told you I only ever attended The Royal Flush once, and I've only ever kissed one man. You.'

Sebastian cringed inwardly at that reprimand.

'And who knows, maybe I'll marry a man who likes to gamble. Then I might be at The Royal Flush every night of the week.' She lifted her nose defiantly in the air, but her lips still frowned.

'That will of course be a matter between you and your husband.'

'So you don't care about me falling into a pit of vice and depravity? You just want me married off to anyone?'

Yes, if it will free me from this torment.

'No, of course that is not the case. It's just that you… well, damn it all, Lucy,' he said, coming to a halt. 'You must know that I am damnably attracted to you, more than is sensible for either of us. And you must know that I cannot marry you.'

She stared at him, her eyelids rapidly blinking as if trying to make sense of his confession.

'Damnably attractive but not good enough to marry,' she finally said quietly.

He chose not to comment on this characterisation. What could he say? She was right, and it wasn't just her past behaviour that excluded her from becoming his wife. He could not take the risk of letting someone like Lucy into his life. The mother he had loved had left him. He would never give anyone the power to hurt him again as she had. The sensible, reliable and dispassionate wife he sought would not do that.

'Yes, the respectable woman and all that,' she added, her voice rising. 'The one you can guarantee will never stray from the straight and narrow and disgrace the family.'

'Exactly. Is that a guarantee you can give?' he asked, knowing the answer was *no*.

'Can you?' she snapped. 'Oh, that's right, you don't think it matters for men, do you?'

She knew his opinion on that, so again he chose not to answer.

'Yes, you are correct,' she continued. 'I have committed the terrible sin of wanting to get some enjoyment out of life, something it seems you do not think women should be allowed to do. While you were off doing whatever you wanted, with whomever you wanted, I was stuck out in that tiny village helping my father with sermons on this immoral world of ours and the folly of indulging in anything pleasurable.'

She poked a finger into the middle of his chest as she gave vent to her annoyance. 'You really can be insufferable at times,' she said, reflecting exactly what he was thinking about her. 'Do you even know what any of your male ancestors got up to? Do you know how many of them gambled, had affairs, contemplated doing away with their spouse?'

Yet again, he chose not to answer.

'Well, do you?' she repeated, glaring at him as she waited for his reply.

'No.'

'Exactly. You men can do whatever you like while expecting women to never, ever do anything that might cause even the least judgemental tongues to wag.'

He forced his voice to remain controlled. 'No one ridiculed me at school because of any behaviour from the males in my family.' He wanted to end this conversation, which had reignited all that anger and pain he experienced because of that constant ridicule and the devastation of being abandoned by the woman who was supposed to love him.

Her expression softened. 'I'm sorry. You should never have had to endure that. I would never want a child of mine to suffer in that way.'

Finally, she had seen the reason why he needed a wife he could trust not to bring shame on the family.

'I would never send my child to a school where such behaviour was allowed. I would never subject my child to such appalling attitudes.'

'Well, my mother wasn't around to ensure it never happened.'

She stopped, drew in a breath and placed her hand on his. 'I can't imagine what would drive a woman to abandon her child.'

Sebastian shrugged and resumed their walk.

'Perhaps you *should* meet up with her before she

returns to America. Perhaps you will find out the real reason why she left, not the one told to you by your father or by those horrid boys at school.'

He circled his tense shoulders but said nothing in response to that preposterous suggestion.

'It does appear to me that by refusing to meet her you are trying to punish her, but…well, perhaps you are also punishing yourself.'

'Nonsense. I'm not trying to punish her,' he stated with more conviction than he really felt. 'And there can be no excuse for what she did.'

'You're not going to know whether that is true until you do meet her. So what do you think?'

'I think this is none of your business.'

'Yes, you're right.' She sighed lightly. 'But what have you to lose? If you do meet her and you find you were completely right, that she is a woman beneath contempt, then nothing changes.'

'Then, why bother doing so?'

'Because perhaps she is not beneath contempt. Perhaps there is a reason why she left you. Perhaps you will be lucky enough to find you have got a mother.'

He wanted to disagree, but how could he do so? She would never know her own mother, and he could see how much that hurt her, whereas he had the opportunity to meet his.

They walked along in silence as he contemplated what she had said. Was his objection to meeting his mother because he did not want to find out that the image he had of that woman, the one he had been holding on to for all these years, was incorrect? He dismissed that thought as quickly as it had arisen.

'I will give it some consideration,' he finally said, although he had no intention of doing so.

'Yes. I think it's about time you were more open to possibilities you have already dismissed.'

He looked down at her and saw her smile, which suggested this statement was a reference to more than just a reconciliation between him and his mother, giving him even more to think about.

Chapter Fifteen

Their promenade in Hyde Park over, Sebastian helped Lucy back into his carriage. Dolly appeared from somewhere, as she was apt to do. While Lucy smiled her thanks for her granting them privacy, Sebastian frowned at the lady's maid in disapproval.

They joined the line-up of carriages and horses leaving the park then drove past the elegant townhouses towards her Bayswater home. The sun was still shining, and Lucy lifted her head to its rays, enjoying its golden glow warm on her face.

Despite his ridiculous stubbornness and his unfortunate attitude to his female ancestors—which she was sure, given enough time, she could change—it had been a delightful day. But then, any time in Sebastian's company was delightful. He had unfortunately reiterated his resolve to not marry her, but again, she was now certain she was more than capable of changing his mind on that as well.

If he found her *damnably attractive*, surely it was

just a small step to seeing her as someone he could not live without and had to take as his wife, despite his misguided objections? All that was necessary now was for him to come to the realisation he did not want an obedient, strait-laced wife who was too timid to even say boo to a goose. What he wanted was her. Then he would see how she would make an ideal wife and mother for his children.

A heavenly feeling fluttered in her stomach.
Sebastian's children.
As if they already existed, a surge of love flooded her heart. Oh, how she would adore those children, just as she adored their father.

She edged closer to him on the carriage bench. They had shared so much today that was personal, it was as if they were now rather intimate, even more so than when they had kissed. He surely must see that.

All too soon, his carriage halted in front of her home. He jumped out, lowered the steps and helped her down. She was pleased to note his hand held hers for a moment longer than entirely necessary then he bent and lightly kissed the back. She couldn't help but sigh at the touch of his lips.

'Will you be attending the Granville ball this evening?' she asked hopefully.

He shook his head. 'I'm afraid not. As you know, I only attend such events when absolutely necessary.'

'Well, maybe it's necessary for you to do so tonight.

After all, if we dance together that is sure to make me a much more desirable catch in the eyes of Society.'

You are so bad, Lucinda Everhart, she thought while smiling at Sebastian. The only man she wanted to appear more desirable to was standing right in front of her.

'I don't believe you need my help in that regard.'

Did the sun just shine brighter? Lucy was sure that it did.

'But if you attend the ball and we dance together, I might get that proposal you so desperately want for me.'

The one I hope to get from you.

'I shall see,' he said, raising Lucy's hopes even higher. He helped Dolly down from the carriage, then bowed to both of them.

They both curtsied then smiling to herself, she took Dolly's arm, and they entered the house.

'Right, let's go through my gowns and see what I should wear tonight,' she said to her companion the moment the footman closed the door behind them.

The two young women raced up the stairs, and just as they had in preparation for the walk, they pulled every item of clothing she possessed out of the wardrobe. Every gown was scrutinised carefully, and they finally decided her apricot gown adorned with embroidered cream flowers was almost what she hoped for.

'It's such a shame it's got all those ruffles around the neckline,' Lucy said with resignation.

'Leave it to me,' Dolly said, taking the gown and disappearing.

While her maid was busy doing whatever she was doing with the gown, Lucy called for the maid-of-all-work to draw her a bath. A male servant brought up a bath and placed it in her dressing room, then all the servants were enlisted in the task of carrying up pots of hot water. Lavender, rose petals and bath salts were added, and once the servants departed she disrobed and climbed into the soothing water.

Lucy lay back in its luxurious warmth and contemplated the night ahead. One where she would dance the night away with Sebastian and by the end of the evening he would come to his senses and make a proposal.

Once the water cooled she climbed out of the bath, just as Dolly arrived, the gown draped over one arm. She held it up for Lucy's inspection. All those annoying ruffles had been removed and replaced with delicate cream lace.

'You are a genius,' Lucy declared. 'I can see why all your previous employers have given you such wonderful testimonials.'

'Thank you, miss,' Dolly said, smiling fit to burst.

Dolly helped her dress, and Lucy discovered the enterprising woman had also altered the full long sleeves so they were now small puffs, giving the appearance that they were almost slipping down, and a man, such as the Earl of Rothwell, could easily slide the fabric off her shoulders if he was so inclined.

She inspected herself from every angle, just as she had done before her walk, and declared the gown perfect.

Dolly selected a pearl necklace and placed it around Lucy's neck. Again it was perfect. It gave the impression of a modest piece of jewellery suitable for a debutante, but drew the eye to her most feminine of assets.

Her lady's maid then picked up combs and a curling iron and set to work on her hair. After much back combing, curling, braiding, plaiting and pinning, a flattering and ornate style adorned her head.

Lucy turned her head from side to side, admiring her Dolly's handiwork. 'How on earth did I ever manage before you came into my life?' she said.

But then, before Sebastian came into her life, Lucy had certainly not cared this much about her appearance.

Excitement causing her body to tingle all over, she arrived at the Granville's ball, on the arm of Aunt Harriet. With what appeared suspiciously like selective vision, her short-sighted aunt spotted her friends on the other side of the room, and with a few words of advice that went no further than *be a good girl and enjoy yourself*, two things that tended to be contradictory, she departed.

Lucy looked around the room for Sebastian. He was nowhere in sight.

'Miss Everhart, you look divine this evening,' Mr Montclair said. 'May I have the honour of the first dance?'

Lucy could hardly say *No, I'm waiting for Sebastian*, so she accepted. Before he had led her onto the dance floor, Lord Coldridge asked if he could add his name to her dance-card. She handed him the small card and pencil. There was nothing to worry about, she told herself as the man scribbled his name on the card. There would still be plenty lines left when Sebastian finally arrived.

Several other men approached her and made the same request, causing anxiety to bubble up inside her. What if Sebastian arrived and her dance-card was full? That would be a disaster.

It would be terrible if all the trouble she and Dolly had gone to, all the hours they had spent in making sure she looked her very best, were to be wasted.

The music began, and Mr Montclair spun her around in the waltz.

'I was exercising my horse in Hyde Park today, and I saw you on the arm of the Earl of Rothwell,' he said.

'Yes, it was such a pleasant day, was it not?'

'It was indeed. And I would be honoured if you would also accompany me on a walk sometime soon.'

'Yes, that would be lovely,' she said as was required, hardly registering his words as she scanned the recent arrivals to see if Sebastian was among them.

The dance over, Mr Montclair led her off the floor

where the second man on her dance-card was waiting. What was his name again? Lucy could hardly remember. She looked around. There was still no Sebastian.

Her new dance partner also asked her if she had enjoyed her walk in Hyde Park. Sebastian was right. All of Society seemed to have been out at the park, to see and be seen.

Throughout the dance she made the requisite small talk, all the while looking around for the man she really wanted to dance with, the man who was nowhere in sight.

And so the evening continued. She danced every dance, chatted politely, stopped for supper and exchanged friendly conversation with the other debutantes, and then danced some more.

Then it was over. No Sebastian. In the early hours of the morning, she and Aunt Harriet travelled home in the carriage. This was hopeless. How was she ever going to convince him that he was in love with her if he failed to put in an appearance?

Dolly helped her change out of her lovely gown, and she climbed into bed, feeling completely despondent.

Next morning she entered the drawing room to discover it full of large bouquets of flowers.

'Isn't it wonderful!' Aunt Harriet declared, smiling with such unbridled joy one could be excused for thinking they had been sent by her aunt's admirers.

Lucy picked out the card from each bouquet and read the messages with an ever-sinking heart. None was from Sebastian, but it appeared he was right: a young lady with no title and a merely adequate dowry was never going to be sought after by the men seeking a bride, but a young lady who had caught the attention of the wealthy, handsome Earl of Rothwell suddenly had a great deal of worth in the eyes of wife-seeking men.

'Oh, sweetie, this is marvellous. It won't be long now before you are to wed. Your father will be so proud of you to have attracted the attention of so many eligible men.'

Lucy smiled weakly as she sank onto the nearest armchair. 'Yes, it's wonderful news.'

'You better change into your finest day dress, as I believe some lucky young lady is going to have to spend the day entertaining potential suitors.'

And that was what Lucy did: she endured a day of making small talk, of laughing at jokes that weren't particularly funny and drinking cup after cup of tea with men who were eyeing her up, judging her and presumably trying to work out why the Earl of Rothwell was interested in her.

By the end of the day, Lucy was completely exhausted, and her jaw hurt from so much forced smiling, but at least she could now relax.

'It looks like we have one more visitor,' her aunt said, still smiling as if the day had been a joy rather than an ordeal.

Lucy knew she should not get her hopes up. Sebastian had sent no flowers, no cards, nothing. But she sat up straighter in expectation, and her smile became genuine for the first time since she had risen from her bed.

The door opened. Her smile froze. Her heart dropped to her stomach as she looked up at the man standing in the doorway.

'Father,' she blurted out. 'What brings *you* back to London?'

Chapter Sixteen

Sebastian re-read the note Lucy had sent to his home. She needed to see him urgently and was desperate for his help and advice but insisted their meeting had to be discreet, private and soon. Sebastian had responded with a note agreeing to meet her at The Royal Flush and had arranged with Nathanial for the office to be made available to them.

As he waited for her to arrive he went over all the things that could possibly cause such urgency and could come to only one conclusion. Somehow her father had discovered they had kissed and now expected them to marry. It was exactly what he dreaded: marrying an unsuitable woman and risking a continuation of the family curse.

But he only had himself to blame. He should never have kissed her. Not at The Royal Flush and most certainly not at Isaac's ball. He would now have to face the consequences of his actions.

He pulled his fob watch out of his pocket, wondering what was keeping her, just as she rushed into the office, her cheeks flushed.

'Where is Dolly, your erstwhile chaperone?'

Why he asked such a question he did not know. Dolly was hardly capable of stopping her mistress from misbehaving. Not that he was placing any responsibility for his behaviour on the maid. The fault was all his.

She looked over her shoulder at the closed door. 'She's at home, but that hardly matters.' Her words came out in a flustered torrent.

'Please, sit down.' He indicated a nearby chair hoping it would help her calm down. She ignored his gesture and commenced pacing around the small office.

'You needed to talk to me?' he prompted.

'Yes, it's terrible. Father has returned to London and insists I marry.'

It was as he expected. Sebastian waited for his jaw to clench or his chest to constrict, for him to experience the usual reaction to devastating news. But his jaw did not tense. His heart did not plummet as if he had let down the Rothwell name. These were all the reactions he should be having to the prospect of marrying a woman he deemed unsuitable. Strange. Instead he felt a curious lightness in his chest, and warmth spread through him. It must be because he was prepared for the news, and now that it had come it was no longer a shock. Surely that had to be the reason.

It couldn't possibly be because he wanted to marry Lucy? Could it? No, of course not.

'I see,' he said, forcing his tone to remain steady. 'I shall of course tell him the blame was entirely mine and you were at all times an innocent.'

'What?' She stopped her pacing, her dark eyebrows drawn together. 'What are you talking about? He doesn't expect *us* to marry. Oh, you thought… No, he doesn't know that we have kissed.'

It was Sebastian's turn to furrow his brow in confusion. 'May I then ask why you are here?'

'I didn't know who else to turn to. Several men have contacted Father and said they wish to court me with the intention of marriage. He is so happy. He expects me to make a choice and accept one of the offers and to marry as soon as possible.' Her eyebrows pulled tighter together, and she looked to him in appeal as if he was supposed to supply some answer.

Sebastian stared down at her, unable to speak, hardly able to breathe. He should be relieved. This was what he wanted…wasn't it? His plan had worked out remarkably well. So why had that tension in his jaw and tightness in his chest decided now was the time to take command of his body?

You're free, he repeated to himself, and yet his body suddenly felt as if imprisoned by the weight of heavy chains.

'And what do you expect from me?' he said, horrified that his voice sounded constricted. He coughed to clear his throat. 'Do you want me to help you make the right choice?'

She stared at him as if he was talking gibberish. 'No, of course not.'

'Then, what is the problem?'

'It's not one problem, it's several.' She lifted her hand, her fist clenched, then extended one finger. 'Firstly, I'm not in love with any of these men, and I don't want to marry them.'

The weight on Sebastian's shoulders lifted slightly.

Another finger lifted. 'Secondly, I don't even want to kiss any of these men, never mind…well, you know, do my wifely duty with them,' she said and laughed awkwardly.

Sebastian should not be relieved by this admission, but against all reason he was.

'And thirdly,' she lifted another finger and then lowered it, her flushed cheeks turning a brighter red. 'Well, there's lots of other reasons as well.'

'I see,' he said, not really seeing at all. 'Who has offered for your hand?'

'Lord Coldridge, Mr Montclair and Mr Barrington.'

'All eminently respectable men.' The weight pressing onto his body returned with a crushing force, and the tension in his jaw ratcheted up another notch.

'But I do not want to marry them.'

'And, as I have already said, what do you expect me to do about it?' Sebastian said with a feigned nonchalance.

Her raised hand dropped to her side. 'I thought, well, maybe you might like to save me from these marriages.'

He waited for her to give a further explanation.

Her cheeks coloured a deeper shade of red. 'You told me you were damnably attracted to me.'

'Yes,' he said slowly.

'And, well, you have kissed me…twice.'

'Yes,' he repeated, certain he knew where this conversation was going but shocked she was finally going to do what he suspected she was planning to do when they first met at his Dorset estate: blackmail him into an unwanted marriage.

She stared up at him, her cheeks still burning as she nibbled on the edge of her lip.

He waited. If she were indeed going to blackmail him, then he was not going to let her off that easily, she would have to spell it out.

'Well, I thought we could…what with the damnably attractive thing, and all that, maybe…'

She came to a halt, turned and looked out the large windows and down at the gaming floor below them. If marriage was what she demanded of him, then he would have no choice but to concede to her demands and join all the other Rothwell earls who had married women who were irresponsible, capricious and imprudent.

And if he needed any further proof that she possessed all three qualities in abundance, her presence here today would provide it. The rational, dispassionate wife he sought would accept one of those proposals and make a sensible marriage.

'Well, I thought perhaps you could have a quiet word with Mr Montclair, Mr Barrington and Lord Coldridge and tell them that marriage to me would not be a good idea,' she said, taking him by surprise.

'Why would I do that?'

She turned back to face him. 'To save me from an unwanted marriage, and...you do owe me. It's all because of you that I'm in this predicament.'

Sebastian could not see how that could possibly be the case.

'If you hadn't paraded me in Hyde Park like some sort of show pony, then those men would not have seen me as a potential bride. Now they think I'm someone of value who can attract the attention of a wealthy earl.'

He could point out she *was* someone of value who *could* attract a wealthy earl but suspected that would not help the situation. Instead he raised his hand, fist clenched.

'Firstly,' he said, extending one finger, 'I did not parade you like a show pony. We merely did what many other couples were doing and took a promenade. Secondly,' he said lifting another finger, 'finding a suitable husband is exactly why you are here in London, and you are lucky enough to get three offers. And thirdly,' he said with a final digit extended, 'I will not be having a quiet word with those three men.'

She sighed as if he were being the irrational one. 'If you told them about, you know, our kiss, the gambling, the sneaking out, and all that, then I'm sure they wouldn't want to marry me.'

'You want me to destroy your reputation to save you from a respectable marriage, and in doing so probably destroy your chances of marrying anyone else in the process, including men you don't consider boring?'

'Hmm, yes, I suppose that's a silly idea, but I don't know what else to do.' She looked towards the carafes on the sideboard.

'Would you like a drink?'

'Oh, yes, please. Just a small one to steady my nerves, as Aunt Harriet always says before she helps herself to a couple of large brandies.'

He poured her a small brandy and one for himself.

She took the glass and turned back to the windows. Sebastian took a long swallow of his own drink. Despite her objections, he knew she would soon be married. Her father would insist on it. That was what his head wanted, but he could not deny it was not what his body wanted and possibly not what his heart wanted either. But soon she would be out of his life, and until she was, he just had to make sure it was his head that remained in charge.

Lucy sipped the brandy, its unfamiliar sting bringing tears to her eyes. Or was it disappointment that was causing her to well up? This had not gone as she had fantasised. Somehow, she had expected Sebastian to save her. She had even, in a secret little part of her heart, hoped that hearing she might soon marry would be enough of a shock to bring him to the realisation that he was in love with her.

And if she were being completely honest with herself, she had even daydreamed of him immediately going down on bended knee, declaring his undying love and telling her he just had to have her as his wife.

He had, she supposed, made a sort of offer to marry her, but only because he thought her father knew of their kiss. That was not what she wanted. She wanted him to love her, just as she loved him, but the simple truth was he didn't.

Making a genuine marriage proposal had obviously not even occurred to him, even when she reminded him that he found her damnably attractive and had kissed her twice. That was apparently not enough.

She went to take another sip of her brandy, changed her mind and stared down at the revellers below. She really was a fool, and thank goodness she had not embarrassed herself even further by telling him what she really wanted or how she really felt.

'Your father is correct, Lucy,' he said, standing behind her, so close she could feel the warmth of his body. 'All three men would make respectable husbands, and you should not ruin your chances of making a good marriage. Even being here, alone with me, could put those potential marriages in jeopardy.'

She forced herself to smile as if her heart had not shattered and turned to face him. 'I know you think I'm being a gormless fool, but I'm not. It's just that my Season has not turned out to be anything like what I expected.'

'Have you not had the fun you were intending to have?'

She looked up at him. 'I have had fun, but not in the way I had imagined.'

He raised his eyebrows to signal for her to explain.

'I had envisaged I would go to lots of balls and dance with copious men and one would stand out as the man I wanted to marry. We would laugh together, talk together, have lots of fun, maybe even share an illicit kiss or two. He would propose, we'd marry and live a fun, happy life together.'

Just as I did with you, minus the proposal and the fun happy life together.

'I'm sorry—'

'No, you've nothing to be sorry about,' she cut him off, her voice full of false jollity. 'You are right. I'm lucky to have three proposals and to be able to make a choice of who is to be my husband.'

Even if none of them is the man I want.

'Perhaps it would have been better if you and I had never met,' he said quietly.

'No, don't say that.' Before she was aware of what she was doing, she placed her hand on his arm. 'I don't regret meeting you, and I don't regret kissing you.'

'Neither do I,' he said, staring down at her with those deep brown eyes. 'I should never have kissed you, and I should regret my actions, but I don't.'

'I suppose I should leave now,' she said placing her glass on the nearby desk but making no move to leave. 'I'll just have to be content that my Season went as well as could be expected. Well, goodbye, then.'

'Goodbye, Lucy.' He lightly ran his finger along her forehead, brushing back a lock of her hair, and she closed her eyes, savouring the caress. His hand moved down to her cheek. He didn't love her, didn't want to marry her, but she had seen that look in his eye before. He wanted her, and by God she wanted him.

If she left now she would never taste his lips again, never feel his caressing hands on her body, never lose herself in his embrace.

'I know I shouldn't have come here,' she said, opening her eyes and forcing herself to be bold. 'But there is one more thing I want to ask you before I leave.'

He made no response, but his finger continued to stroke her cheek, giving her courage.

'I want you to kiss me again, one last time.'

Chapter Seventeen

Sebastian should have been shocked by her request, but he had no time for such a reaction before his lips were where they wanted to be: on hers.

This was wrong. So wrong, but it felt so right to have her in his arms again. And she was right. He, too, wanted to kiss her, one last time.

He wrapped his arms around her body, the body he had been thinking about constantly since the last time she was in his arms, and he deepened his kiss, giving full vent to his unquenchable desire for her.

She kissed him back with a ferocity matching his own. Her hands wrapped around his head, her fingers weaving into his hair, her parted lips crushed against his, her tongue tasting him, tormenting him.

A small mew of pleasure escaped her lips as she rubbed her luscious body against him, causing him to moan with an equally furious desire. He wanted this kiss, but he wanted more. Would it be so wrong to explore her body, with his hands, his lips, his tongue? Of course it would be.

His kisses moved to the satin skin of her neck, kissing and tasting, loving the feel of her soft skin under his lips, while his hand moved over the mound of her breasts.

A deep growl of desire escaping his lips, he did what he knew he mustn't. Still kissing her neck, he flicked open several buttons on the front of her blouse and slid his hand inside, pushing the corset down to cup her full breast.

'Oh yes,' she cried, as his fingers stroked her nipple and it pebbled under his touch.

'Yes,' she repeated as he continued to kiss her neck, continued to excite the tight bud. Her hand moved to cover his, urging him on as her hips arched against his body, in time to his caresses. Her arousal was as obvious as his own, and she too was powerless over the strength of their desire.

Pulling apart the opening of her blouse, he pushed down her chemise, exposing those beautiful breasts to his gaze. He had fantasised about what they would look like, but they were even more luscious than he had pictured, full, firm and desirable, the hard nipples pointing up at him as if to tempt him.

Still tormenting one sensitive tip, he took the other nipple in his mouth, his lips nuzzling, his tongue stroking and gently swirling.

Her gasped breaths turned to low moans, then

groans of pleasure as his lips, tongue and finger continued their sensual dance.

He had already gone too far, but there was more of her body he had to explore, and he knew he would never get this chance again. His lips returning to hers, he took hold of her waist, lifted her up and placed her on the table. Before he had time to question what he was doing, he bundled up her skirt, the folds piled up around her waist.

Was there ever a more erotic sight, than that of a woman's legs encased in silk stockings, held up by garter belts, the naked skin of her thigh just waiting for his caresses?

He looked down into her face. Her eyes were closed, her head thrown back, her lips parted. There was no denying she wanted him as much as he wanted her, but she had asked for his kiss, no more.

As if in answer to his unasked question, her legs parted, and he groaned his thanks. Wrapping his arm around her back, he held her close, kissing her parted lips, as his hand moved up the inside of her leg, loving the soft touch of her vulnerable flesh.

Parting the split in the middle of her drawers, he traced a line along her folds, spreading the slick flesh.

'Oh yes,' she said, her breath coming in fast moans of pleasure.

He pushed one finger inside, her sheath closing around him, wet with arousal. Arching her back, she moved against his hand, and he followed the rhythm of her need, pushing himself deeper as he increased the pressure.

Her silky walls clenched tighter around him. Her moans grew louder, came faster, matching the pace of his caresses. They rose to cries of ecstasy as he increased the rhythm, and in a series of spasms, her feminine muscles quivered around his touch.

She was still panting with pleasure when he lifted her up and carried her to the couch. He could now take what he wanted. There was no question that she wanted him to do so. She wanted to feel him deep inside her, just as powerfully as he needed to relieve his throbbing desire for her.

His body covered hers. Her eyes opened, and she looked up at him, waiting for him to act, waiting for him to show her what lovemaking was really like.

Demanding desire for her pulsed through his body, consuming him, making thought all but impossible. And yet he paused, something deep inside him still telling him this was wrong.

Her hands reached up to the buttons of his shirt, quickly opening then, and her hand slid inside, followed by her lips as she kissed and licked his sweat-slickened chest. He groaned as her fingers traced a line over his shoulders, his chest and down his stomach. When she came tantalisingly close to his erection he took hold of her hand.

This could not happen. With more self-control than he believed himself capable, he removed her hand and lifted his body from hers. She sank back onto the couch and looked up at him, her expression confused. She was so breathtakingly beautiful. Her lips plump and inviting, her naked breasts rising and falling quickly, her skirts around her waist, her legs parted in invitation.

'I want you so much,' he murmured, looking down at the glorious sight laid out before him.

'Then, take me,' she whispered back. 'I'm yours.'

Except she wasn't his and never would be. He looked down at those appealing blue eyes, and reality hit him like a sudden thunderbolt. If he did take her, she would be ruined. He would have ruined her to satisfy his own selfish desires.

Before he could lose himself again, he quickly pulled down her skirt to cover her parted legs.

'We can't do this,' he said, his voice husky with desire. 'We both know this is wrong. You have to save yourself for your husband,' he added, cursing that man who would be the first to taste what he was hungering for with such desperation.

She shook her head, and he bit down hard, clenching his teeth tightly to give himself strength.

'You know that, don't you, Lucy?' he said, hoping she would both agree and disagree. Knowing that if she said one word, made one gesture of encouragement he would be lost, he reached down and with the greatest of reluctance pulled her blouse together, removing the sight of those tempting breasts.

A crash behind him drew his attention. His hand still on her buttons he looked over his shoulder.

'Father!' Lucy gasped out, quickly sitting up, a mere second before Sebastian exclaimed, 'Oh, my God,' knowing that his life had just changed for ever.

'Get away from her, you fiend!'

Lucy stared at her father as if an unwanted apparition had suddenly appeared in the office, which was more or less what had happened.

'My poor, poor girl,' he said, racing over to the couch. 'Thank goodness I arrived in time before this rake had his way with you.'

'No, I...' Lucy pulled herself up into a seated position, unsure how she was going to explain what had happened or if any explanation was possible. While she remained utterly flummoxed, Sebastian continued doing up her buttons with more composure than she would have expected from anyone under the circumstances. She looked at his white shirt, pushed aside, half the buttons undone, his muscular chest still exposed, and wondered whether she should be following his example but suspected that would do more harm than good.

Her father grabbed hold of her arm, pulled her to her feet then stood between her and Sebastian, as if protecting her from a wild animal.

'Father, it's not what it looks like,' she said to his

quaking back, even though it was exactly what it looked like.

'Do not defend him, my dear. The man is a rake and beneath contempt.'

'No, it wasn't like that,' she said, wondering how she could possibly explain to her father what it was really like. *Marvellous*, *ecstatic*, *earth-shattering* were the words that sprang to mind, but she doubted that was what her father wanted to hear.

'Sir, I apologise,' Sebastian said, and Lucy wanted to tell him he had nothing to apologise for. It wasn't his fault her father had burst in and ended what was a sublime experience.

'I don't want your apologies. I just want you to stay away from my daughter. Practise your seductive wiles on some other poor, defenceless girl. You will not ruin my daughter.'

'But, Father—'

'And what is that?'

Lucy peeked out from behind her father to see what he was alluding to.

'Have you been plying my daughter with alcohol?' He was pointing at her barely touched brandy balloon. 'Is that how you intended to have your way with her? You are even lower than I had thought.'

'No, Father. I—'

'Come, Lucinda. Let's leave this den of iniquity.'

Before she could utter another word, the clergyman

once more grabbed her arm and all but dragged her across the office.

'I'm sorry,' she threw over her shoulder before her father slammed the door behind them.

'Do not apologise to that bounder,' her father said as he rushed her down the stairs, his hand still holding her arm in a vise-like grip. 'You, my poor, poor, misguided girl, have done nothing to apologise for.'

They all but ran through The Royal Flush, and a few patrons looked in their direction, but most were too absorbed by their game of chance to pay them any heed, or perhaps young ladies being dragged off the premises by irate fathers was not an unusual sight.

They raced out the door, where the carriage was waiting, door open. Her father pushed her inside and signalled to the driver. They took off down the alleyway at a breakneck speed as if escaping the gates of hell.

'Um... I'm sorry about all that,' Lucy said, wondering how on earth she was going to excuse or explain her behaviour, which in her father's eyes would be inexcusable and beyond explanation.

'It is I who should apologise to you,' her father said, shaking his head sorrowfully.

'You? Why? What did you do wrong?' The only thing her father had done wrong was interrupting what had been an experience so wonderful that it had previously been beyond her comprehension. Sebastian had stopped before he had given her the ultimate pleasure, something every inch of her body was yearning for, but she was sure she could have convinced him to continue. That is, if her father had not burst in and ruined everything. But she doubted that was what he was apologising for.

'I should never have left you in London. I should have known that men like him would try to take advantage of your innocence.'

If Lucy told him she was the one to ask to be supposedly *plied* with alcohol, he would not believe her. Nor would he believe she had been the one to ask to be kissed and then had continued to encourage Sebastian, even as he hesitated. And she would have continued to encourage him, if her father had not arrived at such an inopportune moment.

She had desperately wanted one last kiss from him, but once his lips were on hers it had been impossible to stop. He had said she'd be ruined if they continued, but what did she care of that? She had wanted all that he could give her, and hang the consequences.

'Thank goodness I arrived in time.'

Despite what she really thought Lucy knew it wisest not to express her frustration. Instead, she asked, 'How did you know where I was?'

'What? Yes, that was most fortuitous. I went to your room to ask you whether you had decided which of the young men who had offered for your hand you had decided to accept and found your room empty. I confronted that lady's maid but the dim-witted girl said she knew nothing of your whereabouts.'

There was nothing dim-witted about Dolly, and this display of loyalty was another reason why Lucy would be giving her an exemplary reference at the end of the Season.

'No, I didn't tell Dolly where I was going. She is not to blame.'

He continued the sorrowful shaking of his head. 'No, of course not. How could she ever know you would be lured to such a house of vice?'

'Hmm' was all Lucy could say in answer to that question.

'Then I found the note from that cad, inviting you to meet him in that pit of decay.' His face became more distressed. 'Oh, my poor, naive girl. How were you to know what he would be planning? You couldn't have known he had the seduction of an innocent on his mind.' He reached over and lightly touched her arm. 'Does he have you in some sort of thrall? Is that why you were led astray?'

Lucy nodded. That was certainly one way of explaining it.

'Oh, Lucinda,' he all but wailed.

'I am so sorry to disappoint you, Father,' she said, taking his hand and meaning every word. She had no regrets about what happened between her and Sebastian, but she did not wish to hurt her father, and she regretted seeing him in this state.

'And to think I was once hoping that you would marry that bounder and was disappointed when he did not see you as *compatible*.' Her father almost spat out the last word. 'Not compatible to marry, but certainly compatible to seduce and to ruin your chances of making a good marriage to a respectable man.'

Ruined. That was exactly what Sebastian had done, but not in the way her father meant. After what she had just experienced, how could she ever consider marrying another man? She loved Sebastian. She wanted Sebastian to make love to her. He was the only man she wanted and could not possibly consider marrying anyone else.

She sat up slightly straighter on the carriage bench. 'So I suppose after what just happened I won't be able to marry any of those men who asked for my hand?' she said, hoping her father would agree immediately and that would be the end of the matter.

'I don't know,' he said dolefully. 'We'll discuss that at a later time. Right now, you must be in such shock, my dear. All that is important is to get you home where you are safe and secure.'

'Yes, Father.' Lucy smiled to herself. She had gone to see Sebastian, desperate to find a way out of marrying those men she cared nothing for, and it looked like he had inadvertently provided it. She had not received the proposal from him she had secretly hoped for, or even a declaration of love, but the look in his eye when he had taken her to the pinnacle of ecstasy was surely the look of love.

She closed her eyes briefly, remembering the intensity in his eyes as he gazed down at her. That could be nothing else but the look of love. When he had kissed and caressed her, it had been more than just a physical act. She had felt worshipped, as if his lips, tongue and hands were showing her how much he cherished and adored her.

And she had responded, not just to the desire building inside her but to the exquisite wonder of being in love and feeling loved.

Sebastian must also be aware of that now. He must know that he loved her.

While he was kissing and caressing her, he had surely said so, not with his words but with his body. He had shown her he was as hopelessly in love with her, as she was with him.

The carriage pulled up in front of their townhouse. Her father took her arm and led her up the path as if she were an invalid. Their footman opened the door, and a fretting Aunt Harriet was standing in the hallway, dressed in her nightgown, winding her long grey plait around her agitated fingers.

'Oh, thank goodness, you found her. Are you all right, Lucy?'

'No, she is not,' her father answered for her. 'I caught her just in time before that scoundrel—'

'Oh no.' Aunt Harriet's hands covered her mouth,

and she swayed slightly. 'Oh, but I thought the earl was such a nice, kind gentleman, and the other chaperones said he was a man of the highest integrity.'

'It seems the man managed to delude us all,' her father said. 'I won't tell you what he was about to do to my daughter. It is not something that a woman's ears should hear, but rest assured, I caught him in time. It was only because I am a peaceful man of God that I didn't give the reprobate the good thrashing he deserves.'

Thank goodness her father did not try. It would have been embarrassing for all concerned.

While her father was a frail man, Sebastian was fit, muscular and in his prime. She rubbed her fingers lightly together remembering just how fit and strong he was, how his shoulder, chest and stomach muscles felt under her caresses. Oh, how she'd like to stroke them again, with her fingers, her lips and her tongue.

She stifled a sigh and tried to focus on what her aunt and father were saying.

'I blame myself,' her aunt said, echoing what her father had said earlier. What was wrong with these people? Why were they so anxious to feel guilty for something that was all her own action? Something about which *she* did not have the slightest bit of guilt. 'I should have paid more attention at that ball he attended and said no to that walk in the park. I could see he was interested in Lucinda but thought he had honourable intent.'

'No, no, it is not your fault,' her father consoled Aunt Harriet. 'It is all mine. But I am here now. From now onwards I will be fully committed to protecting my daughter's virtue from men such as the Earl of Rothwell.' Her father shook his head dolefully. 'I should have known what he was like. I'd heard rumours about that family but believed it was a case of *Judge not lest you be judged*. If I were a cursing man, I'd curse myself for ignoring all I'd heard and being dazzled by his title and wealth.'

'You have nothing to admonish yourself for,' Lucy said. She reached out and took her aunt's hand. 'Either of you.'

'Oh, you are such a good, good girl,' her aunt said, causing guilt to rise up inside her. Not guilt for what she had done tonight. She would never feel guilty about something that had been wonderful, but for causing such distress to her father and aunt.

'Now, go to bed, my dear, and try to get some sleep,' the reverend said. 'I'll get your maid to bring you some warm milk. Hopefully that will go some way to calming you down after such a traumatic experience.'

'Yes, Father. I am rather tired and am sure I will be able to sleep.' *And dream of Sebastian's hands caressing me, his lips kissing me, of him finishing what he so cruelly halted before I had been given the ultimate satisfaction.*

'She is such a dear, sweet girl,' she heard her aunt say as she walked up the stairs.

'Indeed she is,' Reverend Everhart agreed. 'Sweet and innocent, and I am determined she will remain that way until she is safely married.'

Lucy halted at the top of the stairs. Drat it all. Despite everything that had happened tonight, her father still had plans to marry her off. She could only hope that Sebastian would now, after what they had shared, finally realise he just had to save her from such a fate.

Chapter Eighteen

Sebastian knew exactly what he had to do. He would have done so last night but judged it best to let the reverend's anger settle somewhat and for the man to get a modicum of perspective regarding the situation in which they found themselves.

Not that he blamed the man for his outrage. It was a completely justifiable reaction to what he had seen. And what Sebastian was about to do was the one and only way he could put right the wrong he had committed. It was something he should have done after he had kissed her at Isaac's ball, and it was remiss of him to have not done so. It was apparent now that he would not be the one to break the Rothwell curse after all. He was not even married yet and he was already immersed in scandal.

He arrived at the Everhart home unannounced after breakfast and handed his card to the footman. The man walked off down the hallway, and as Sebastian expected to be turned away, he broke with protocol, entered the house and followed the man into the drawing room.

'What is the meaning of this?' Reverend Everhart said, rising to his feet, an open newspaper falling from his lap.

Sebastian flicked a quick look at Lucy sitting beside her startled aunt then turned all his attention back to the father. 'You and your daughter have been greatly wronged, and I have come to put things to rights.'

'You may leave us,' the reverend said to the footman.

The man bowed and departed.

'I'm surprised you have the audacity to show your face in this house after...after what you did to my sweet daughter,' he said, the moment the door clicked shut.

'I have come to offer for Miss Everhart's hand,' he said, the words he had hoped never to have to say coming out easier than he would have expected.

Father, daughter and aunt all stared at him, but no one spoke.

'How dare you?' the clergyman finally said seething, his normally pale face becoming florid. 'I would not allow a man as debauched as you anywhere near my lovely Lucinda. You are a Lothario of the worst order.'

'I have offered to marry your daughter,' Sebastian repeated. 'I don't believe a Lothario would do such a thing.'

The older man was not appeased by this counterargument and fixed an angry stare on Sebastian. 'And how would you treat my daughter if I did consent to such a vile marriage? With contempt? Would you keep her as your wife while you ran around with your mistresses and continued seducing any young lady unfortunate enough to come into your orbit?'

Sebastian gritted his teeth and reminded himself that the reverend loved his daughter, cared for her well-being and believed she had been wronged, which of course she had been, and it was up to him to put things right.

'I can assure you that your daughter will be treated with the utmost respect, and I will not be running around with any mistresses.' He could add that he did not seduce young women, but after what the father had witnessed, he was never likely to believe him on that count.

'Hmph,' the vicar said. 'You are no doubt an experienced liar. How else would you have got my daughter in such a compromising position?'

Again, Sebastian knew it would be a waste of breath to try to correct this assessment of his character.

'As you know, I am a man of substantial means,' he said instead, sticking to the point of this conversation. 'I can keep your daughter in comfort and style, and she will be a countess.'

'Are you trying to buy my forgiveness now?'

'No, I am merely stating the advantages of such a marriage.'

The father huffed out his distaste.

Sebastian had tried. He had been rejected. He was quite within his rights to leave now and to do so with a clear conscience. But instead, he remained, trying to think of other reasons why he should be allowed to marry a young woman he had long ago decided was not the countess for him.

'Perhaps we should not be so hasty to dismiss him, Father,' Lucy said. 'As you say, *Judge not lest you be judged* and all that.'

'Quite right, Lucinda. I forget myself.' He nodded to his daughter. 'You were wronged, and yet you still show humility and piety.' He turned back to Sebastian. 'That is the type of girl you tried to seduce, you blackguard.'

'May I have a few moments alone with the earl?' she said.

'Absolutely not,' her father shot back. 'The man cannot be trusted.'

'But you and Aunt Harriet will be in the next room. I'm sure I'll be completely safe.'

Sebastian resisted the temptation to roll his eyes. Of course she was safe. What did they take him for? But he knew the answer to that question.

'If anything untoward happens, I can always call out for your help.' Was Lucy stifling a smile? He could see nothing funny in this situation.

The father eyed Sebastian as if he were evil incarnate. 'Are you sure, my dear?' he asked his daughter.

'I'm certain, Father.'

He lifted one long, bony finger and pointed it in Sebastian's direction. 'We will be just outside the door, so do not try any of your tricks.'

Sebastian gritted his teeth. What did the man expect, that as soon as the door was closed he would leap across the room and ravish his daughter?

'I will not forget it for one second,' Sebastian said, reminding himself once again that he was dealing with an outraged father.

'Come, Harriet,' the father said, his gaze still fixed on Sebastian as if he were a dangerous predator who had been set loose in their drawing room.

The aunt skirted around the edges of the room, seemingly not wishing to be in too close a contact with a man such as Sebastian, then skittered out the room, followed by the father. He turned at the door, gave Sebastian one last threatening look then slowly closed the door.

'You don't have to marry me unless you really want to,' she said quietly so those listening at the door would not hear.

'It is the right thing to do, Lucy, the honourable thing. You know that as well as I do.'

The edges of her lips pulled down, as if the right thing, the honourable thing, were not to be admired.

'And that is why you wish to marry me?'

He frowned. That was surely obvious. 'Of course it is. I should never have kissed you, and I most certainly should not have done more than kiss you. Now I have to pay the price.'

Her blue eyes grew enormous. 'The price?' she spluttered out.

That was perhaps not the best way to phrase it. 'I'm not saying that marriage to you would be disagreeable, it's just that…' He threw his hands up, knowing this had all been discussed before and there was no reason for him to once again mention the Rothwell curse. 'We'd both agreed that a marriage between us was not what either of us wanted.'

'And yet you kissed me. More than once and did a lot more besides.'

Shame gripped him. 'Yes. I should not have done that. I am sorry. I should not have given into temptation.'

'So why did you?'

'I think we both know the answer to that.'

'I want to hear you say it.'

Sebastian pulled in an exasperated breath. This was not the conversation he had been expecting to have. He had anticipated a quick acceptance of his proposal and for this to be all over without any interminable discussion. And he certainly had not expected any resistance from anyone in the Everhart household to what was the best outcome to this delicate situation in which they found themselves.

'Well?' she prompted.

'You know that I am attracted to you, Lucy. Kissing you was something I was incapable of resisting, much to my shame. I should have resisted, but I couldn't. And when you put up no objection, well, I continued well beyond what could ever be forgiven.'

'Oh, so it is all my fault, is it?' she said, standing up and placing her hands on her hips.

'I didn't say that. It is hardly your fault that you are so beautiful and desirable.'

For a moment that stern expression softened slightly, before returning again looking just as condemning. 'So I'm to blame for being beautiful and desirable like some sort of siren that drags men to their death.'

'Marriage is hardly death.'

'You make it sound like it is. At least, the idea of marrying me. With all this talk of shame, paying the price, doing the unforgivable.'

'That is not what I meant,' he said, unsure how he had got himself into this tangled argument and even more unsure how to get out of it. 'My God, you are exasperating, Lucy. I'm trying to make this situation right. I'm offering to marry you.'

'Yes, I'm not deaf. I did hear you telling my father that you are prepared to do the honourable thing. It's so good of you to sacrifice yourself in that manner.' She narrowed her eyes slightly. 'Or are you worried that my father will spread rumours that you are some sort of rake and you will be seen as no better than all those countesses you despise?'

'I know he won't do that. Even if he wanted to besmirch my name he would not jeopardise his sweet, innocent daughter's reputation.' He hadn't meant to, but he found it impossible to keep the sarcasm out of his voice when he described her as *sweet* and *innocent*.

That was a mistake. She glared at him in much the same way as her father had. 'You really do think I am a loose woman, don't you?'

'To be quite frank, I do not know what to think. You arranged to meet me last night, said it was a matter of some urgency and came unaccompanied.'

The glaring stopped, and her cheeks coloured slightly.

'And despite what your father thinks, I do not make a habit of luring debutantes to my lair so I can have my wicked way with them,' he continued before she could throw any more accusations at him. 'You are the only debutante I have ever kissed, and certainly the only one I have...' He circled his hand in the air, not wanting to go into any descriptions about what happened between them last night. 'But none of that matters now. I did kiss a debutante. I know what the consequence of such behaviour is, and I am here to put things right and take you as my wife. I am not here to discuss who is or isn't to blame.'

The look of acrimony returned. Why on earth was she so angry with him when all he was trying to do was what was right? As there was no way he would ever understand the workings of her mind, he saw it as circumspect to wait until her anger at him settled so they could discuss this as rational human beings presented with a problem that had an obvious solution.

'Answer me one more question,' she said quietly. 'If Father had not burst in last night, would you still be asking to marry me?'

'That hardly matters. He did burst in.'

'So it was the fact that we were caught that has led to you asking me to marry you?'

He paused and contemplated her question. What would he have done if her father had not entered? Would he still be here asking for her hand? It was a hypothetical question but one he was unsure how to answer.

'Well, I think your silence answers that question quite clearly.'

'What more do you want from me, Lucy?' he asked, surprised to find himself pleading for something he had never wanted in the first place. 'This might not be what either of us wanted, but I believe we should make the best of the situation. And it's not as if there isn't a strong physical attraction between us. That's more than many people of our class have when they marry,' he added, hoping that would make her see the sense of this arrangement. 'And last night you said you did not want to marry any of the other men who had offered for your hand. This gets you out of those marriages as well.'

'So for all those reasons I should accept your proposal?'

'Yes,' he said, hoping she was finally starting to see things logically.

She took a step towards him. 'You want me to accept your proposal, even though you are going to have to lower your standards by marrying a woman like me.' She began ticking off points on her fingers, much as she had done last night. 'I should accept your proposal, even though I am not the right sort for your oh-so-respectable countess. I should marry you even though you believe I will bring shame and scandal on the precious Rothwell name, just like all the other countesses before me.' Before continuing, she clenched her hand into a fist.

Sebastian cringed, not wanting to say so, but yes, those were all things he had been thinking when he realised he was going to have to marry her.

'You think my father is a deluded numbskull when he says I am sweet and innocent, don't you?'

Again Sebastian felt it safest not to answer, even though that was exactly what he thought.

'Well, I *am* innocent. I have already told you that I have never kissed any man other than you. I have never wanted to kiss any man other than you. I have never wanted any other man to hold me or to caress me, but last night I wanted you to touch every inch of my body. And yes, I wanted you to make love to me.'

'Then—'

She held up her hand to stop his words and stared him directly in the eye. 'But I most definitely will not be marrying you, and as there is no more to be said on this subject, I would like you to leave.'

Sebastian stared at her, wanting to once again repeat that he found her the most exasperating, illogical, irritating woman he had ever met.

'Lucy, I—'

'Leave. Now.'

She turned her back on him, giving him no choice but to stride out of the room.

Chapter Nineteen

The temptation to accept his proposal had been all but overwhelming. It would mean being married to a man she loved but who did not love her. Lucy could not do that, so she had to turn him down.

He had said he desired her, but how long would desire last if there was no love? How long would it be before he resented her? How long before he believed she had manoeuvred him into a marriage he did not want?

She did not know the answers to any of those questions. All she knew was that she wanted Sebastian but did not want the kind of marriage he was offering her.

The door through which Sebastian departed was flung open. Aunt Harriet hurried into the room and took her in her arms, followed by her scowling father.

'Oh, my poor, dear child,' Aunt Harriet said, stroking her cheeks. It was only then that Lucy realised she had started to cry.

'Silly me,' she said, brushing away those annoying tears.

'So you saw the blighter off with a flea in his ear,' her father said, puffing up his gaunt body as much as he could and looking in a threatening manner towards the door. 'Good for you. That's the way.'

A concerned Aunt Harriet led her to the divan as if she were poorly.

'Don't waste any of your tears on him, sweetie,' Aunt Harriet said, stroking her back. 'There are so many much more worthy men out there.'

'Quite right, Harriet,' her father said, starting to pace. 'There are all those other young fellows who have offered for your hand. Any one of them is worth ten—twenty of that earl.'

'Isn't that right, sweetie?' her aunt said. 'All is not lost. You will soon get what your heart desires.'

The tears coursing down Lucy's cheeks flowed more freely, and her aunt's look became quizzical.

'That is what you want, isn't it?' Aunt Harriet asked. 'To marry someone else? You didn't want to marry the earl, did you?'

'Don't be absurd, Harriet,' her father answered for her. 'She may have succumbed to the man's charms and good looks on this one fateful occasion, but she is sensible enough to have seen through them now and knows not to make that mistake again.'

He looked down at Lucy as she tried to discreetly wipe away those tears. 'We all need to put this entire unpleasant episode behind us.' He nodded once as if that put an end to the matter. 'And you can now focus on those good, upstanding men who would make ideal husbands.'

Lucy squeezed her eyes together. She had forgotten all about Lord Coldridge, Mr Montclair and Mr Barrington.

'Father, would you be terribly disappointed in me if I asked to return to Greyton?' Lucy could hardly believe what she was saying, but it was what she wanted. She did not want to continue with the Season. She did not want to stay in London. And she certainly did not want to be courted by any other man when all she could think about was Sebastian.

'That would be wonderful,' he replied, showing a surprising amount of excitement for a man who was usually dour in the extreme. 'We can all return to where we belong, and you can go back to helping me with my sermons and my ministrations to my parishioners. There's no end of good works you can become involved in. An unmarried lady never has to be bored, especially when her father is the local vicar.' He looked at her aunt. 'Don't you agree, Harriet?'

Her aunt did not appear convinced. 'Are you sure that is what you want, Lucy? To leave London? To forgo the rest of the Season?'

'It is. And can we please leave today? Now?'

Once, the prospect of leaving London and the excitement of the Season and going back to that dull village would have filled Lucy with horror, but right now she didn't care what she did, as long as she would not see Sebastian again. She wanted to be busy so she didn't have time to think about what she had lost, and she could think of no better way of doing so than in helping her father. Although she suspected, no matter how much she tried to fill up her days with supposed good works, she was not going to forget about Sebastian Kingsley anytime soon.

Sebastian was in a state of disbelief and was burning up with so much aggravation he hardly knew what to do with himself.

He shifted on the carriage bench, agitation making him restless. The drive from Bayswater to his Knightsbridge townhouse was taking far too long. The unspent energy coursing through his body had to be used up or he was sure he would go mad. He banged his hand on the roof of the carriage to signal the driver to stop and jumped out of the cab before it had come to a complete stop.

'Take the carriage home,' he called to the driver. 'I need to walk.'

The carriage rolled off down the leafy street as he strode off at a rapid pace, overtaking nannies wheeling large black perambulators, footmen walking dogs and people out for a gentle stroll.

'She said *no*,' he muttered under his breath. 'Unbelievable.'

For her sake he had turned his back on a vow he had made the day he had inherited the earldom. She not only did not appreciate the sacrifice he was making but had thrown it back in his face.

She had even had the audacity to behave as if marriage to him would be so intolerable she could not possibly bring herself to consent.

What on earth was wrong with the woman?

She was willing to give her body to him but not marry him. Unbelievable.

He increased the pace of his walking. It was surely all for the best. After all, this was not the first time he had been astounded by her mercurial behaviour, and that had been one of the many reasons why he had never considered her of the right calibre to be the next Countess of Rothwell. Last night and this morning she had proven that this assessment of her character was correct.

Mercurial, impetuous and irresponsible. Those were among the long list of faults that had initially ruled her out, and she had just shown him she possessed them in abundance.

Along with a beauty that took his breath away, a laugh that soothed his spirit and a smile that caused warmth to fill his heart.

But those qualities were surely not enough to counter her shortcomings. And it mattered not. She did not want to marry him, even if it would save her reputation, elevate her to one of the highest ranks in Society and make her one of the wealthiest women in the country.

'Unbelievable,' he repeated to himself as he rounded the corner. If he had made that proposal to any other young lady she would have replied with a resounding *yes*.

But not Miss Lucinda Everhart.

What was she going to do now? Marry Barrington, Montclair or Coldridge? The fury simmering under the surface boiled up, making his body burn with barely containable rage. Well, they were welcome to her. They could deal with her capriciousness, her recklessness and her foolhardy behaviour.

He bit down harder, refusing to think of what else those men would have if they married Lucy. A young woman who laughed easily and who had a daring spirit and an irresistible body that he doubted he would ever forget.

He came to a sudden halt as an image of how she looked, lying on the couch, entered his mind. Of her blouse parted, her breasts exposed to his admiring gaze, her skirt bunched up around her waist, her long legs, still wearing those white silk stockings and blue garter belt, spread and waiting for him.

He resumed walking even faster. He would not think of that, nor of the way she'd looked at him, with unbridled desire and longing.

A groan escaped his lips, causing the couple he was overtaking to look at him in concern. If he were to avoid driving himself insane, that was an image he was never going to be able to think of again. Nor would he think of how he would never have the chance to finish what they started last night, would never again have her lying before him, waiting for him to make love to her.

His teeth were now clenching so hard his jaw was aching. What he had to focus on was how that same woman had just rejected his proposal of marriage.

And as for that fool of a father, he thought, clasping onto a subject less distressing. Sebastian would admit he was only trying to protect his daughter, but if the man opened his sanctimonious, censorious eyes he would see that a marriage to Sebastian *was* the best way to protect her. Accepting his proposal would mean marriage to a man who would treat her with respect, who would care for her and who would elevate her to the position of countess.

Yes, he could see that the reverend would have been shocked and outraged by what he saw last night, but surely he should have given Sebastian some credit for trying to make amends in the most noble of ways. Wasn't that what most fathers expected, for the man who had supposedly ruined the daughter's reputation to make everything right through marriage?

Instead, what did Sebastian get? Outrage and rejection.

He was better off away from Lucy and that preposterous family.

He turned the corner into his street and stopped. What he needed now was the company of rational, sensible men. He would summon his friends, Isaac and Thomas, to their club. Whiling away time at The Eldridge, playing billiards, discussing politics and the achievements of their sporting heroes would take his mind off other unwanted thoughts.

He started walking again then stopped. That would not do. His two friends had changed since they'd become happily married men and were unlikely to provide him with the same sympathetic ears they once had.

He carried on, thinking. Instead, he would join Nathanial at The Royal Flush and pass some convivial time in the company of his half-brother. His heart sank, and he came to another halt. The last place he wanted to visit was the office at that gambling den. He did not wish to be confronted with that couch and remember all that happened on it—all that had nearly happened—and the face of Lucy's irate father storming in on them.

It looked like it would have to be an evening spent at the type of haunts where a man could drive away thoughts of a vexatious woman in the company of carefree women who knew how to make a man forget his troubles. His heart sank further. He would not be doing that either. No woman had interested him since he had met Lucy.

He strolled more slowly towards his townhouse. How was he going to drive thoughts of her from his mind and blot out the memory of last night and this morning's unexpected rejection he did not know, but he was going to have to find a way.

He entered his home, a maelstrom of emotions waging a war inside him, his agitated state not diminished by his vigorous walk.

'Sir, there is a woman waiting for you in the drawing room. I could not stop her, and she refused to leave her name.'

Sebastian stared at his footman in surprise. Had Lucy taken a carriage to his townhouse while he was walking? It was unlikely that she would come to her senses so quickly, but anything was possible with a woman as fickle as her.

'Very well, Samuel,' he said, as he handed his hat and coat to the servant.

Smiling to himself he walked towards the drawing room, curious as to what she would now say after the insults she had thrown at him.

He entered to find an older woman standing in the middle of the room.

She stepped forward, her hands outstretched as if for an embrace. 'Hello, son.'

Sebastian froze in the doorway. He had not thought this day could get any worse. It was now apparent he was wrong.

Chapter Twenty

'What do you want?' Sebastian said to the woman he refused to call *Mother*. She had lost the right to be addressed in such a manner when she abandoned him twenty-five years before.

She took a step towards him. 'I had to see you before I returned to America.'

'Well, you have seen me now.' He stepped away from the open door and with a sweep of his hand indicated the way out of the room.

'I know you are angry with me, Sebastian. I know you don't want to see me, but please, if you would just give me a few moments of your time.'

She did not deserve even that, but he pointed towards the divan and asked her to take a seat. If nothing else, her presence would provide a distraction from his thoughts of Lucy.

'Would you like tea, or would you prefer something stronger?' Given all he had heard of his mother he suspected drinking when it was barely past noon would not be unusual for her, and after the tumultuous morning he'd had, he could do with a stiff drink.

'Tea would be lovely,' she said, tucking her skirt underneath her and sitting down.

He rang for tea and sat across from her, saying nothing, just waiting for her lies to begin.

'You've grown into a finely built man,' she said, smiling at him. He could say that if that was true, it was despite her not because of her, but he had no desire to enter into an argument with this woman. All he wanted was for her to say her piece and leave.

The maid entered with the tea service. They sat in silence while she poured two cups and handed them to his guest and Sebastian. Neither made any move to drink their tea, placing them on nearby tables and waiting in silence until the maid left.

'Why did you leave me?' he asked. Despite his determination to say nothing to this woman, the words escaped his mouth. It was a question he had been asking himself since he was a small, lonely boy. A question he suspected he would not like the answer to.

She sat forwards in her chair. 'You have to believe me, Sebastian. I never wanted to leave you.'

He snorted out a dismissive laugh. 'I don't *have* to believe anything you say. All I know to be true is that you *did* leave me.'

'If I'd had a choice I would never have done so.'

He shook his head slowly. He was not surprised that she would not take responsibility for her actions.

'I suppose you're going to say it was Father's fault,' he said, his words laced with sarcasm.

'Yes, I'm afraid it was.'

'Oh, pray tell. How did Father force you to leave your young child? How did he make you run off with your lover to start another family?'

'Quite easily.' She paused, looked down at her hands then back at him. 'It wasn't as you think, or as your father no doubt told you.'

Sebastian crossed his arms, waiting for whatever attempted justification she had for doing the unjustifiable.

'The marriage between your father and me was an arranged one, and there was no love on either side.' She placed her hand on her stomach as if stilling her nerves, but Sebastian would not be fooled by this act. 'Your father chose to spend as much time as he could away from the estate, usually in London, but I had no such choices. I was a woman in my early twenties with no one to talk to, and my loneliness was so intense it felt physical.'

'So you took a lover,' Sebastian said. He would not feel pity for the woman who had abandoned him to be with that lover.

'No, I found a friend. Joseph, the estate manager, took pity on me, and we spent time together, talking and laughing. When I was with him I remembered what it was like to be happy again.' She smiled in remembrance.

'And so you took him as your lover.'

'No,' she shook her head sadly. 'But when your father found out we were spending time together, I could not convince him we were merely friends. The idea of a man befriending a woman because he felt sorry for her, or even because he just enjoyed her company, was something your father would never understand. He decided we must be lovers and threw me out of the house.'

Sebastian stared at her. 'Are you claiming Father made you leave, that you did not leave of your own accord?'

'I would never have left you. I loved you with a strength I would not have thought possible if I had not felt it. I would have gladly sacrificed my happiness to be with you. I would have done anything your father asked of me, but he would not let me anywhere near you.'

Sebastian's heart clenched painfully in his chest, but he fought not to be swayed by her words. He had felt such intense anger towards her for so many years he was not about to let it go now.

'I had nowhere to go,' she continued. 'My family had abandoned me, taking the earl's side. Your father also dismissed Joseph from his service, so he, too, was without a home. His family kindly allowed us to stay with them in their humble little cottage while I tried to work out what I was to do and how I was to get you back.'

She gripped her hands together tightly in her lap. 'We even made an attempt to kidnap you, but your father ensured that was impossible. He had you guarded at all times. Then he sent you away, and I had no idea where you were.'

Sebastian stared straight ahead, not knowing if she was telling the truth or whether she was merely a convincing liar.

She looked down. 'Then your father filed for divorce. I went to see a lawyer who told me my case was hopeless, and I would never be able to defeat him in court. Who would believe the word of a woman against that of a man, and one who was a respected earl? Plus, I had been living with the man everyone assumed was my lover. It was then that Joseph and I decided to leave for America.'

'Rather than stay behind and try and fight for me?'

She wiped the edge of her eye. 'I had already lost. The lawyer said no court would ever grant custody of a child to an adulteress, and I knew if I stayed they would take Nathanial from me as well.'

'Nathanial?' he blurted out. 'But he was born in America. He's your lover's son, your second husband's, not Father's.' Her story was starting to unravel. The woman was obviously a liar.

'When your father turned me out, I was pregnant, with his second son. He never knew, and I never told him. If I had remained in England and appeared in court to fight my case, he would have eventually realised I was pregnant. He could be so vindictive. Whether he believed Nathanial to be his son or not, he would have taken him out of my care. I could not risk losing two children.'

She shuddered a deep sigh. 'So we ran to America. Joseph and I soon became more than friends. He is such a good, kind man, and I finally had a marriage based on love and mutual respect. I would have been completely content with my new life if it were not for having been forced to abandon my firstborn child.'

He stared at her, stunned at this revelation. 'No, that can't be true. Nathanial has said nothing about any of this.'

She smiled. 'Surely you've seen how much he looks like you and your father. The dark hair.' She touched her chin. 'That dimple which he inherited from your father.' Her smile faded. 'Thankfully, he is nothing like the old earl in nature, perhaps because he was raised by Joseph and always thought of him as his father.'

'And he was raised by a mother,' Sebastian added, bile once again rising up his throat.

She leant forward and reached for his hands. 'Not a day went by when I did not think of you, Sebastian. Not a day passed when I did not hope and pray you were happy, that you were loved and cared for. I wrote countless letters to you, even though they kept coming back unopened.' She bit the edge of her lip. 'When they continued to be returned after your father died, I realised it must be you who was now sending them back and that you, perhaps rightly, could not forgive me.'

Sebastian sat back in his chair, the anger he had held on to for so many years deflating, but he did not know with what to replace it. He had not known about the earlier letters, and when letters started arriving after he inherited the title and estates, fury had stopped him from opening them. He had assumed they were little more than begging letters from a woman who realised her son was now a wealthy man.

'I can tell you can't forgive me, and perhaps you are right to be still angry with me. But please, Sebastian, I beg of you, when you do take a wife, make sure you marry for love. Then hopefully you will be the one to break the Rothwell curse.'

'What?' He leant forward. 'What do you know of the Rothwell curse?'

'Of course I know about it.' She gave a mirthless laugh. 'Your father led me around the portrait gallery when our marriage was first agreed upon by our parents, as if warning me about his expectations regarding my behaviour.'

Sebastian inwardly flinched, remembering how he had done the exact same thing with Lucy.

'He told me about each woman's transgressions and the scandal she had caused. Has he not told you about them?'

'Yes, he told me all about the behaviour of those

women,' he said more sternly than he intended. 'My father often recounted the sorry story of our scandalous family history.'

'But I suspect he did not explain that all those so-called scandals were the result of generation after generation of Rothwell men marrying women they did not love, then abandoning them in the countryside to deal with their loneliness and unhappiness.'

He flinched again. Her words were so close to those Lucy had said when he had informed her of what he had hoped for in his future countess.

'Many of those women were so desperate for some affection, for some happiness, that they took it where they could find it,' she added.

'No, that's not right. What about Grandmother? Are you saying she didn't almost gamble away the estate, or are you saying she did so because she needed someone to hug her and pay her a bit of attention?' he said, his voice dismissive.

'Your poor grandmother was a deeply miserable woman. Like all the Rothwell countesses, her marriage had been arranged, and she was stuck with a man who cared nothing for her. She had no interest in gambling until after she married but was often invited to a nearby estate to take part in their gaming evenings. I doubt if she would have gone if she weren't so desperate for company. She hardly knew the rules of the games they were playing, and she was taken advantage of. The rumour that the Prince of Wales was her lover and he paid her debts was unlikely as she rarely left the estate, and there is no record of him visiting. It was more likely he had heard what had happened and put a stop to it.'

This was nothing like the story he had been told repeatedly by his father, and now he was unsure which version was the truth. 'And I suppose all those women who had affairs were innocent as well,' he said with biting sarcasm.

She shrugged. 'Who knows? But I have always had my doubts about the story of the countess having affairs with men on both sides during the Civil War. It would be difficult for a woman shut away in the countryside to meet a commanding officer on one side of that war, never mind men both. It was more likely that the earl was trying to play both sides off each other. I suspect he made up that story to staunch rumours about his duplicitous strategy.'

Sebastian stared at her, unsure what to believe. 'The rumours of attempted murders? Arson? Embezzlement?'

She turned her hands, palms upwards. 'Again, we only have the husbands' words for what happened, and as society and the courts are always on the man's side, especially if he is an earl…'

Her words faded, and she remained silent for a moment, as if remembering her own experiences with the legal system.

'As for embezzlement, women have little access to

money even now, so if any embezzlement happened, it is more likely it was the earl who was at fault, and once again the wife got the blame.'

'Hmm,' he said, forced to admit that a woman's lack of access to finances was credible.

'And as for the first countess, the one who apparently gained the earl his title and all the lands that make up the Rothwell estate by becoming Henry VIII's lover, well—'

'Don't tell me. That was all fabrication as well.'

'No, I suspect that was true. But at that time what choice would a young woman have if the king noticed her? And if her marriage was as loveless as every other marriage in that cursed family, it would not surprise me if her husband hadn't happily handed her over to the lascivious king so he could increase his wealth.'

She smiled sadly at Sebastian. 'After all this time I doubt you want to take any motherly advice from me, but please, Sebastian, make a good marriage, one in which you and your wife will be happy. Marry for love. Marry a woman who loves you and brings you joy, or else you risk ending up like every other Rothwell earl, angry, bitter, blaming your wife and claiming that the Rothwell line is cursed.'

Sebastian stared at his mother, unsure what to say. What did you say when everything you believed had been undermined, when the premise under which you had lived your life had been shown to be false, when your world had seemingly come crashing down around your ears?

All his life he had accepted what his father had said and blamed his mother. He had believed himself to be unloved. As a child he had craved that love. As he'd grown older, he'd berated himself for still desperately wanting the love he had never had and never could have. As an adult he'd seen such yearnings as fanciful, seen love as an indulgence that was not for him. His role was to break the curse, and the only way he could do that was to marry a woman who, like him, put duty ahead of emotion.

Now his mother was telling him that the curse, if he could still call it that, was caused by generations of Rothwells not marrying for love.

Thoughts whirled around in his confused mind as he tried to fight off the uncertainty that such a revelation had caused.

'Is there anyone you do love or could love?' she said quietly. 'Someone who could make you happy?'

An image of Lucy's smiling face appeared in his mind.

'I can see from your expression that there is someone.'

'I did meet a young lady this Season, but she is wholly unsuitable.'

'Unsuitable? How?'

'She is unpredictable, wayward and obstinate. These are not the qualities I want in my wife.' Damn it all, there was that bombastic voice again, the one Lucy never failed to tease him about.

'And yet you still love her?' his mother said, smiling. She waited, but Sebastian chose to neither confirm nor deny that statement. Love? That was an emotion he had told himself to never expect, and certainly not from a wife.

'Maybe she's not unpredictable, wayward and obstinate, but spirited, spontaneous and resolute,' she continued. 'All qualities I think would be admirable in a countess and a woman worthy of your love.'

'I did not say I love her.'

She made no response, just looked at him and waited.

'All right. Yes, I am attracted to her, more attracted to her than is wise. So attracted it has caused me to act out of character on occasion.' That was an understatement, but he did not wish to inform his mother of the true extent of his uncharacteristic behaviour.

She waited.

'And yes, unfortunately I find myself thinking about her more than I should.' He released an exasperated huff. 'I can't get her out of my thoughts, damn it all.'

'But do you love her?' his mother repeated quietly.

Images of Lucy swam before him, of her laughing with such unfettered pleasure, teasing him for his pomposity, looking at him with intense desire and affection. He closed his eyes, determined to push them away, along with the burning emotions they ignited.

If he let those emotions consume him, then surely he would be left vulnerable to pain, the way he had been as a lonely child.

That was why he needed to marry a woman who would never breach the barriers he had erected around his heart.

But instead he had met Lucy, an unconventional young lady who had turned his world upside down and made him forget who he was and what he wanted from his marriage.

He opened his eyes. 'Yes, I do love her,' he finally said, those barriers tumbling around him.

'Then, if she returns your love, you should marry her.'

'I have already proposed, but she has turned me down.'

'Oh, Sebastian, I am so sorry.' She rose from the divan, crossed the room and sat beside him, taking his hands in hers.

'I'm afraid I wronged her terribly,' he added.

'By proposing?'

'Yes, I made a ham-fisted job of it and insulted her terribly. I behaved as if offering her marriage and the chance to become a countess was a great honour for her.'

'Then, it was to her credit she turned you down.'

He nodded, hardly able to believe what he had said to such a lovely, giving, open-hearted young woman. He had not only made it seem like she was the one to benefit from such a marriage but he had given her every impression that he was reluctant to take her as his wife, whereas being married to Lucy would be the greatest honour that could be bestowed upon him.

'But I urge you, Sebastian, make things right before it's too late. Let her know how much you love her. Let her see that she is loved and cherished.'

He nodded slowly, unsure of how he was to do that.

His mother smiled at him, understanding his confusion. 'You need to tell her how you feel. Speak from your heart, not your head,' she said, placing her hand in the middle of his chest. 'Love is so precious, Sebastian. You can't let it slip away.' She looked up at him, tears in her eyes. 'If she is a woman worthy of your love, then you should fight for her. If you don't, you'll regret it for the rest of your life, and that will be your curse.'

Sebastian nodded, knowing everything she said was true. He could only hope that it was not too late.

'You're right, Mother. I will.'

She smiled through her tears, and Sebastian wrapped his arms around her.

She hugged him back, and he could feel her tears against his neck.

'Oh, my son, my lovely son, I've dreamt of doing this every day for the last twenty-five years.' She sniffed and wiped away a tear as she looked into his eyes. 'And I can't wait to meet the young woman who has captured your heart.'

Chapter Twenty-One

After spending the evening in the surprisingly delightful company of his mother and brother Nathanial, the next morning Sebastian found himself outside the door of Lucy's Bayswater townhouse unsure what he was going to do or say, but determined to follow his mother's advice and speak from the heart. He had to hope it was not too late and that she had not accepted a proposal from any of those other men offering for her hand. If she had, then somehow he was going to have to convince her that he would make the better husband, not because he was the better man but because he could promise her his eternal love.

The door was opened, not by a footman in smart livery but by a man in a suit. 'I didn't expect to get a response so quickly, and I haven't even advertised yet,' the man said.

'I'm here to see Miss Lucinda Everhart,' Sebastian said, confused.

'Oh, I see. I'm the landlord. The Everharts cancelled

their tenancy yesterday and have moved out. But if you're interested in renting a spacious four-bedroom home for the rest of the Season, with ample room for entertaining, then I have just the place for you at a very reasonable rate.'

Sebastian could hardly believe what he was hearing. They had left? Lucy had gone? Lucy, who was so determined to enjoy the Season had left before it was over? Had his atrocious behaviour driven her away? Had she fled because she wanted to get away from him?

'I can even give it to you at a reduced rate as the Season is almost over,' the landlord continued.

Sebastian politely declined but thanked the man and returned to his carriage. There was only one place they could have gone: back to Cheshire. He racked his brain to remember the name of the village they hailed from. *Greystone? Greyport? Greyton*—that was it. It would surely not be hard to find the vicarage in such a place.

Telling his driver to make haste, he returned home and informed his valet they needed to pack for a journey, then the two men headed for the station. The train journey gave him time to think about what he was going to say, although apart from *I'm sorry* and *I love you*, no other words presented themselves.

Speak from the heart his mother had said, so hopefully it would not matter that he was so ill-prepared for making what was to be the most important speech of his life.

When they arrived at Greyton, he left organising accommodation to his valet, asked a passing local where he'd find Reverend Everton's vicarage, then headed off immediately, across the village green and past rows of thatched cottages. He paused outside a modest two-storey brick cottage beside a stone church, his hand on the wooden gate and took a moment to compose himself.

Perhaps it was a mistake to have nothing prepared, because now he had no idea how he was going to express everything he had to say. The words were all just a jumble rolling round and round inside his head, refusing to form sentences that made any sense to him, so were hardly likely to make sense to Lucy or convince her that she should become his wife.

Speak from your heart, not your head.

With more confidence than he felt, he pushed open the gate, walked up the stone pathway and knocked on the door.

A maid opened and smiled brightly at him. 'Yes, sir. What can we do for you?'

This was a good start, but then, it was a vicarage. The maid was probably used to strangers coming to seek counsel from the reverend and had not been informed about the man who had been told to never contact Lucy again.

'I have come to see...' After all that had happened,

it would not be appropriate to ask to see Lucy alone, and he also needed to put things right with her father, so that was where he would start. 'I'd like to see the Reverend Everhart on a matter of some importance.'

'Certainly, sir. Who shall I say is calling?'

'Sebastian Kingsley, the Earl of Rothwell,' he said, hoping that name meant nothing to the maid and she wasn't about to change from a sweet, friendly woman into a raging harridan who would slam the door in his face.

'Yes, my lord,' she said instead and bobbed a quick curtsy. 'Please follow me.'

Another good sign. He followed the maid into the parlour. She coughed lightly to draw the reverend's attention. 'The Earl of Rothwell to see you, sir.' She gave another quick bob in Sebastian's direction and disappeared.

While the maid was friendly, the look on the vicar's face was anything but. His thin white face turned red as he stood up, gripping the edge of the wing-back chair as if the floor was moving under his feet.

'What is the meaning of this?' he boomed in a voice that would carry to the end of any church. 'I have made my opinion of you clear. Leave this house.'

'I have come to apologise.'

The man's face turned a darker shade of red.

'I have wronged you and wronged Lucy. But, sir, I love your daughter, and I want to make her my wife.'

'*Love,*' the reverend shouted out as if it were the

most despicable word he had ever heard. 'Men like you do not know the meaning of the word *love*.'

'You're right. At least, you were right until I met Lucy,' he said, smiling as he mentioned that lovely name.

'Enough of your nonsense,' the clergyman thundered. 'I know what you are up to. My daughter came to her senses, and that was an insult to your pride. That is why you want her. That is why you are professing this so-called love. You want to turn her head yet again. You are worse than the worst of debauchees. Most rakes would know when they are beaten. They would not continue to pursue the innocent young woman they had already tried to ruin.'

'No, it's not like that. I wish to—'

'Accept that you have failed. Thanks to your debauched ways, my Lucy has seen the wisdom in remaining in the countryside, where she is safe, away from ruinous men such as yourself. She quite sensibly will not be attending the rest of the Season, or any other Season, and she certainly will not be mixing with the likes of you.'

Sebastian drew in a breath through his teeth as guilt and shame welled up inside him. How could he have been so callous as to hurt such a young woman, one who loved life so much, who wanted to embrace all the fun and pleasure the world had to give?

He knew how much joy living in London had given her and how the country life was not for her. And yet to get away from him, she had chosen to, as she had said before, 'be stuck away in the Cheshire countryside'.

But he hung on to one sliver of hope, revealed in the reverend's tirade.

'So she hasn't accepted any of the other proposals?' he asked, his body tense.

'Not that it is any of your business, but she has sensibly decided the life of an unmarried daughter of a vicar is much more rewarding. She will be dedicating herself to helping me in my work with the parishioners.'

Sebastian released his held breath. At least he had no rival for her hand, and his appalling behaviour hadn't driven her into the arms of another man. While he doubted a woman as vibrant and vivacious as Lucy would really be happy to live the life of a spinster, nothing would be gained by pointing that out to her angry father.

'May I at least speak to her?' he asked, suspecting he knew the answer.

'No, you most certainly may not,' her father boomed back at him.

'In your presence of course,' he added, although making a heartfelt admission to the woman you love while her enraged father glared at you would hardly add to the romance of the occasion.

'You will not be going anywhere near my daughter, either in or out of my presence, do you hear?' He lifted his cane as if he intended to give Sebastian a thrashing.

Sebastian thought it wisest to depart before that happened. If the man did try to assault him, Sebastian feared the unfamiliar exertion might cause the old man to have a heart attack.

'Goodbye, sir,' he said with a slight bow of his head and departed.

'And let that be the last we ever see of you,' the reverend shouted to his departing back.

Sebastian paused in the entranceway, the maid nowhere in sight, as he contemplated what he was to do next. How does one speak from the heart when there's no one to speak to?

A door slowly opened, and Lucy's aunt Harriet peeked out and waved her hand to signal for him to approach. When he reached the doorway behind which she was hiding, she whispered something to him.

He lowered his head to hear what she was saying.

'Lucy went down to the village to distribute some money from the alms boxes,' she said in a barely audible voice. 'After that, she planned to take a walk beside the stream,' she pointed in the direction Sebastian should go. 'That is where you will find her.'

He gave his thanks to the older lady and all but ran out the front door.

Lucy walked slowly beside the gently flowing stream, the warm sun on her face. It was a beautiful day, but she hardly noticed the sparkling water or the weeping willows dipping their green bows into the babbling brook.

Despite the idyllic setting, she had never felt more miserable. Her father had claimed nature had a soothing effect on the soul, but she was yet to feel its restorative benefits.

Distributing the much-needed alms to poorer parishioners had briefly taken her mind off her own troubles. How could she think of her own sorrows when other people's concerns were so much greater than her own?

But as soon as she left their modest homes, her own despondency crashed down on her.

Despite her misery, she had made the right decision when she had told her father she wished to leave London. Not so long ago, the idea of returning to Greyton and working with her father would have been as unlikely as a Sunday without church bells, but now it was the best option available to her.

It was far preferable to being married to Lord Coldridge, Mr Montclair or Mr Barrington. It would be cruel to marry one man when you were constantly thinking about another. All that would result from such an arrangement was for two people to be miserable rather than one.

And the life she was now embarking on was preferable to being married to a man she *did* love who did not love her in return. She placed her hand on her stomach in a fruitless attempt to relieve the tension that thoughts of that one-sided love always evoked.

Yes, her decision to flee back to the countryside had been the best and only option. To continue with her disastrous Season would only compound her sorrow. One regret, among so many, was that, without a Season to prepare for, Dolly's contract had come to an end. Lucy told her father not to worry about writing a reference, as she would take that task off his shoulders and do so herself. As promised, she wrote Dolly a reference that could get her entrance into the finest houses in England, but it was all for nought. Dolly informed her that she had been offered a position at The Royal Flush, which she had accepted.

Without her confidante to talk to, Lucy had surprisingly found herself turning to Aunt Harriet, who provided a surprisingly good source of comfort.

She listened without judgement to all Lucy had to say and was not even shocked when Lucy admitted to being the one to instigate those kisses. Her aunt had merely wrapped her in her arms and let her cry out her sorrow at what a mess her Season had been.

And it *had* been. In every way, her Season had been a complete failure, even though everything she had hoped for had happened. She had danced. She had laughed. She'd had several illicit kisses, received offers of courtship and even a proposal of marriage.

And if she hadn't made the fatal mistake of falling in love with the wrong man, it might have been a complete success.

She released a long, sad sigh. Now she had chosen to live the life of the vicar's unmarried daughter.

That was certainly not the life she had envisaged for herself when she'd set off to London full of such high expectations, but it was one she was determined to accept with as much grace as she possessed, even if grace was something she had hitherto not been blessed with an abundance of.

She broke off a small twig, tossed it into the stream and watched it spin around then float away.

Didn't people say time healed everything? She was sure she'd heard that somewhere. And it had only been a couple of days since she had seen Sebastian, so she could not expect miracles. Like all other injuries, a broken heart must take time to mend, but surely eventually it would heal. She had to believe that, as the years passed, she would forget Sebastian and she would find some happiness in helping her father's parishioners; otherwise, the anguish possessing her would be more than she could bear.

She continued walking along the stream, around a bend and towards the stone bridge that would take her to the path that led back to the vicarage.

She stopped in her tracks.

Was she going mad? In her melancholic state had she conjured up an image of Sebastian?

'Lucy,' he said, crossing the arched bridge, his hands reaching out towards her.

She tentatively walked up the curve of the bridge, unsure if that was a wise idea. Whether this was a crazed image or not, surely her heart would heal sooner if she did not engage with him.

'Lucy,' the image repeated as she moved closer.

'Sebastian,' she said tentatively and waited for him to disappear in a puff of smoke, the way she had once seen a magician make his assistant disappear.

'Your aunt Harriet told me where I would find you.'

'She did?'

He reached out for her hands, and even though she knew it was unwise, she could not stop herself from placing her hands in his. And oh, didn't it feel good! His warmth seeped into her, coursing through her body like a blazing fire on a cold winter's day.

This was real. The man she loved was really standing in front of her.

'I had to see you,'

'You did?' she said, knowing she was sounding somewhat gormless.

'Yes. I had to talk to you.'

She resisted the temptation to once again say *You did?*

'I had to apologise.'

'Apologise?' She cursed herself for her inability to string together sensible, coherent sentences.

'Yes, apologise for that insensitive proposal. Apologise for judging you so harshly. Apologise for being a fool.'

'That's rather a lot of apologies.'

He smiled, and her heart melted inside her chest. How could she have not fallen under the spell of a man with a smile like that?

While a sensible young lady would just accept those apologies graciously and walk away, Lucy could not. She'd never been particularly sensible and wasn't about to start now.

'Perhaps we should take a seat,' she said instead and walked towards a stone bench in the middle of the arched bridge, positioned to allow strollers to rest and look out over the stream and the surrounding countryside.

Sebastian sat beside her, and Lucy was sure her pounding heart was drowning out the sound of the gurgling water beneath them and the birds tweeting in the trees.

'So, I believe you had a series of apologies you wished to make,' she prompted him as much for something to say as to hear what those apologies were.

'Yes, firstly I want to say I'm sorry for my ridiculous criteria regarding who I was to marry.'

She turned to face him. 'What? You mean choosing a bride who will break the Rothwell curse?'

He screwed up his face as if wounded. 'Yes. I was a fool in so many ways.' He nodded slowly. 'But after speaking to my mother I have come to realise how wrong I was, how quick I was to judge and how I had condemned women for actions I would easily forgive in a man.'

'Oh, Sebastian, you've met with your mother! That's wonderful.' She placed her hand on his arm. 'Isn't it?' she added with more caution.

'It is. Nathanial was right. She is a kind, loving woman. And you were right. I did need to talk to her to find out why she left me.'

'And I take it she answered your questions,' she said quietly.

'She did. I discovered she never wanted to leave me but had been forced to do so by my father, out of some sort of mean-spirited punishment towards the woman he thought had wronged him.'

Lucy was tempted to take him in her arms. He had suffered so much as a little boy because he thought he had been abandoned by his mother. Hopefully, their reconciliation would help heal those wounds.

'She also told me about the so-called Rothwell curse.'

'Was it as bad as you thought?'

'It was worse.'

'Oh.' She removed her hand and placed it in her lap.

'It appears generation after generation of Rothwell countesses have suffered terribly. They've entered loveless marriages, been all but abandoned by their husbands, then shamed and dishonoured in a manner far in excess of any scandal they might have caused. It was those loveless marriages, and certainly not some curse or some fault with the Rothwell countesses, that led to all those supposed scandals.'

'I'm pleased she put that straight,' Lucy said, wondering where that left them.

'Yes, my mother's revelations made me see that you were right,' he said, turning slightly on the bench to face her. 'I judged the women in my family harshly but never considered what the males' behaviour had been like. And if those men were anything like me, then they were callous imbeciles who did not deserve the women they married.'

'That's a bit harsh.'

He shook his head. 'No, not in the slightest.'

'So you're not going to make respectability the only criterion on which you choose your future wife?' she asked, trying to keep her voice light.

'No. Although, even that is something I need to apologise for. I should never have suggested you were anything other than perfect in every way.'

'Me? Perfect?' Her voice came out in an embarrassing squeak, but that was no surprise. *Perfect* was not a word she would use to describe herself.

'I have judged you so harshly and so unfairly, Lucy, right from the moment we first met.' He smiled sadly, as if remembering that first meeting, which was yet another occasion where Lucy's behaviour had been far from perfect.

'Well, perhaps not when we first met. On that occasion, if I did judge you, it was to judge you the most beautiful, enchanting, vivacious young woman I had ever met.'

Lucy smiled, liking the sound of that.

'It was on our second meeting that I judged you more harshly than you could possibly deserve. I cannot believe I dismissed you as someone out to compromise me into marriage. And then when we kissed for the second time, instead of seeing it as proof of my attraction for you, I saw it as proof that you were less than respectable, even though you had done nothing I had not done myself.'

Lucy closed her eyes, remembering that kiss, the touch of his lips, the feel of his arms around her, the heat of his body.

'I am so sorry,' he continued. 'I was clinging to those ridiculous beliefs about how my future wife should or should not behave, beliefs that were not only false but unfair.'

He looked out at the river. 'I now know why I was so determined to see you as an unacceptable countess. It was so much easier to do that than to admit to myself how I was feeling. I thought it was easier to close down my heart than to open it up and leave myself vulnerable to the possibility of pain greater than what I believed I could endure.'

Lucy nodded, knowing full well what such pain felt like.

He once again turned back to face her. 'And, Lucy, I

am so sorry for that appalling marriage proposal. You had every right to turn me down, and your father had every right to throw me out of the house.'

'As you're making apologies, I suppose I should make one or two myself.'

'No, you have nothing to be sorry for.'

'Well, I did put you in a rather awkward position, and when Father found us, he would of course see you as a rake.'

'And quite rightly too.'

'No, quite wrongly. I went to The Royal Flush to find you. I deliberately made sure we would be alone because, well… I was hoping you would kiss me again. I had been thinking about nothing else since our first two kisses. And well, deep down, I had been hoping that when you heard I had other offers of marriage, you would fall to your knee and declare your love for me and insist I marry you.'

'Oh, Lucy, I—'

'And we both know it was me who tried to seduce you,' she interrupted, before he could once again take all the blame. 'Or, at least, encouraged you to seduce me, or something. And if I really was perfect, I would have told Father you were not to blame, but, well… because you didn't love me and didn't really want to marry me, I chose to take the coward's way out, say nothing and let him continue to hold you entirely responsible.'

'And that is also what I came here to do today.' He once again took hold of her hands.

'What? To seduce me?' Lucy knew she should be outraged, but the reaction in her body, while outrageously strong, was very keen on that idea.

He smiled. 'No. To declare my love for you.'

She was momentarily disappointed, hearing the word *no*, then the second part of that sentence hit her like a crashing wave strong enough to knock her off her feet. 'You love me?'

'With all my heart and soul.'

'Oh,' Lucy gasped, once again becoming inarticulate and gormless.

He lightly touched her cheek. 'I thought you the most beautiful, enchanting, vivacious woman I have ever met the moment I saw you. Our first kiss confirmed that suspicion, and every moment I have spent with you has only reinforced that fact. You are simply wonderful, and I have wasted so much time with all my foolish prejudices and misconceptions.'

Her hand shot to cover her mouth.

'When I proposed, I said I was doing it because it was the right thing to do. I lied. At least, I lied to myself. I was pretending I was being honourable when in reality I was being selfish. I wanted to marry you for my own benefit because I love you, even if I hadn't realised it at the time. I wanted to marry you, and I still want to marry you, because my life without you in it is dull and colourless.'

Her hand still covering her mouth, Lucy stared at him wide-eyed, hardly able to believe he was actually saying the words she so longed to hear.

'And you were right to turn me down,' he continued, causing Lucy to shake her head. 'You were right when you said my proposal suggested I was lowering my standards by asking you to marry me, when what I should have said was I would be honoured if you would stoop so low as to marry an arrogant fool such as me.'

Lucy's eyes grew even wider as he moved off the stone bench and down onto one knee. 'Lucy, you say you are not perfect, but you are. You're perfect for me. I love you, and nothing would make me happier than you doing me the greatest honour in the world and becoming my wife.'

Lucy nodded.

'Imagining my life without you in it is like trying to imagine the world without sunshine, without laughter, without joy. I want you in my life. I want to be part of your life. I want to hear your laughter every day, see your sunny smile, feel the joy that only you can bring.'

She continued nodding, her smile growing wider with every word.

'I promise I will do all I can to be worthy of your love, to prove to you every day that you are my ideal countess. Will you marry me, Lucy?'

'Yes,' she whispered, once again wondering whether this was a fantasy she had conjured up to soothe away the anguish she had been feeling since she had first turned down his proposal.

'Oh, my darling, you can't imagine how happy that makes me.'

On that he was wrong, as no happiness could be greater than what she was feeling right now.

'So now that we've got that out of the way, are you going to finally seduce me?' If this was a fantasy, she might as well make it an even more memorable one.

He laughed as he rose from his knees. 'It would be my pleasure,' he said, then his arms were around her, and he was kissing her.

Lucy had her answer. This was no fantasy. Even her fervid imaginings could not bring to life the exquisite feel of his lips on hers, that intoxicating masculine scent or the way her body responded to his touch.

She sank into his arms knowing this was where she belonged, in the arms of the man she loved. She could spend an eternity here, but all too soon his lips withdrew from hers, and with her still in his arms he looked down at her.

'But we still have one problem.'

Yes, there was the danger of someone coming along the path and finding them. She looked around for a secret spot where they could continue in private.

'Your father hates me. He will never give his consent for us to marry.'

'Yes, there is that, I suppose.' She screwed up her nose in thought. 'I'll just tell him this was all my fault, that I pursued you, tried to seduce you, you resisted, then when you wanted to do the right thing, I rejected you then finally accepted you.'

She looked up into his eyes. 'In other words, I'll tell the truth. I really am rather frightful, aren't I? Are you sure you want to marry me?'

He laughed and lightly kissed the end of her nose, causing her to smile. 'Marrying you is what I want with all my heart and soul. But you are certainly not to blame, and you cannot say that to your father.'

He sent her a mischievous smile that she definitely liked the look of. 'I have an idea.'

'What?'

'We could elope.'

'Elope?' she said her eyes growing enormous, hardly able to believe he had suggested such a thing. 'How scandalous.'

'Yes, you're right.' The smile died, and his brow furrowed. 'You deserve a big white wedding attended by all in Society, one that will make your father proud.'

'No, I love the idea of starting our married life with a scandal.'

He shook his head. 'It was a foolish idea. Your father would never forgive us.'

'I know my father well. Once we have entered the state of holy matrimony, he will accept that we are married. And once he gets to know you, he will come to love you as the son-in-law he always wanted.'

He looked unconvinced, but Lucy knew this would

be true. How could anyone who knew Sebastian not love him?

'Just trust me,' she said. 'Oh, and kiss me again, or I might change my mind about this wedding.'

'Oh, Lucy, I do love you,' he said, and laughing he picked her up and swung her around, before doing what she asked and kissing her again.

Chapter Twenty-Two

With a lightness of spirit Sebastian had never experienced before, he wasted no time and headed back to London to apply for a special licence to marry. Once the paperwork had been set in motion, he was so full of energy he found it all but impossible to contain it. He wanted to stand on top of the highest building and shout out to all of London that he was in love, in love with the most wonderful woman in the world, and despite being possibly the biggest buffoon to ever seek a wife, for some reason that marvellous woman was in love with him.

Instead of doing that, he made haste round to Nathanial's club to tell his brother the good news.

He burst into the office and once again found his brother hard at work behind his desk, Lucy's lady's maid unaccountably standing behind him and acting as some sort of secretary.

She bobbed a quick curtsy, picked up a pile of letters and departed.

Sebastian shook his head slightly at the encounter then turned back to his brother. 'Nathanial, brother, I'm in love and I'm to marry,' he said, suspecting he sounded like a lovesick fool but not caring in the slightest.

Nathanial stood up and walked round the side of the desk, his hand outstretched. Before he could shake his hand, Sebastian took him in a hug. That was surely the only way one should greet one's brother.

'So you're to marry Lucy Everhart then, are you? Congratulations.'

'How do you know?' He was sure he hadn't mentioned that he was in love with Lucy and wanted to marry her. He looked towards the door. Had Lucy contacted her former lady's maid and imparted the news?

'We all know which young lady captured your heart,' Nathanial said, laughter in his voice. 'I saw the two of you here at the club, and then at Thomas's card evening. And as for you being alone here in this office...' He waggled his eyebrows up and down in a comical manner. 'We've all discussed it. We all knew she was the one, and we were just waiting for you to come to that realisation.'

'We?'

'Thomas and Isaac, and of course their wives. And Dolly was hoping the two of you would come to your senses eventually.'

Under normal circumstances Sebastian would not

appreciate being the subject of such gossip and speculation, but today it only added to his pleasure.

'It seems everyone else knew I was in love before I did.' He continued smiling at his brother, even though he was sure he was looking, as Lucy would say, rather gormless.

'I believe Isaac and Thomas are both in London, so this calls for a celebration,' Nathanial said.

The four men were soon gathered in the bar of The Eldridge, toasting the happy occasion to come with champagne.

'You haven't told us the date,' Thomas said as he signalled to the steward for another bottle. 'Grace will want to know in plenty of time so she can get a new gown made.'

Isaac nodded. 'Yes, fabric must be chosen, designs debated, hats selected.'

'That's the thing,' Sebastian said with a frown. 'Lucy's father thoroughly disapproves of me. He thinks I'm a corrupting influence on his daughter and hasn't given us permission to wed. Not only that, he's banned me from seeing her and all but told me never to darken his doorstep again.'

The three men stared at him in disbelief then burst out laughing.

When the laughing died down, Thomas asked him what they were going to do.

'We're going to elope.'

This caused another round of disbelieving looks.

'I suspect Grace will find that both terribly romantic and terribly disappointing,' Thomas said.

Isaac nodded his agreement. 'Yes, Adelaide will miss the chance for a new hat and gown, marking the happy occasion and all that.'

'Well, give your wives my apologies,' Sebastian said. 'But we have to do it this way.' He smiled at Lucy's reaction when he had suggested it. 'After all, there's no better way of starting a marriage than with a scandal.'

Thomas and Isaac nodded and smiled, remembering the complicated and somewhat scandalous ways their own marriages had started.

'Speaking of which, I must be going.' Sebastian placed his hand over his glass before Thomas could refill it. 'The paperwork must surely be completed by now, and I've got an elopement to stage.'

'It's off to Gretna Green, is it?' Thomas asked.

'No, I've telegrammed the vicar at the church near my estate, and it's all organised for tomorrow afternoon.' He quickly downed the last of his champagne and stood up.

The three men raised their glasses in toast. 'Best of luck,' Nathanial said. 'And next time we see you, you'll be a married man.'

They cheered as Sebastian hurried out of the club. With as much haste as possible, he took a cab back to the Faculty Office, picked up his licence and took the next train up to Cheshire, anxious to become a married man as soon as possible.

That evening, Sebastian found himself back in Greyton, preparing for an event that he would have once considered an impossibility. But that was before he had met Lucy Everhart and the impossible became a reality.

Thanks to his surprisingly resourceful valet, who had procured a ladder for him and worked out a way in which it could be transported on a carriage, Sebastian made haste to Lucy's cottage so he could carry off his bride into the night.

The carriage was parked at the end of the lane, where the driver did his best to keep the horses as quiet as possible, lest their snorting and whinnying disturb the silence of the quiet village and woke the occupants of the vicarage.

Carrying the ladder, he moved as stealthily as possible down the lane, crept around the back of the cottage and propped it up against the side of the house. Luckily it was long enough to reach the first floor. Smiling to himself he climbed the ladder. All going well, tomorrow he would be a married man, and Lucy would be his wife.

A cough broke through the silence of the night, and Sebastian almost slipped off the ladder. His heart jumped to his throat, and ideas spun wildly in his mind on how to explain his bizarre behaviour to the reverend.

'I'm standing beneath you.' Lucy's quiet voice came out of the dark. He looked down and made out the shape of his wife-to-be, dressed in her travelling cloak and carrying a large suitcase.

He scrambled back down the ladder, disappointment strangely coursing through him. 'I was going to make a grand, romantic gesture,' he whispered when he reached the bottom.

'What? To Aunt Harriet? That's her window you were heading towards,' she said, stifling a laugh.

Sebastian had to stifle a laugh of his own, and as quietly as possible he lowered the ladder and placed it beside the house. He was tempted to take Lucy in his arms, but they needed to hurry, so he picked up the suitcase and took her hand, and they raced up the lane to the waiting carriage.

The driver quickly stowed her case while Sebastian helped Lucy into the carriage. As quietly as it was possible for horses to be, they moved down the lane and out onto the village's sleepy main street. As soon as they were far enough away from the vicarage, the driver commanded the horses to increase their speed, and they galloped towards the station, where they would catch a train to London, then on to his estate in Dorset.

This was really happening. He was eloping. Lucy would soon be his bride.

As if they were both sharing the same thought,

matching smiles spread across their faces, then she was in his arms and he was kissing her.

Sebastian could hardly believe he had risked losing her, had risked never having her in his arms, never tasting her sweet lips again. Knowing she would soon be his, that he would be hers, he kissed her, not with the aching desperation he had done so in the past but with a loving gentleness.

It was a kiss that expressed how much he adored her, how he had finally come to accept she was the only woman who could ever be his countess.

She sighed gently, as his kisses moved to her soft neck.

'I love you, Lucy,' he murmured between each taste of her satin skin.

'And I love you,' she whispered back.

He was still kissing her when the carriage pulled up at the station. He would gladly stay where he was, with his lovely Lucy in his arms, but there was no time to waste. He helped her out of the carriage, and hand in hand they raced along the platform, just in time to catch the train to London. They settled into their compartment, and released equally deep sighs of relief. There was no way her father could stop them now.

'I do believe that Father was right,' Lucy said with that cheeky smile he loved so much. 'You really are a bad influence on me.'

'Do you agree with him that I have led you into sin?'

Her smile grew wider. 'Oh, I do hope so.'

If it hadn't been for the passengers and staff walking past their compartment, Sebastian was sure he'd be leading her into sin right here, right now, but that would be a step too far. They would have to wait until they were alone and were husband and wife.

'It's tempting, isn't it?' she said, looking towards the window in the door that led to the passageway, echoing his thoughts. 'But I think that would be a scandal too much even for me.'

He laughed, reached over and took her hand. 'I'll send your father a telegram when we get to the station near my estate, so he doesn't worry when he wakes up tomorrow and finds you gone.'

'Will you tell him you've abducted me and dragged me off into the night so you can have your wicked way with me?'

'Yes, I think it's probably best to tell the truth.'

She laughed and lightly swatted his arm.

'I *will* tell him the truth,' he said, his expression serious. 'I will tell him we are in love and by tomorrow we will be married. By the time he gets the telegram, it will be too late to stop it.'

'And we will be married.'

'Yes, we will be married,' he echoed.

He gave her hand a small squeeze. 'And I could tell him I intend to make you very, very happy to make up for what a buffoon I've been.' He shook his head, unable to believe that he had not seen immediately that she was the one for him. No, that wasn't true. He had seen it immediately: he had just refused to admit it.

'So if you're planning to make me very, very happy, perhaps you can start now.' She looked towards the door leading to the passageway. 'Make me happy even if it does cause a scandal.'

With that he moved to the bench beside her, took her in his arms and kissed her, not caring if anyone was watching.

The train arrived at the station, and Sebastian's carriage was waiting, and once the telegram had been sent, they made their way to his estate, where a room had been prepared for Lucy.

With the greatest reluctance they parted company so they could get some rest before their wedding the following day.

Sebastian was unsure if he was going to be able to sleep, knowing that the woman he loved was in the next room. He consoled himself with the thought that tomorrow she would be his bride, and their new life together would begin.

He pulled up his shirt, just as the door adjoining their rooms opened, and Lucy entered, wearing her nightdress, her hair loose around her shoulders.

Sebastian stopped what he was doing and stared at her, his shirt half-on, half-off. Had he ever seen a more beautiful sight?

'I thought we should start our life together with yet another scandal,' she said, smiling and biting the edge of her lip.

* * *

How could she possibly sleep when she knew the man she loved was just one door away? The answer to that was: she couldn't. So Lucy had turned that doorhandle and entered his room.

And looking at him now she knew she had made the right decision.

Her eyes swept up and down his body. She had felt those muscles in his chest when he had held her; now she could see them in all their glory. But what she really wanted was to touch them, explore them with her hands, her lips, her tongue.

When her gaze returned to his, she could see the depth of his desire burning in them, desire for her. That awareness sent a hot throb of anticipation pulsing through her body, and she held her breath, eager to discover what was to come.

'Are you sure?' he asked, his voice thick with desire. 'It's only one day. We can wait until we are married, if that is what you want.'

'What I want is you,' she said quietly. 'Now.'

He crossed the room, cupped her chin and kissed her more gently than she had expected. 'I imagined you like this from the first day I saw you.' He ran his hand through her long hair. 'I'd pictured you with your hair tumbling around your shoulders.'

His eyes stroked down her body, encased in the thin muslin nightdress before returning to gaze into her eyes. 'I've also repeatedly thought about seeing you naked,' he murmured.

Lucy's heart pounded harder in her chest with a mixture of nerves and excitement. Hoping her fingers weren't shaking, she pulled at the ribbon at the neck of her nightgown. The fire in his eyes burnt fiercer, giving her confidence and a strange sense of power. He desired her. He wanted her. He was hers.

She pushed the nightgown off her shoulders, and his kisses covered her naked skin. 'Take off your nightgown,' he commanded as he continued to kiss her neck.

He stood back as she pulled up the light fabric, lifted it over her head and tossed it to the side. Naked in the soft candlelight, she stood in front of him, any embarrassment, any shyness pushed away by the look in his eye.

'You are perfect,' he murmured.

Her nipples tightened under his gaze, and she did feel perfect: perfect, desirable and sensual.

Then his arms were around her, his kiss this time hard, demanding, as the warm naked skin of his chest rubbed against the sensitive peaks of her breasts. In one quick move, he scooped her up and carried her to his four-poster bed, laying her in the middle. Standing at the end of the bed, his passionate eyes never leaving her, he pushed off his undone shirt and pulled off his trousers.

Her gaze stroked his naked body.

You, too, are perfect was the thought that formed in her mind as her gaze moved up and down that hard, muscular body, but she was beyond speech. And this perfect man was about to make love to her, about to express the love he felt for her with physical pleasure.

She reached out her hands to him, her inner core throbbing with a need that only he could fill.

He joined her on the bed, his body covering hers, as he once again captured her lips, parting them and exploring her with his tongue. He tasted so good, smelt so good, felt so good.

Her hands wrapped around his head, and as if under a will of their own, her legs parted, and she rubbed the inside of her thighs against his legs.

His lips still on hers, his hand moved to cup her breasts, which swelled under his touch, the pebbled tips so tender Lucy was unsure where pleasure ended and aching need began.

Lying back, she surrendered herself to the sensation of his caresses as his lips left hers, and he kissed a line down to her waiting breasts. When he took a hard nipple in his mouth, her moans became cries of ecstasy. The tension gripping her body mounted with each stroke of his tongue, his licking, nuzzling, sucking taking her higher and higher, until pleasure crashed over her, sending quivers rippling through her body.

Before she had time to recover from the intensity of that experience, his kisses moved lower, trailing down her stomach. It was glorious, but he didn't stop there. His lips moved even lower.

Was he really going to kiss her there? That surely was too scandalous.

A slow, sultry smile crossed her lips. Yes, scandalous. Deliciously, deliriously scandalous. She parted her legs wider, letting him know that it was something she certainly had no objection to and something she wanted, desperately.

His kisses reached the mound of hair. His hands moved between her thighs, parting her legs even wider. Kneeling between her legs, he looked down at what she was exposing to him. This was so wicked, so wanton, so wonderful.

'You are beautiful,' he whispered, before kissing her in the most intimate of places. A gasp of pleasure escaped Lucy's lips. A gasp that turned to moans, as his tongue moved along her folds, causing the heat to surge between her thighs, as his tongue and lips nuzzled her sensitive bud.

Just as Lucy was sure she could take this wild torment no longer, her muscles contracted then released as wave after wave of pleasure shot through her, starting at the site of his tongue and consuming her body.

'That was…that was…' She faltered, words inadequate to explain what she had felt.

'Do you want more?' he said, smiling up at her.

'Oh, yes, please.'

His body once more covered hers, and she felt him hard at her opening. Her heartbeat once again increased its pounding, loving the thought of him being inside her, of them joining and him relieving the pulsing need that was once again throbbing deep within her.

She wrapped her legs around his waist, her hands cupping his buttocks, pushing him towards her, urging him to do what she knew he must want to.

'Tell me if it hurts and I'll stop,' he whispered in her ear.

'I will,' she said, knowing she would not. Nothing could stop her now, not even pain.

Slowly he pushed himself into her, his eyes fixed on hers, as if waiting for her to put up a protest.

'Yes,' she murmured. 'Don't stop.'

He pushed in deeper. She watched his face, loving the pleasure this was giving him, the pleasure he was taking in her body.

Then she was lost, lost to the wild sensations building up in her body, lost to the heat of passion consuming her, lost in the power of their primal connection. Her moans became cries, then she called out his name, louder and louder with each deep, hard thrust.

When an intense shudder ripped through her body, she all but screamed his name one more time and was sure she'd also told him again how much she loved him, before she collapsed under him, feeling completely sated, completely loved and completely in love.

Chapter Twenty-Three

After a night spent racing across the country, then expressing their love for each other again and again, Sebastian and Lucy barely had time for sleep. Yet the next morning, instead of being exhausted, Sebastian was exhilarated. He would happily spend the entire day in bed with Lucy, but they had a wedding to get to.

He jumped out of bed and rang for a servant to run baths for the two of them, then gazed down at Lucy, still asleep. She looked glorious, her tangled hair spread out over the pillows, the tousled sheets wrapped around her beautiful, naked body. And to think Sebastian would be waking up to that sight every day for the rest of his life.

She opened her eyes, looked up at him, smiled and held out her arms towards him. It was a tempting invitation.

'Have you forgotten what today is?'

'Mmm,' she responded, moving sensually, making it even harder to ignore what he really wanted to do.

'Wedding? Remember? The vicar will be waiting, and I think you probably should put some clothes on.'

'Spoil-sport,' she said, with a laugh, before pulling herself off the bed and looking around for her discarded nightdress. Spotting the crumpled pile of muslin in the corner, he picked it up and handed it to her, then watched as that beautiful body disappeared from view.

'Right. Bathe, dress and then we'll head straight for the church.'

'Yes, sir,' she said in a sleepy voice. He turned her towards the door adjoining their rooms and, with a light slap on that glorious bottom, sent her on her way.

Once he was bathed and dressed in the morning suit he had worn when best man at his friends' weddings, he waited at the bottom of the stairs for his bride.

She appeared at the top of the stairs, dressed in a white gown.

'Virginal white,' she said, smiling at him when she reached the bottom of the stairs. 'It's not entirely appropriate, but no one will know except you and I.'

Sebastian suspected the servants may have been woken by her loud moans and cries last night but saw no reason to mention that.

'It's the same gown I wore for my presentation to the queen, minus the quivering ostrich feathers.'

'And hopefully minus the fits of giggles.'

She lifted one finger. 'That I cannot promise.'

He kissed her lightly on the lips and took her hand, and they rushed out to the waiting carriage.

'Should we have waited for your wedding night?' he asked as they rode along the hedge-lined country lanes. 'Would you have preferred to go to the wedding altar a virgin?' It was a pointless question as there was nothing they could do about it now, but Sebastian did feel some guilt at not controlling his desire for her for one more night.

'Absolutely not,' she stated emphatically. 'We had waited far too long already, and I for one want to get these formalities over and done with as quickly as possible so we can get back to bed and we can officially consummate our marriage.'

He laughed at her reaction, which was so typical of the woman he loved.

The carriage came to a halt outside the church.

'Let's hurry, then and get this thing over and done with,' he said, taking her hand as they raced up the path, leading to the stone church where the vicar would be waiting to make their union official.

Sebastian opened the door. They both stopped in their tracks, struck by the sight before them.

The scent of lilies, roses and lavender filled the air from the enormous bouquets of flowers that adorned the church. The aisles were decorated with garlands of white hydrangeas strung in graceful loops, and a group of happy guests were sitting in the front pews, rows of smiling faces turned towards them.

The organ player struck up the 'Wedding March.' Sebastian and Lucy looked at each other with the same surprised expressions, then smiled and together they walked up the aisle towards the waiting vicar.

Lucy had said she wanted to get this thing over and done with so they could officially consummate their marriage, and that was undeniably what Sebastian wanted as well, but as the vicar read out the marriage vows he also had to admit that everything the man said rang true, and it was an honour to solemnly declare his love for his bride. And to do so in front of his friends and family made this day even more special.

Finally, the clergyman declared them husband and wife, and Sebastian kissed his wife, the woman he would share the rest of his life with, his lovely Lucy.

The guests gathered around them at the church door, and they were showered with pink rose petals.

Lucy was soon surrounded by the female guests, including Sebastian's mother, who took her in her arms.

'I am so happy to see my son has married for love,' she said, lightly kissing Lucy's cheek. 'And I'm sure you two will be extremely happy.'

'And I am so pleased to meet you,' Lucy replied, a tear in her eye. 'And I do hope you will become a part of our life.'

His mother once again embraced her, and Sebastian found himself wiping away a tear of his own.

'Congratulations,' Thomas said, shaking his hand,

followed by the same gesture from Nathanial and Isaac.

'How did this all happen?' Sebastian said to the three men, pointing back at the church.

'That was Adelaide and Grace,' Thomas replied. 'When we told our wives about your planned elopement, they sprang into action. London's flower shops were stripped of their goods, wine merchants were contacted, food was procured, telegrams were sent to get your servants ready, and we were all bundled onto a train, the luggage cart filled to the brim with everything deemed essential for a wedding day.'

Thomas and Isaac looked affectionately towards their wives, who were talking to Lucy and giving her repeated hugs. 'I think most military commanders could learn a thing or two from our wives,' Isaac said.

Thomas laughed. 'Yes, if a military campaign were organised by those two it would go a lot more smoothly. The troops would certainly be a lot better fed.'

'And every soldier would have a flower in his lapel,' Isaac added, patting the orchid in his own buttonhole.

Lucy and the other two wives, along with his mother and the ubiquitous Dolly walked over to join them.

He looked at Nathanial, who gave a shrug, and Sebastian suspected there was a tale to tell about what was happening between his brother and his wife's former lady's maid, but now was neither the time nor the place to discuss that.

'I'm so happy for you,' his mother said, kissing Sebastian's cheek. 'The new countess of Rothwell is everything I had hoped for, and I am so pleased that an earl of Rothwell finally married for love.'

'As am I,' Sebastian said, taking Lucy's hand.

They all made their way back to the estate, where his friends' wives had also worked their magic and arranged for a hasty wedding breakfast. The dining room had been miraculously transformed with more bouquets of scented flowers, and the tables were set with white linen, crystal and silverware.

Somehow his servants had also kept these arrangements secret from them, and their smiles showed they had thoroughly enjoyed being in on the conspiracy.

Courses were served, toasts were made and much laughter filled the dining room. It really was a happy occasion.

Just as the dessert was being served, a footman entered and whispered in Sebastian's ear.

He gritted his teeth and looked over at Lucy, who was sharing a joke with Dolly.

'What is it?' she asked, her smile fading.

'Your father has arrived.'

Before the words were hardly out of his mouth, the reverend burst in, his dour face a burning red in what was becoming a familiar manner, followed by an anxious-looking Aunt Harriet.

'Leave this to me,' Lucy said, standing up and walking around the table.

Sebastian would do no such thing. He followed his bride and together they waited for the storm that was certain to erupt.

'What is the meaning of this?' Lucy's father said in a loud voice, bringing the sound of chatter, laughter and silverware on china to a halt. 'Does your corruption of my daughter know no bounds?' he added, pointing an incriminating finger at Sebastian.

'Father, I—' Lucy said.

'Reverend Everhart, I can assure you—' Sebastian said at the same time.

Lucy placed a warning hand on Sebastian's arm. Unlike him, she knew her father and how to placate him.

'Father, I am so pleased you were able to make it in time so you could celebrate this sacred occasion,' she said.

Her father's eyes bulged, and his florid complexion grew darker, and she worried he was suffering apoplexy.

'As you can see, I am now a married woman. Sebastian and I have been joined in holy matrimony, in a church, by a vicar.' She indicated the man wearing black with a white clerical collar and happily eating his strawberry tart, oblivious to the drama taking place.

The man finally stopped eating when he noticed

everyone had gone silent and was staring in his direction. He lifted his champagne flute.

'To the happy couple,' he said, before downing a significant part of the full glass.

Everyone repeated his toast and took a drink, and Lucy turned back to her father, whose face was still burning red.

'Father, please don't be angry. I am married to the man I love.' She threaded her arm through Sebastian's. 'And have you not often informed your parishioners that wrath is one of the seven deadly sins?'

She could also say that lust was on that list, as her father never failed to remind his unfortunate parishioners, and it was mutual lust that originally brought her and Sebastian together, but that certainly would not help calm her father's agitated state.

'Lucy, you know I only want what's best for you. I only want you to be happy,' he said mournfully.

'And you have got that wish, Father. I am happy.' *So happy it's almost a sin.* 'And Sebastian is what is best for me.'

Her father glared at Sebastian through narrowed eyes, then turned back to Lucy. 'There's still time to have the marriage annulled,' he whispered. 'Before it's consummated.'

Lucy was unsure if that were entirely accurate, but again, it was not something she should discuss with her father.

'Father, I love Sebastian. He loves me. We are now husband and wife.'

That narrowed gaze turned once again to Sebastian.

'I do love your daughter,' Sebastian added. 'And I promise I will do everything in my power to make her happy every day of her life and never have reason to ever regret marrying me for one moment.'

The father looked from daughter to son-in-law and then back again. 'Well, I suppose under my daughter's improving influence you might eventually become a better man.'

'I already have,' Sebastian said, wrapped his arms around her and kissed her waiting lips.

Her father made a few huffing noises at such a flagrant display of affection.

'Now, if you'd like to drink to our health, I believe there is fruit punch as well as champagne,' Sebastian said, his arm still around her.

A footman miraculously appeared, and her father took a glass of punch, while Aunt Harriet helped herself to a glass of champagne.

'Perhaps you'd like to join the vicar and talk about things theological,' Lucy said, guilt nipping at the edge of her happiness, but she pushed it away with a promise to make it up to the cheerful vicar.

Her father wandered off, looking slightly lost now that his anger had been deflated.

'Oh, sweetie, I am so happy for you,' Aunt Harriet said, taking Lucy in her arms and kissing her cheek, then hugging an astonished Sebastian. 'I knew he was the man for you the moment I saw you dancing together at your inaugural ball, and I was right,' she added.

'You were watching?' Lucy asked, in surprise. Her memory of that event was of a distracted aunt talking to the gaggle of chaperones.

'Like a hawk,' Aunt Harriet said with a girlish giggle. 'And I'm hardly likely to not notice you took the air just at the same time as the earl?'

Both Sebastian's and Lucy's eyes grew wide at this admission.

'I was a bit surprised when he made that awful proposal.' She sent Sebastian a scathing look. 'And I had thought momentarily that he wasn't quite the man I had thought him to be.'

'Didn't we both, Aunt?' Lucy said and winked at Sebastian. 'But it seems we were both wrong, or at least we were both right…or something.'

'Indeed we were.' Aunt Harriet raised her glass to Sebastian and went to take another sip but noticed her glass was empty and went off in search of the footman who was serving the champagne.

Lucy and Sebastian stared at each other then both laughed.

'So did you tell my father the truth?'

Sebastian raised his eyebrows in question.

'When you said you were going to do everything in your power to make me happy every day of my life?'

'Of course, and I am sure I will enjoy doing so.'

'But what about every night?'

'I could hardly say that to your father, could I?' He leant down and whispered in her ear. 'But making you happy every night of your life, making you cry out in ecstasy, making you writhe beneath my touch will be my continued goal and my continued pleasure.'

'I like the sound of that.' She looked over at the guests, still laughing and chatting. Her father and the vicar had been joined by Sebastian's mother who was thankfully distracting her father from lecturing the poor man on some theological argument. Aunt Harriet had taken a seat next to Dolly and was chatting to her and Nathanial. Isaac and Thomas were deep in conversation with their respective wives.

'How much longer do you think they are going to stay?' Lucy asked.

'I have no idea, but I doubt if anyone would miss us if we crept away and officially consummated this marriage.'

With that, he took her hand and led her out the dining room and up the stairs to their bedchamber so they could begin their life together as husband and wife.

* * * * *

MILLS & BOON®

Coming next month

HIS CINDERELLA DUCHESS
Tina Gabrielle

Brent leaned forward in his chair. 'You do recall the arrangement you proposed? You want a child. I need an heir for the dukedom. For either to happen, we have to share a bed.'

She felt her cheeks burn hot. She was by no means blind to his attractiveness. Still, mention of bedchamber visits made her heart thump hard in her chest. 'I understand but I still want a proper courtship.'

'How long?'

'Three months from the wedding.' She knew this was lengthy but meant it to be a point of negotiation.

He shook his head. 'A week.'

'A month.'

'A week.'

She pushed back her chair and stood. 'You are being inflexible. However, since the banns of marriage must be read aloud in church for three Sundays prior to the wedding, I'll agree to a three week courtship.'

He rose, walked around his desk and stopped before her. She stood her ground and raised her chin, trying to assess his unreadable features. To her surprise, an unwelcome surge of excitement at his nearness made her pulse leap.

He leaned casually against the desk. 'Banns are not required if a special license is obtained.' His voice was level.

She gaped. 'A special license? But…but that requires the Archbishop's consent himself.'

'I know.' An unmistakable hint of arrogance tinged his voice.

Continue reading

HIS CINDERELLA DUCHESS
Tina Gabrielle

Available next month
millsandboon.co.uk

Copyright © 2025 Tina Sickler

COMING SOON!

We really hope you enjoyed reading this book.
If you're looking for more romance
be sure to head to the shops when
new books are available on

Thursday 28th August

To see which titles are coming soon, please visit
millsandboon.co.uk/nextmonth

MILLS & BOON

afterglow BOOKS

THE CODE FOR LOVE

Her perfect plan has a gorgeous glitch...

NEW YORK TIMES BESTSELLING AUTHOR

ANNE MARSH

✈ International

⛅ Grumpy/sunshine

🤝 Fake dating

OUT NOW

To discover more visit:
Afterglowbooks.co.uk

FOUR BRAND NEW BOOKS FROM
MILLS & BOON MODERN

The same great stories you love, a stylish new look!

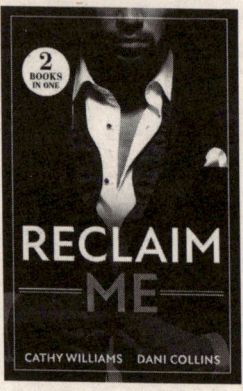

OUT NOW

Eight Modern stories published every month, find them all at:

millsandboon.co.uk

LET'S TALK
Romance

For exclusive extracts, competitions and special offers, find us online:

- **f** MillsandBoon
- **X** @MillsandBoon
- **◎** @MillsandBoonUK
- **♪** @MillsandBoonUK

Get in touch on 01413 063 232

For all the latest titles coming soon, visit
millsandboon.co.uk/nextmonth

OUT NOW!

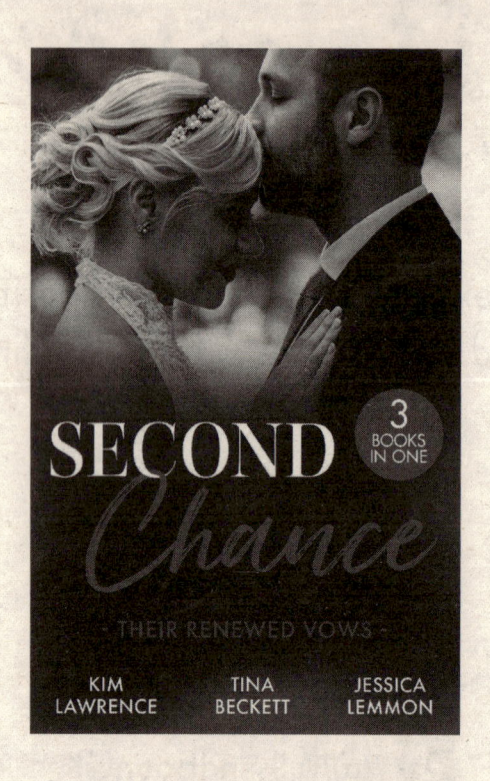

SECOND Chance

THEIR RENEWED VOWS

3 BOOKS IN ONE

KIM LAWRENCE

TINA BECKETT

JESSICA LEMMON

Available at millsandboon.co.uk

MILLS & BOON